Praise for N:
Blackbird Sisters mysteries

"Nancy Martin writes about Philadelphia high society like no one else. With romance, humor, sex and money. What more could a debutante want?"
—Sarah Strohmeyer

"Sing a song of suspense, a pocket full of wry, Nora's funny Blackbirds make you laugh until you die."
—Mary Daheim, author of *The Alpine Obituary*

Dead Girls Don't Wear Diamonds

"If you're looking for a light, comic mystery with a touch of romance, *Dead Girls Don't Wear Diamonds* fits the bill."
—*Romantic Times*

How to Murder a Millionaire

"Welcome the Blackbird sisters, Philadelphia aristocracy, born to money, now widowed and strapped. . . . *How to Murder a Millionaire* is clever, good-humored and sharply observed."
—*The Philadelphia Inquirer*

continued . . .

"A Main Line Philadelphia backdrop, a self-deprecatingly funny former debutante, and a cast of wonderfully quirky characters combine for a thoroughly entertaining mystery that also provides some red-hot sexual tension between the heroine and her tough-guy protector. Can't wait for the next installment in this smart and sophisticated new series."
—Jane Heller, bestselling author of
The Secret Ingredient

"Nancy Martin has a rich, engaging, and funny hit in *How to Murder a Millionaire*. With a scandalous mystery, hot romance, and the delightful to-the-manor-born Blackbird sisters, Martin also treats us to a rare peek into Philadelphia's exclusive high society where all is not Grace Kelly. It's a book to curl up with and savor. You won't want it to end!"
—Sarah Strohmeyer, author of *Bubbles Ablaze*

SOME LIKE IT LETHAL

A BLACKBIRD SISTERS MYSTERY

Nancy Martin

A SIGNET BOOK

SIGNET
Published by New American Library, a division of
Penguin Group (USA) Inc., 375 Hudson Street,
New York, New York 10014, U.S.A.
Penguin Books Ltd, 80 Strand,
London WC2R 0RL, England
Penguin Books Australia Ltd, 250 Camberwell Road,
Camberwell, Victoria 3124, Australia
Penguin Books Canada Ltd, 10 Alcorn Avenue,
Toronto, Ontario, Canada M4V 3B2
Penguin Books (N.Z.) Ltd, Cnr Rosedale and Airborne Roads,
Albany, Auckland 1310, New Zealand

Penguin Books Ltd, Registered Offices:
80 Strand, London WC2R 0RL, England

First published by Signet, an imprint of New American Library,
a division of Penguin Group (USA) Inc.

First Printing, April 2004
10 9 8 7 6 5 4 3 2 1

This book is dedicated to my hero, Jeff Martin. For twenty years, you were the best thing that ever happened to me. And the last ten haven't been too bad either. Luv ya.

ACKNOWLEDGMENT

Thanks to the wonderful people at Malice Domestic, who know how to make a newbie feel welcome.

Chapter 1

After my newly widowed sister Libby gave birth to her fifth child, she decided to become a goddess.

"It takes effort," she advised me when I went into her bedroom to shake her awake one cold November morning. "But it's just what you need, Nora."

"I'm too busy taking care of your family," I said, passing her the squirming body of her newborn son. "When you finish transforming yourself, could you make some peanut butter sandwiches for the kids?"

"I can't," she said, taking the child. "I've given up peanut butter as a sacrifice to Placida."

"Who?"

"My goddess within." Libby began unlacing the ties on one of her exquisitely embroidered nightgowns in preparation of feeding her frantic son his overdue breakfast. "Placida is the deity of tranquility, sexual adventure and weight loss."

I sighed. "Libby, you had a baby just five weeks ago. And you can't expect to lose weight without getting out of bed once in a while. Giving up peanut butter is a good start, but if you quit watching all those episodes of *Trading Spaces* and get some exercise—"

"You don't understand the goddess process, Nora." Libby plumped the lacy pillows around her voluptuous figure and sat back with a beatific smile as the baby clamped on to her breast like a starving Yorkshire piglet. "You must open yourself to the possibilities so the goddess may flow from within you. It's a mental path to all kinds of fulfillment. Why, just last night I had an erotic dream about Dr. Phil."

As she nursed her perfect baby I looked at my demented sister, with her beautiful skin glowing and her hair in a vixenish sort of tangle and her body all soft and glamorously flaunted, as if ready to be ravaged at Versailles by a Bourbon king. The Blackbird white complexion and auburn hair—which had been passed down through the generations, along with a very peculiar family crest and a seventeenth-century Blackbird blunderbuss—looked demure on me but distinctly more erotic on Libby. After childbirth, women weren't supposed to look as if they'd been airbrushed by *Playboy*'s most gifted photographer, but here was Libby looking divine while I felt as if I'd been beaten with a shovel.

I said, "If I strangled you with your own nursing bra right now, it would be justifiable homicide."

"I'm re-centering my life!" she cried. "Don't rush me! I must gather my cosmic resources, prioritize my most primal joys and learn to validate my sacred inner magic so I can evolve into the goddess of my mysterious potential. Such a powerful psychological makeover takes time."

"Well, the kitchen floor needs a makeover, too. How about using a mop while I'm out?"

She sat up and widened her eyes in pretty dismay. "Where are you going? Good heavens, you're not having clandestine morning sex with That Man, are you?"

Although clandestine sex might tempt me I knew I shouldn't leave Libby's children alone in her custody for any reason whatsoever. Sixteen-year-old Rawlins had taken to suspiciously disappearing late at night with a group of friends who collectively had enough body piercings to start a surgical supply store. The thirteen-year-old twins Harcourt and Hilton were closeted in the basement, making a Santa Claus movie that involved bloodcurdling screams every three minutes, and five-year-old Lucy had invented an imaginary friend who graffitied the living room walls with grape jelly when I wasn't vigilant. The baby, who still had not been bestowed with a name by his goddess mother, couldn't bear to be anywhere but in my arms, except when he was trying to deplete his mother's milk supply.

To top everything off, Libby was lactating with more volume than a dairy cow, so one of my jobs was bottling and freezing the overflow to contribute to a breast milk bank at a Philadelphia foster child agency. Which meant there were even more children who depended on me while Libby lolled in postpartum splendor, dreaming of talk-show hosts and cockamamie deities.

I had no time for anything, including clandestine sex.

"That Man," I said, "is fishing in Scotland."

She settled back against her pillows and muttered, "Yeah, sure."

I turned in the doorway. "What's that supposed to mean?"

Libby smoothed the fair hair on her baby's head. "Honestly, Nora, if you believe your mob-boss boyfriend has gone fishing, I'm marching straight out to find a bridge to sell you."

"Oh, not that again."

"Do I need flip charts to explain it? Michael Abruzzo is a dangerous man mixed up in so many shady businesses—"

"Name one."

"That new chain of gas stations," Libby said promptly. "Gas 'n' Grub? They're popping up all over the place."

"What's wrong with selling gasoline and sandwiches? Besides the indigestion?"

"They're cash businesses, Nora. Even you must know what that means."

"He's making a living?" I said, tartly, bringing up a sore subject, since my parents blew the last of the Blackbird fortune and sailed off to a tax-evader's paradise where they spent most of their time rehearsing for the weekly mambo contest.

Libby covered her baby's ears lest he learn about high crime at such a tender age. "Michael Abruzzo is laundering money."

"Oh, for crying out loud—"

"The papers say he's under investigation."

"He's always under investigation. Because of his family, not himself."

"Well, this is a new one, and he's the star of the show. I heard it on the news last night. It's probably why he's fled the country."

"He hasn't fled! He's taking a vacation."

"Think about it, Nora. If you had ill-gotten gains, you'd want a place to pass the dirty money to an unsuspecting public in small batches. That's why he started Gas 'n' Grub. *Vanity Fair* had a big article about money laundering last month. Pizza shops: now, those are a gold mine for criminals."

"Michael is not a criminal."

Which I believed most of the time.

"He looks like a criminal," Libby declared. "A sexy criminal, I'll admit, with, okay, a sort of fallen-angel magnetism that some women find attractive, but—"

"I'm leaving now," I said before she could go into her riff about consorting with the devil. Somehow I wouldn't mind so much if I actually enjoyed a little consorting, but lately I'd been stuck refereeing her children. "I'll be back in two hours."

"Where are you going?"

"I told you. I'm covering the hunt breakfast for the newspaper. And Emma's riding, remember?"

Neither of us had quite gotten the hang of my employment yet. Before I was widowed, I'd spent my adult life being married to a doctor and devoting my time to good works and the Junior League, so when the family fortunes evaporated on tropical breezes, I didn't have a respectable resume for job hunting. But an old family friend who owned a Philadelphia newspaper had found me a position as an assistant to the society columnist. The job required me to attend parties and report on clothes, guest lists and the details of so-called high society entertaining. It was work for which I was singularly suited, having been brought up in a tax bracket where the oxygen was very thin and party planning was an art form. I wasn't going to earn a Pulitzer any time soon, but the job helped me pay down the heart-stopping tax debt on Blackbird Farm.

This morning's assignment was the hunt breakfast at an exclusive fox hunting club just off the Main Line. And I needed to be there shortly after sunrise.

Libby eyed me. "Are you going to talk to Emma?"

"I'm going to try."

"Maybe I should come along."

"I think I can address Emma's situation in a calm and rational manner on my own."

"Are you implying that childbirth has rendered me incapable of rationality?" Libby asked. "I'll have you know there are actually studies that prove motherhood makes you smarter. So you have something to look forward to."

My sister Libby had plans to make everyone's lives perfect. She decided that I only needed children to reach a state of serenity, and she rarely missed an opportunity to remind me of the maternal rewards that awaited me if I paid closer attention to the expiration date on my ovaries.

"After five weeks in the household from hell," I said, "I'm having second thoughts about having a family of my own."

Libby appeared not to hear me. "I think I will go along with you this morning."

"You're kidding, right?"

"We should present a united front. Yes, I'll definitely come. I have an invitation around here somewhere." She disconnected her son from his food source and began to burp him while she imagined the party. "It might be a nice reentry into the world for me, too. All those handsome men on horseback!" The look in her eye reminded me of a pyromaniac lighting a match.

"Don't start, Libby."

"Don't start what?"

"Chasing unsuspecting men as if they were helpless rabbits doomed for the stew pot. You're in a hormonal fever right now. You're a danger to society. I'm not taking you with me. Besides, my car will be here in five minutes, and you'll never be ready."

"I'll follow you later," she said. "Run along."

"What about the baby?" The idea of my lactating sister descending on an early morning party made me fear for the safety of my fellow guests. "And the rest of the kids?"

She waved me off. "There's plenty of my milk in

the fridge, so he'll survive. I'll call a neighbor girl to keep an eye on the mayhem. I want to see you in action. You're always stumbling into excitement, and Placida thrives on exciting events. See you there!"

My driver, Reed Shakespeare, was waiting in the driveway in the predawn darkness when I went tearing outside. He worked for the limousine service Michael owned—one of his many businesses—that had been hired by my newspaper to deliver me to assignments. A part-time college student and barely out of his teens, Reed took his job very seriously. Now experienced with my various moods, especially when I was escaping one of my sisters, he calmly handed me a paper cup of tea—skim milk, no sugar, just the way I liked it—along with the morning newspaper for me to read in the backseat. He opened the rear door for me. He hadn't decided to allow me to sit up front yet, and I was determined to prove myself worthy. But it obviously wasn't going to happen this morning.

"Good morning, Reed. Look, I'm sorry, but we're going to have to take the puppy along."

Reed looked pained.

A small pointed nose poked out of my handbag, and an unholy growl rumbled from the depths of the leather Balenciaga.

Reed said, "You used to say you didn't want a dog. You were really firm about that."

"I couldn't refuse your mother, could I? When you think about it, Reed, you're the reason I have Spike in the first place. You have nobody but yourself to blame."

"You could have refused."

"Refuse your mother? Reed, get real."

Rozalia Shakespeare, a woman of awesome inner strength and a voice perfectly suited to belting spiritual hymns to the highest church balconies, had pushed the puppy into my arms not long after Reed was released from a hospital stay. The bullet that had put him there had been my fault, although his mother felt otherwise. I couldn't refuse her gift.

For months people had been telling me I needed a dog, but I assumed they meant something large, drooling and protective. Instead of a territorial Doberman, however, I was now using my best handbag to carry around a puppy no bigger than a teapot who thought he was a weapon of mass destruction. Spike had a predatory glitter in his slightly cockeyed gaze and a quick and bloodthirsty bite, not to mention other personal habits that made him unpopular with most human beings. After only a month in my possession, he'd sunk a perfect imprint of canine teeth into the left hand of a man I despised and peed on his foot at the same time. Which was the moment I decided to keep him, despite his flaws. Spike, that is, not my old enemy Jamie Scaithe.

But Reed wisely didn't trust the puppy, no doubt because Spike was the offspring of Mrs. Shakespearc's beloved rat terrier–poodle–rattlesnake mix and a legendary neighborhood mongrel that had been featured on Animal Control's Most Wanted list for two years.

Spike popped his head out of my handbag and told Reed in no uncertain terms to back off.

Reed retreated hastily. "That dog is dangerous."

I patted Spike's bristly head and tried to wedge him back into the bag. "He's very sweet when you get to know him."

"I can't ever figure out what you're going to take a shine to," Reed said.

"Can we take him along this morning or not?"

"Do I have a choice?"

"Of course. But any minute my sister will come out here demanding to go with us, so hurry up and decide."

That information galvanized Reed into action, and he opened the car door. "Let's go. Just keep that monster away from me."

I got into the backseat, and Spike climbed out of my bag. He gave me a smiling puppy yawn before nestling in my lap for an angelic snooze.

Reed pulled out of Libby's driveway as if being chased by a rifle-wielding maniac, then drove me out of Bucks County across the back country roads.

Reed had been driving me around for nearly six months, and so far we seemed suited for each other. I wished I could drive myself, but I was still struggling with an annoying tendency to faint at critical moments. I couldn't be trusted behind the wheel, so Reed had a part-time job between taking classes at a community college.

In about half an hour, the sun began to lighten the horizon and we reached the Tri-County Horse Club.

I thanked Reed and left him to study his textbooks in the car. With Spike tucked securely into my handbag, I threaded my way through the expensive cars that had brought their owners out from the Main Line to the bucolic countryside.

I rounded a boxwood hedge and came upon Hadley Pinkham.

He was leaning photogenically on the nearest fence, with the faded autumn hues behind him making the most of his tanned coloring in the early morning light. He wore a rumpled tuxedo that advertised the fact that he hadn't been home yet after a night carousing on the town. He had removed his tie, however, and wrapped his fringed silk scarf rakishly around his neck to keep off the morning chill. His absurdly handsome face was sharply cut with a long, narrow nose, a flexibly cynical mouth and a dash of fair hair that spilled with false boyishness over what he euphemistically called a high forehead. He carried a glass of something amber in his right hand and a slender cigar in the fingertips of the other. With his sleeve pulled back just so, he showed off a wristwatch that cost more than some oceangoing yachts.

Hadley looked me up and down and said, "My God, Nora, you're the only decently dressed woman here. Everyone else makes it look like Ralph Lauren's warehouse just blew up. You look stunning, kitten. Is that a Claude Montana?"

"Yes, thanks, Hadley, you glamour-puss." I'd put on a twelve-year-old jacket bought in Paris during one particularly lush winter of my marriage, along with my faithful black Calvin Klein skirt and a pair of spike-heeled, fawn lace-covered boots that Grandmama Blackbird purchased in 1965 and were, thank heavens, making another miraculous fashion comeback. Underneath it all were my threadbare long johns and a turtleneck sweater from Old Navy. The final look was more Hepburn than horsey, I knew, the kind of fashion juxtaposition Hadley could appreciate. "That's high praise, coming from you."

"Fashion is blood sport, kitten. And you are positively mopping the floors with everyone else. Now say something nice about me, and we're even."

I laughed and kissed his Bijan-scented cheek. "Hadley, you're the most beautiful man here."

"I'm simply oozing sex appeal, aren't I? All right, I'll go into this party if you'll promise not to abandon me to any woman with jewelry that pictures dogs or horses. My God, who is this?"

"Spike. Be careful, he bites."

Hadley sipped from his glass and listened respectfully to Spike's tenor snarl. "If I looked like that, I'd be bad-tempered, too. What kind of dog is it?"

"Today I'm calling him a Romanian weasel hound."

"Well, keep him chained, kitten. He looks hungry. Tell me about you, now. Are you sleeping with anybody these days? It's too boring if you're not."

"I'm not, so you'll have to lie in wait for someone else."

He took my hand and tucked it into the crook of his arm. "You're fibbing. I heard you're dating a menace to society who makes everybody under forty go weak in the knees."

"What about the over-forties?"

"The old folks are all horrified. Now dish, kitten, or I'll be forced to torture you with that god-awful sausage that's always on the buffet at these morning things. Just because the club's board has arteries clogged beyond hope doesn't mean the rest of us have a death wish, right?"

I'd first become aware of Hadley Pinkham in our childhood days at the croquet club where his father and my father crossed mallets and swizzle sticks every season. Even then, Hadley had charmed his way into my cousin Brophy's birthday party because my aunt had secured a real elephant for everyone to ride. To the delight of adults and children, Hadley wrapped a waiter's apron around his head and waved from the howdah like a maharajah, and thereafter Hadley had been a mainstay of my social scene. Now a gay blade about town, he was considered the best dance partner, the most urbane dinner companion and the man at the bar most likely to draw a laugh. Of course, his own swizzle stick didn't perk up for women, but Hadley had something better than sex.

He was *fun*, dammit.

He could talk clothes better than your best girl-friend, sports better than your college boyfriend and art better than your bluestocking grandmother. You could call him up on a Saturday afternoon for a blitz of shoe shopping and tea, but he never wanted to share your dessert. He knew the best people, played the cleverest hand of bridge and frequented the most chichi shops, spas and nightclubs.

And he always, always got through the velvet rope.

"Now, Nora," he said as we approached the wel-come table. "I haven't donated to the cause, so you're going to have to smuggle me in."

In front of us, a gaggle of debutantes was accepting invitation cards to prevent the hunt breakfast from being gate-crashed by marauding suburbanites in jeans and sneakers. I handed over the vellum card I'd re-ceived in the mail. If I had not been a member of the press, I'd have also palmed a discreet envelope containing a donation. As my card was carefully exam-ined for authenticity, Hadley set about charming the girls, who giggled and blushed and never asked to see his invitation. The glass in his hand was a prop, I realized. The girls assumed he'd already been in the party because he had a drink. I couldn't hold back a smile as Hadley bowed to his audience and took my hand again as we slipped into the party, smooth as you please.

"Tell me about your boyfriend, Nora," he said, strolling away in handsome triumph. "Does he make you do deliciously bad things on his waterbed?"

"He's in Inverness at the moment, Hadley. He's gone fishing."

"Oh, Lord, the outdoorsy type! Well, then, I'm not the least bit jealous. My idea of a good time is room service at the Ritz, not standing up to my sporran in a Scottish loch. When are we going to meet him?"

Maybe never, I thought, and my answer must have shown in my face because Hadley laughed. "Afraid we'll eat him for lunch?"

"Not even close," I said.

"How in-ter-esting. Well, it's good to hear you're back in circulation, kitten, whoever the reason. I can now say that I always thought your husband was a shit. Of course, all you Blackbird girls choose the wrong men, which is why you always end up widows, I suppose. I'm sorry he's dead—well, not too sorry—but dying was the best thing he could have done for you."

"Thank you for sharing, Hadley, but forgive me if I don't find that sentiment comforting."

"I tell it like it is, baby." He gave me a placating kiss on my temple. "Now, go forth and have your little fling with the outlaw before you settle down with one of our own kind."

"Nobody is an outlaw," I snapped with more force than I intended.

His eyebrows lifted. "What a good sign! I never saw you get this touchy about your husband."

"Nobody ever felt the need to share idiotic opinions about him when he was alive."

"No? I wonder why not. Well, you suffered in splendid silence, which was heartbreaking for those of us who knew you when you used to hide Miss Markham's dancing slippers. I'm glad to hear you get snippy."

My relationship with my husband was too complicated for me to understand even now, nearly two years after the night his cocaine dealer shot him in a slushy South Philly alley, so I wasn't going to analyze my feelings with the likes of Hadley.

I said, "You're still a juvenile delinquent, Hadley."

He laughed again. "I know! And you love me anyway!"

We rounded more English shrubbery, and he stopped dead, aghast at the building that reared up ahead of us. "Sweet heaven, will you look at the new club? I haven't been here since the renovations. Who hit the lottery?"

Once a rustic farm owned by the Strawcutter family—of the dog-food-fortune Strawcutters, of course—the land had been donated as a tax write-off decades ago to some avid equestrians to create a club where members could play polo, practice their dressage or follow the club's pack of hounds over the countryside. Lately, the club had enjoyed the stock market success of its members, and with a post-dot-com flood of cash, the original fieldstone house had been quadrupled in size and renovated into a full-fledged country club with all the amenities. The resulting castle might have been plucked from Prince Charles's back yard and plopped down in the Pennsylvania meadows, but it had industrial air-conditioning, a massive event kitchen and rooms of every size and configuration for entertaining. And just in case an attacking Norman horde had to be repelled, the central turret sported narrow windows perfect for longbows or cauldrons of boiling oil. Multiple chimneys on either end bespoke massive fireplaces within, perfect for roasting mastodon or warding off chilblains.

On the double doors, a brass plate read TRI-COUNTY HORSE CLUB, EST. 1895, which was an outright lie. The date signified the first time an elderly Strawcutter climbed on a plow horse to chase a neighbor's mutt out of his cornfield.

I said, "I hear they bought the dining room carpet from the old Pressley Hotel. It's sixty feet long."

Hadley stared at the new building. "Talk about contemptuous consumption! Is it true the faucets in the little boys' room cost four thousand apiece?"

I smiled. "What about your house, Hadley? How many gold faucets do you have at the Pinkham Arms?"

He laughed, having dubbed his family's Main Line estate after a crumbling hotel himself. "Well, at least ours are old."

Old, indeed. Five generations of Pinkhams lived the good life thanks to the proceeds of their grandfather's book of stunning photographs of the civil war. George Franklin Pinkham, the famous pioneer photographer and descendant of a fine American landscape painter, had chronicled the battles and aftermath of the war between the states in a book that still— more than one hundred years after Appomattox—appeared on best-seller lists at Christmastime.

Beyond the club's mansion we could see the polo field, the dressage ring and the long twin barns with the cobblestone stable yard running between. A white tent stood at one end, sheltering the festive buffet. Guests already milled in the yard, drinking their spiked coffee from silver handleless cups. Waiters in gray morning coats and white gloves glided among the crowd, warming up their drinks while keeping the hungry ones away from the food until the hunt arrived from the field.

I could see the gathering was primarily people who didn't belong to the club but who came out of their Main Line homes one cold morning every year to claim they'd attended the prestigious annual hunt breakfast. The women—most wearing ungainly and unseasonable hats—were trying not to get their high heels stuck between the Rhode Island cobblestones underfoot. The men, ruddy-faced and falsely hearty, nearly all looked as if they would much rather be on a Palm Beach golf course as long as they were awake at such an ungodly hour on a November Saturday.

Hadley and I remained on the brick path above the yard.

"See what I mean about the clothes?" he asked. "Have you ever seen so much tweed outside the Cotswolds?"

A horn blast split the cold air. As everyone turned to watch, the hunt appeared over the crest of the hill and burst out of the morning mist, the vivid colors of hounds, horses and people brilliant against the fading autumn foliage. The master of the hounds led the tongue-lolling pack, and the members of the hunt followed to the muffled thunder of hooves on turf, sitting triumphantly high in their saddles after a good morning's gallop. The horses, blowing clouds of steam, were magnificent in the morning sunlight. Their coats—black, chestnut and mottled gray—gleamed with glorious sweat. The scarlet coats of the men glowed against the backdrop of frosty ground. The women, in shades of black and crisp navy blue, some even riding sidesaddle with full skirts and handsome bowler hats, seemed to leap from the pages of a romantic picture book. Spotted hounds with their tails still high flowed like a living river around the master. Steel bits jingled, voices called and laughed. The heavy smell of upturned earth and coming snow swept over the crowd.

I said, "Admit it, Hadley. It's a beautiful spectacle."

He drained the last of his drink. "You forget I'm allergic to the picturesque."

As if disagreeing with him, the crowd on the ground burst into spontaneous applause. From my handbag, Spike gave a yip of agreement.

The annual hunt breakfast was an event that both celebrated the beginning of formal hunting at Tri-County and raised money for the local humane society. Years earlier, the club had abandoned hunting live animals and instead dragged a scented bag for the hounds to follow over hill and dale for the sport of the chase. Giving a donation to the humane society seemed a natural extension of their decision to become a bloodless hunt.

For a chaotic half minute, the hounds mingled with the oohing crowd in the stable yard. Then the whip called them back to him, and the pack eagerly went off to their kennel. I could see their building from where I stood. It had been the summer playhouse of some Strawcutter granddaughters back before the crash of '29, making the Tri-County hounds the only dogs in the world who slept in a splendid replica of a Bavarian despot's castle.

"Is Emma riding today?" Hadley asked. "Doing her Sheena, Queen of the Asphalt Jungle imitation? No, I take that back—Emma is everything and more than Sheena."

"Yes, she's here somewhere. I hope to catch her."

Reminded of my secondary purpose for attending the breakfast, I looked for Emma amidst the riders. But the kaleidoscope of people and animals prevented me from catching a glimpse of my wayward younger sister.

Some of the riders dismounted and led their horses off to the barns, while others who didn't stable their animals at the club headed for the cluster of trailers parked near the polo field.

Below us in the yard, a tall, elderly man swung down from his saddle and threw the reins at his private groom, uttering a curse that turned heads.

"Tottie's still working that Boarman charm," Hadley observed.

Thornton "Tottie" Boarman had been master of the hunt for as long as I could remember, but he'd recently stepped down from that illustrious position, citing business obligations. He didn't look too happy about his first hunt as retired master.

Hadley said, "I hear he's got more trouble than his personality these days."

"I heard that, too," I murmured.

Hadley gave me a raised eyebrow. "His margin was called by the stock exchange. He's lost a bundle of his own money, not to mention oodles of dough belonging to his clients. Where did all that cash go? Pretty serious stuff for a man who wouldn't outlive a prison sentence."

"With half the Main Line losing money on his investment schemes, he's probably lucky to still be alive now," I agreed.

Tottie shoved past his groom and marched up the brick walkway toward us, ripping off his top hat as he strode. He was tall, with a vain man's mane of flowing white hair and a prominent knob of a chin. At that moment, his heavy features were set in a tense scowl, bushy white brows practically concealing his steely blue eyes. His boots rang out on the bricks underfoot as he climbed toward us. He had the stiff gait of someone who'd spent many years spurring horses over fences. . . . or kicking his employees around. His reddened fingers ripped at the buttons on his scarlet coat.

"Good morning, Tottie," Hadley sang as the old man approached. "Lovely morning for a ride."

Tottie looked up and frowned deeper. "Pinkham," he rasped in disgust. "The only thing you'd ride shouldn't be seen in the light of day, you pervert. Get out of my way. I've got to take a piss."

Tottie brushed past me as if I were invisible. Thank heavens.

"Don't knock it until you've tried it," Hadley replied mildly. "You okay, Nora?"

I caught my balance on Hadley's arm. "Fine, no thanks to him. You'd think he might make an effort to be likable to the one person in town who definitely didn't lose a fortune on one of his deals."

"Tottie's an equal opportunity bastard. But he'll probably get his comeuppance. Unless he bolts for somewhere sunny that won't extradite him for stealing millions of— Oh, sorry, kitten. Does that cut your heart out?"

"I'm learning to accept that my parents were idiots, Hadley. At least the money they stole came from our trust funds, for the most part, not from anyone else."

"Except for pocket change," Hadley corrected. "I hear they picked a few deep pockets before they— Well, it wasn't your fault. It's just too bad you're a church mouse as a result of their flight to financial freedom. How are you faring in your first job?"

"I'm enjoying it, as a matter of fact. Speaking of which," I said, "I think it's time to get started. Care to join me?"

Chapter 2

We mingled for a bit before my sister Libby chose to make her entrance. I caught sight of her chugging toward us in a monstrous hat bedecked with autumn leaves and, yes, pheasant feathers. Combined with her postpartum bosom, which threatened to jiggle out of her jacket as she steamed up the cobblestones, she made quite a sight.

"Libby!" Hadley looked as affronted by her appearance as an Episcopal preacher who'd accidentally wandered into Hooters. "It's time we had a discussion about birth control."

"Hello, Hadley," she gasped, kissing his proffered cheek. "Thank you for sending the silver spoon for my new baby. You have the most beautiful manners when the mood strikes you."

"I wish I'd sent a diaphragm instead. Is this what childbirth does to you? You look like Dolly Parton just outwrestled a Windsor."

"Up yours," she said, still breathless. "Nora, how can you walk out here in those heels? I'm absolutely crippled by these shoes. Have you seen Emma yet?"

"No, but I'm sure she's here somewhere. She intended to drive her trailer over last night."

"Yes, it's parked right out front. Didn't you see it? And that enormous horse of hers is tied up to the tailgate without his saddle."

"Well, she's probably—"

"I mean, he hasn't been ridden," Libby said with significance. "Obviously Emma didn't go out with the hunt this morning."

Hadley glanced between us. "Unsettling news?"

Nothing should have kept our younger sister from taking her horse, Mr. Twinkles, out onto the field to prove to everyone that, in three counties, they were the boldest, fastest team over fences. I realized Libby wasn't out of breath from walking. She was upset.

"Do you suppose . . . ?" Libby asked.

Our eyes met, and we shared the same thought.

"Tch, tch," said Hadley. "What's Emma done now? Not aiding and abetting an adultery, I hope?"

"Just what the hell do you mean by that?" Libby demanded.

"Or has she been drinking again?"

"Hadley—" I began.

"I saw her at Moonglow last week. She'd had enough vodka to float a Russian submarine."

"Listen to me, you worm," Lilly began.

I stepped between them. I was sure neither one could throw a punch worth ducking, but I wasn't taking chances because I certainly didn't want to get stuck taking care of her children if my sister ended up hospitalized. "It's all right, Hadley. We've been a little concerned about Emma lately, that's all."

"Oh?" he asked. "What's going on?"

"None of your beeswax," Libby said. "Nora, I'm going to look for Em. You can stay with Sir Lance a Little, if you like."

She threw a glare at Hadley and stormed away.

"Well, now," he said.

"Drop it," I advised. "Or you'll be invited to the goddess intervention she has planned."

"How positively obstetrical that sounds. Say no more."

"Good. Shall we get a drink?"

"You read my mind." Before we could stroll into the crowd, however, Hadley's attention was caught by a movement in the shrubbery. He said, "Good heavens, is that a person lurking in the bushes? And what in the world is she doing?"

I followed the inclination of his head and spotted a corduroy-clad figure hiding among yews just a few yards from the walk.

Hadley asked, "Who is it?"

I recognized the woman and sighed. "Gussie Strawcutter."

"What a good example of how money can't buy everything. How much do you suppose she's worth?"

"A few hundred million," I guessed, feeling a rush of sympathy for Augusta Strawcutter. She had been saddled with the unfortunate nickname Gussie at an early age, when she had been precious enough to carry it off. But now she was the most socially inept woman I knew, and was often called "Gloomy Gus" by even her closest acquaintances. Seeing her once again standing wistfully on the edge of a party made my heart twist.

"Well, surely she could buy herself a decent haircut. But maybe she's trying to appeal to her customers."

"Hadley, you are a very naughty man."

Gussie Strawcutter, heiress to the Strawcutter dog food fortune, would eventually become one of the wealthiest women on the East Coast. Although Gussie didn't look capable of managing her own hair, let alone a national conglomerate, she was reportedly assuming more and more of the company's affairs as her father, locked away in an institution now, slowly succumbed to Alzheimer's disease.

I took a longer look at her crouching behind the tree and decided maybe Hadley was right. She did look a bit like a Chow Chow. A whoosh of reddish-gold hair stood out from her head in a frizzy halo, and her underslung jaw and wide mouth lent a certain canine pugnaciousness to her face. I felt Spike stir in my handbag and clamped it shut, just in case he felt the urge to attack.

"Isn't she our age?" Hadley asked. "I vaguely remember her in an etiquette class my mother forced me to attend."

"I can't imagine you ever needed an etiquette class, Hadley."

"I spilled some wine between courses when I was seven or eight, so it was off to learn how to mind my manners with Monsieur Muumuu, that ghastly fat Frenchman who always wore caftans—remember him? Poor Gussie was hopeless even then. I think she threw up during the lesson on seafood forks."

"Let's go talk to her, Hadley. Put on your good behavior, please."

I thought our footsteps might have warned Gussie of our approach, but she spun around at last and gasped at finding us so close.

"Oh!" She pushed her glasses up on her nose and blushed.

I saw at once that she had been crying. "Gussie, are you hurt?"

She shook hr head and dashed the tears from her face. "I'm fine. Nothing's wrong."

"But—"

"Really, I'm fine. Just some dust in my eye, that's

all." Desperate to come up with the correct greeting, she tried them all in a rush. "Hello, good morning, what a nice day, thank you for coming."

Hadley blinked at the denim skirt and bulky corduroy jacket that bunched up on her behind and did no favors for Gussie's square, athletic figure. "Gussie, dear, does that coat actually have a plaid lining?"

"Stuff it, Hadley. Gussie, the club looks unbelievable. Your family must be astonished by the changes."

"What? Oh, the changes, yes."

"How long ago did your family donate this property to the club?"

"My great-grandfather got rid of it. It was a drain on our resources."

Family history was obviously less important to the Strawcutters than to my family.

I tried again to draw her out. "Do you often visit here?"

"Not much."

"But your husband hunts, doesn't he?"

Gussie knew she was failing a social quiz. Nervously, she tried to smile, which revealed poppy seeds in her teeth. "Yes, he loves horses."

Her husband, Rush, was everything Gussie was not—sweet-tempered and attractive in a gangly, geek-grown-up kind of way. He had a shy smile and usually traveled with a motley pack of small dogs he'd adopted. Rushton Strawcutter was also unusual because he had taken the last name of his wife's family upon marriage. Since the Strawcutters were synonymous with dog food nationwide and Rush had enthusiastically plunged into the family business, it seemed logical for him to ditch his own name to join the Strawcutter clan. With all the personality Gussie lacked, he was probably a welcome addition to the company.

"I haven't seen Rush yet today," I said, still trying to coerce Gussie into a conversation. "Did he enjoy the hunt this morning?"

"I don't know. I—I'll go look for him."

"It's hopeless," Hadley muttered out of the corner of his mouth.

"I didn't mean— Wait, I'll go with you, Gussie."

She blushed again and turned away. "Oh, no, no. I'll go by myself."

With a little gasp that might have been a strangled sob, she rushed away toward the barns.

"How can a woman with so many advantages be such a loser?"

"You're heartless, Hadley. I've never seen her so emotional."

"I know. She actually had some personality for once."

"I'm going after her."

"Then this is where we part ways, because I'm dying for a drink. Bye, kitten. Mention me in the newspaper."

Hadley strolled away. Spike finally succeeded in wrestling his head out of my handbag and gave Hadley a parting snarl. I gripped his collar and held tight.

Gussie Strawcutter had hurried off through the crowd and disappeared, so I took a deep breath and plunged into the party. Time to get to work on my article for the paper. Spike peered out from under my elbow, doing his best impression of a moray eel lurking for unsuspecting prey.

In spite of the cold morning, people seemed to be enjoying themselves. I saw flushed faces and plates of breakfast treats circulating. Friends called my name, and I joined their group. Jane Frampton and her brother Donald, treasurer of the humane society and avid dalmatian fancier, were full of high spirits and demanded to know what had become of me since I'd last seen them at the autumn zoo fund-raiser. We chatted, and I asked about Donald's involvement in today's event. He filled me in on details. I made notes with pad and pen.

Then Donald guided me through some milling horses to the petite woman who'd organized the breakfast. Thomasina Silk was as cool as a martini in the midst of entertaining nearly two hundred people and scores of horses. A veteran horsewoman who had given up riding after breaking her back in a legendary fall at the Devon Horse Show, a healed but frail Thomasina didn't ride anymore. She bred quality Hanoverian jumpers and was the behind-the-scenes powerhouse at Tri-County. Dressed in a ladylike knee-length tweed skirt and fitted jacket with a discreet show of lace at the collar and cuffs, she finished checking the forelegs of a noble-looking beast and dismissed him with a hearty slap on the rump. Dusting off her hands, she gave me the lowdown on the fund-raiser.

"What kind of dog is that?" Thomasina squinted at Spike when he displayed his teeth with diabolical flair. "A wire fox? Jack Russell?"

"A miniature pit bull," I told her, straight-faced. "Not recognized by the kennel club yet."

"Not very friendly, is he?" Her brows pinched suspiciously. "Are you taking him to obedience class?"

"I've been a little busy."

She shook her head and reached into her pocket for a business card. "If you don't make an effort now, you'll regret it for the rest of his life. Call me at that number and I'll set you up with a trainer I know. She's the best for hopeless cases."

"Thanks."

Thomasina grabbed my arm just in time to yank me out of the way of a huge chestnut horse that lunged at the end of the reins held by a pixie hardly big enough to reach his massive shoulders.

"Sorry!" The girl laughed, her gimlet eyes still alight with the excitement of the hunt. "Come on, Genghis!"

It was Merrie Naftzinger, I realized, all grown up since I'd attended her eighth birthday party at the Four Seasons a few years ago. She wore a bowler hat and sported blue rubber bands on her braces.

An idea hit me.

"Merrie," I said, "how about having your picture taken for the newspaper? You and Genghis?"

"Hi, Miss Blackbird! Sure, you can take our picture. If I can get him to stand still a minute."

Thomasina stepped forward with a businesslike air that Genghis recognized immediately. I dashed off to find the *Intelligencer* photographer, and by the time we came back, Genghis was standing at attention and Merrie looked flushed and pleased. I herded Thomasina and Donald into the photo, too, and in seconds the deed was done. I thanked the photographer and everyone concerned, reserving special attention for Merrie.

"Come see my dad," she said. "He's over in the barn."

Keeping a safe distance from Genghis's lethal-looking hind legs, I followed Merrie across the cobblestones to the east wing of the barn. We skirted groups of people and various heaps of riding gear that cluttered the walkway. Canvas chairs stood outside most of the stalls, with thermoses and heavy clothing in evidence. Some horses were already stabled, and put their heads out of the Dutch doors to watch the action. Riders busily attended their mounts. The scents of sawdust, saddle soap and exertion overpowered the cold air.

Tim Naftzinger was stripping off his mud-spattered scarlet coat, obviously having just finished cleaning up his horse.

I had first met Tim years ago when he'd been a medical school classmate of my late husband, who had introduced Tim even then as "one of the good guys." Now Dr. Naftzinger was a respected pediatrician, and I knew he was destined for great things. We hadn't seen much of each other in the last two years, which had been no accident. Tim felt guilty, I think, for not saving my husband from the drug life. I couldn't help feeling the same way, despite all the friends who urged me to believe I couldn't have made a difference when my husband turned into a cocaine-burning comet that blazed off on a trajectory to oblivion.

Tim saw me behind Merrie and went still. "Nora," he said, a nanosecond too late. "Great to see you."

"Hi." I put my hand out to shake his. "I just commandeered your daughter for a newspaper photo. I hope you don't mind."

He managed a smile. "Not a bit. I hope she didn't break the camera."

"Da-ad!" Merrie laughed and disappeared into the next stall with her horse.

"Merrie's all grown up," I said. "She's going to be tall, just like her father."

"Fortunately, the rest of her looks come from her mom."

I smiled, too, but felt a pang. "How is Caroline?"

Tim shrugged. "About the same."

His wife's coma had lasted almost a year now, I calculated. They had been skiing, and she'd skidded on ice and struck a tree. Tim still looked as shell-shocked as he had at the beginning of his ordeal.

I said, "I went to see her in August. I just sat and talked for an hour."

"That was nice. Thanks."

There must have been a time when Tim and I could make conversation. Maybe we had talked about the med school softball tournament or whether we should go sailing on the weekend or maybe run up to New York to see a play. I couldn't remember. Before Merrie was born, Caroline collected early pewter, and I occasionally tagged along with her to estate sales. We'd meet our husbands at the end of the day for cozy dinners. But eventually Todd became unreliable and Tim had checked his watch often at our restaurant tables, while Caroline talked with too much vivacity to cover my pain and embarrassment. Merrie's birth had given Caroline and Tim a graceful excuse to stop our weekend socializing altogether, and when Todd died, essentially so had our relationship.

Now, with both our spouses gone, there seemed nothing to talk about without bleeding all over each other.

Merrie bounded out of the stall and clipped a nylon web in place of the door. She put her bowler in her teeth and struggled to get a scrunchie around her ponytail.

I went over and took the hat from her mouth. "Here, let me help. Did you have a great ride today?"

"Wonderful! Genghis went over every fence, even the coop. Did you see us, Dad?"

"Sure did, Mer. You looked like a pro."

"All those lessons with Emma are really paying off. Do you ride, Miss Blackbird? Like your sister?"

"Nobody rides like Emma."

Tim laughed. "Nora was the one who fell off her pony in the middle of Orchard Pond once."

"I'm still thawing out," I told Merrie. "Has Emma been teaching you to play poker as well as jump fences?"

She finished her ponytail with a flourish. "No, just working on my riding. She's been great, hasn't she, Dad?"

"Yes," said Tim.

I said, "She hasn't made you ride Mr. Twinkles yet, has she?"

"Oh, no, he's too wild for me. But we've been working with Genghis." She gave her horse's nose an affectionate rub. "Dad says we won't have to sell him to the glue factory after all."

Tim smiled.

To me, Merrie said, "Emma says he might be ready for eventing next summer. She's going to take us around in her trailer. That is, if Dad says it's okay."

"We'll see," said Tim, making no promises. "Are you ready for some breakfast?"

"I'm starving!"

"Me, too," said her father. He slid his arm affectionately across Merrie's shoulders. "Finish taking care of Genghis, and we'll eat."

Merrie looked at me. "Would you like to come with us?"

Tim stiffened almost imperceptibly.

"Actually, I should go talk to more people."

"Okay, maybe we'll catch you in the tent."

When she dashed into the box stall, I said to Tim, "She's a delightful kid."

He didn't meet my eye, but continued to untangle a bridle. "Yeah, she's great."

"I'm glad Emma's been able to work with her. Sounds as if they get along really well."

"I'm just glad Merrie's learning how to ride safely. It's a dangerous sport."

Of course Tim would be concerned about his daughter's well-being. He, more than most anyone, knew how fast life could change. "I'm sure Emma takes every precaution."

"Emma's been wonderful," he said.

"I hear you've been nominated for Chief of Pediatrics at your hospital. Congratulations."

"Oh. Yes. I'm one of several nominees."

"Good luck. I'm sure you're the man for the job."

Neither of us had a chance to say anything more.

We heard screaming.

From the direction of the other stable wing came shouts for help and one long, hysterical, babbling shriek. Tim and I turned together and Spike wriggled his head out of my bag.

He barked when he saw Libby stumble into view.

Rushing toward us, she looked dreadful. Windblown and terrified, she'd lost her hat somewhere, but one of the pheasant feathers was sticking out of her hair. She screamed as if she'd been stabbed.

I ran to Libby and caught her shoulders. "What's wrong? What's happened?"

She gasped. "Come quick."

She grabbed my arm and I went with her, my heart slamming in my chest. I heard Tim and Merrie behind us, and we all ran across the stable yard.

A cluster of people had already gathered outside a stall door. By the way they were bumping into each other and rushing around, I could see something was very wrong. There was shouting, and someone called for an ambulance. Libby shoved through the crowd, dragging me with her. Someone tried to bar our way, but Libby gave him a push and he gave up. We blundered inside the stall.

A knot of people were bent over a figure in the fresh straw.

On the other side of the stall, Emma lay flat out, her booted legs spread at a vulgar angle, her clothing dirty, her beautiful face completely blank and very white. Blood smeared her hands and jeans.

"Oh, God," I said. "Please, no."

I don't remember how I reached her body, but I went down on my knees in the straw and felt for her pulse. Her head lolled away from my hand. Spike jumped out of my handbag and seized Emma's shirt-sleeve in his teeth. He began to yank. Behind me, Libby went into hysterics.

With probing fingertips, I found a pulse in Emma's throat. When I called her name, she did not respond. Spike let go of her sleeve and began to yap.

Inches from her hand in the straw, as if dropped when she had passed out, glittered her silver flask. Libby snatched it up. The cap was missing. The flask was empty.

"She's not dead," Libby prayed above me. "She's not dead, she's not dead."

Farther away in the straw lay Emma's riding crop. She had taped the handle to fit her grip, and I recognized it. The leather looked wet and dark.

Suddenly, Tim was there. He shouldered me aside and knelt in the straw, reaching competently to help my sister. He called her name and smacked her cheek with enough force to make me gasp. But I thought I saw Emma's eyes roll back in her head. I put my hands on her shoulders and shook her. "Em!"

Over Libby's sobbing, I heard other people arrive. Someone pulled me to my feet to give Tim room to work. A voice began talking to 911 on a cell phone, and the stall started to spin around me. The air was very hot and hard to breathe.

Thomasina Silk came over, agitated and very white. "Tim. Tim, it's Rush Strawcutter. I think he's dead."

I tried to draw a breath and couldn't.

"Tim!" Thomasina tried again. "Did you hear me? There's blood everywhere. He's been hit in the head. I think Rush is dead."

Still bent over Emma, Tim said, "Then I can't do anything for him."

"What about Emma?" I said.

Tim looked up at me, but he seemed to telescope to a distant place. "Hold her," he said to someone far away. "She's fainting."

A black wave slammed over me and I was swept away.

Chapter 3

At the hospital, the ER staff immediately whisked Emma into a treatment room. Libby and I were escorted more slowly to another cubicle, where a young nurse and a doctor with a goatee fussed over me. While they tried to determine the cause of my faint, a patient-care representative brought frequent updates on Emma's condition. Alcohol poisoning was the most serious concern.

"They're pumping her stomach," was the first report.

"She's coming around a little."

Then, "The doctor's with her. She's awake and talking."

And finally, "Your sister's quite a handful, isn't she?"

I felt as if I'd been hit by a truck. The weight of calamity was so heavy it made me dizzy, and I could barely sit up. Surprising the hell out of me, my sister Libby pulled herself together first and spoke firmly to my doctor.

"She faints all the time. It's nothing new and nothing serious."

"Any loss of consciousness is serious."

"Not with Nora. She's very tenderhearted. It's all emotional. I'm emotional too, of course, but my constitution is stronger. I had a baby just a few weeks ago, and you don't see me looking wan, do you?"

"Certainly not."

The doctor had an earring as well as the neat goatee. He had slender hands, too, and he toyed with a Cross pen as he contemplated the state of Libby's health. He said, "You're vibrant."

"Vibrant!" Libby smiled, and her hand strayed unconsciously to the upper slope of the Himalayas barely contained by her jacket. "What a charming word. You're charming, Dr. Quartermaine."

"And you," he responded solemnly, "are enchanting."

"Oh, my goodness! Look at me, I'm leaking again!" She clutched her breasts and blushed. "I can't help myself sometimes. It's so embarrassing, but I can't stop the flow—"

"It's quite natural," the doctor said calmly, but I thought I detected a quiver in his pointed beard as he passed her a handful of tissues.

She stuffed them into her bra to stop the torrent of milk. Any minute she was going to start telling him about her personal goddess, so I said, "I'm fine, too. I don't need coddling."

But Libby began acting like Florence Nightingale. "Let me take care of her, Dr. Quartermaine. I know just how to settle her nerves."

The doctor listened attentively and approved of her plan.

Libby insisted on taking me to her favorite spa.

"Don't be ridiculous," I objected when we were alone again. "I'll be fine in five minutes. It's just a stupid fainting spell."

"That handsome doctor says to get you out of here."

"For God's sake, stop acting like you want to play with his stethoscope. I'm not leaving Emma."

"You can't take care of Emma if you're a mess yourself," she argued. "Now, come on."

I was woozy and in no shape to make decisions for myself, and Reed was completely bulldozed by my sister's imperious commands, so the spa is where we ended up. Reed pitied me so much that he took charge of Spike.

At The Pink Windowbox, Libby helped me get undressed and into a plush cotton candy-colored robe. I felt like Camille when she guided me to a table behind a large potted plant in the corner of the spa's serenely pink dining room. In minutes, Libby had the whole staff scurrying to take care of us. A pot of herb tea was rushed to our table. Libby frowned over the lunch menu and ordered me a grapefruit and a piece of broiled fish with lemon. For herself, she requested a chicken quesadilla with extra cheese and a beer. "Because I'm nursing," she announced to the waitress.

"No kidding," said the girl, who from her perspective had a breathtaking view of Libby's cleavage.

"No tip," Libby warned.

When the waitress hurried away, I said, "Libby, this is completely ridiculous. I'm not an invalid."

"You're as pale as paper. Besides, I can't take care of Emma, so I'll take care of you instead. I have a motherly nature. You can't fight instinct."

"We should be with Emma."

Libby poured tea for me. "Dr. Quartermaine said it would be better to come back when Emma's fully conscious."

I planted my elbows on the table and put my head in my hands. I couldn't even fake normalcy. "Oh, God."

Libby softened and gave my elbow a shake. "Let's get you healthy. Then we'll think of a way to help Emma."

The waitress came, and Libby received her beer with pleasure.

When we were alone again, I said, "This is very bad, Lib. Rush Strawcutter is dead, and Emma had blood all over her."

"I know."

Libby took a slug of her beer and glanced around the restaurant to make sure nobody could overhear us. Then she leaned closer and dropped her voice to a whisper. "I spoke to Emma for just a minute in the emergency room. She doesn't remember anything. She'd been drinking last night, and she passed out. She told me that much before the police showed up."

I had just swallowed a sip of tea, and the mention of police made me choke on it. Libby gave me a karate chop between my shoulder blades.

"Yes, the police," she said when I had myself under control again. "What did you expect? Rushton is dead, and it wasn't an accident, either. He'd been hit on the head."

"By whom?"

We looked at each other.

"No," I said. "Even drunk, she'd never."

Libby didn't answer, and I wobbled to my feet. "I need a telephone."

"What for?"

"I'll be right back."

When I returned from the spa lobby, I sat down at the table and pulled the pink robe closer around my shoulders. Shivering, I wrapped both hands around my teacup. I felt as if I'd barely survived an earthquake.

"Well?" Libby asked.

"I called a lawyer." My teeth rattled against the rim of the teacup, so I put it down again. "Emma's in a lot of trouble."

We both sat, thinking about our little sister.

We had tried. Libby and I had both talked to her in recent weeks, to try making her see that drinking wasn't an answer to her pain. But Emma hadn't slowed her headlong downhill plunge long enough to listen to a single word. Mind you, we'd all three lost husbands. Libby had even buried two. It was the curse of Blackbird women. But in the two years since her husband had been killed in a car accident, Emma had tried every way she could think of to forget the man who'd been her soul mate. Lately, she'd taken to alcohol.

The only thing clear in Emma's mind was that she didn't want anyone's help—not from her sisters or the various men who followed her around like fraternity boys on the trail of the campus bad girl.

"Oh, stop," she had ordered me with disdain when I broached the subject. "I'm in control."

She wasn't even close.

And with history having a tendency to repeat itself, I was terrified of losing my sister as well as my own husband.

Drinking tea, I tried to imagine how we were going to get through the next few days. I needed an expert strategist to think it through.

"One of Mr. Abruzzo's lawyers?" Libby asked.

"What?"

"You called one of Mr. Abruzzo's mob lawyers?"

"He's not— Yes, as a matter of fact. He's going to the hospital now. He'll make sure Emma is protected."

The waitress brought our food, the sight of which made my stomach sour.

Libby began tearing apart her quesadilla. "One weird thing."

"Yes?"

"There was a big white envelope in Rush's hand."

I stared at her. "What?"

Libby ravenously bit the corner off a wedge of cheese-packed tortilla. "While the paramedics checked you out, I looked at Rush. He was in the straw, just like Emma, except there was— Well, he was a mess, let me tell you. Normally, I have a tender stomach for gore, but Placida must have been with me. They hadn't moved the body yet, and I saw it—a white envelope. Kinda squished, but I noticed it." She licked melted cheese from her thumb.

I tried to understand what she was telling me. "What kind of envelope? You mean like the invitation? Or a Christmas card? A utility bill?"

She took a more ladylike nibble. "No, more of an oversized envelope, maybe eight-by-ten, like a small-ish manila envelope, only it wasn't manila. It was white. I noticed it because it was an unusual thing to see in a horse barn. I mean, there was Rush, dressed for fox hunting, except he had this nice white—"

"Had he gone hunting?" I asked. "Could you tell if he'd been riding?"

Libby frowned. She was an artist, and I trusted her to remember visual details. At last she shook her head. "No. He was wearing his riding clothes, but they were clean. And he was still wearing his street shoes."

Fox hunters, we knew, rarely drove their cars wearing their best riding boots.

Emma, I recalled, hadn't changed into her formal riding habit. She'd been wearing jeans.

I said, "Was it Rush's blood all over Emma? Or was she cut anywhere?"

Libby shook her head. "Just her mouth and a little around her eye—not enough to cause all that blood. That doesn't mean it was Rush's. Don't think negatively, Nora. It's bad karma."

"But it's logical. What about her riding crop? Did you see it in the straw?"

"Yes. Nobody touched it until the police came. They took it immediately."

I didn't want to think about what Emma's riding crop had been used for. "Does Emma even know Rush? Were they friends?"

Libby slid her eyes sideways at me. "Are you asking me if she was sleeping with him?"

"Oh, for God's sake, Lib—"

"Emma has a gazillion boyfriends. It's not out of the question that she and Rush—"

"He's married. She wouldn't date a married man."

"She hasn't been herself lately. In a lot of ways."

I pierced a tiny bite of fish with my fork but didn't raise it to my mouth. In the center of our table, a soft candle flickered. A barely audible strain of Mozart wafted in the air. Around us, The Pink Windowbox oozed comfort and luxury. But I didn't feel remotely relaxed. My brain was humming.

"What do you know about Rush Strawcutter?" I asked.

"Only that he married Gussie, which was odd. Nobody ever thought Gussie could snare a man. Didn't they meet at a big dog show? I remember hearing something like that. She was there as a sponsor and he was . . . I forget. They fell in love over basset hounds, didn't they?"

"I don't think Gussie likes any kind of dog."

"Oh, right, that was the joke. Their company makes dog food, but Strawcutters don't have pets."

"Until Rush came long. He always has—had—a few

pound puppies with him. They rode around in his station wagon."

Libby drank more beer. "I bet Gussie dumps them at the humane society before nightfall. She always struck me as the heartless type."

"That's a mean thing to say. Poor Gussie."

"But what an odd couple. She's such a schlub, but I always thought Rush had a winning quality."

"Oh, heavens, you didn't make a pass at him, did you?"

"He wasn't my type. And he was married, after all." A crumb of quesadilla tumbled down the curve of her bosom and disappeared into the bottomless crevasse. Libby glanced down and wisely decided a rescue effort was hopeless.

I tried to recall seeing Gussie and Rush together. Plenty of men had made a run at Gussie over the years, of course. With the Strawcutter fortune behind her, she was an obvious catch. Gussie rejected them all. But Rushton had gone more slowly than the others, I remembered, and somehow he'd won her over.

"They had the longest engagement on record," Libby said. "Four years, maybe. It probably took that long to soften up Gussie. Remember?"

"And at first he was reluctant to take a job with Strawcutter Industries, right?"

"He probably didn't want to look like a gold digger. What's the male equivalent of a gold digger? Well, Rush took the job, after all, so what does it matter?" Libby chowed down on her lunch.

I put my fork on my plate. No matter how he'd started at Strawcutter Industries, Rush had worked hard. He hadn't chafed under working for his wife, either, as Gussie's father gradually let go of the business.

Libby noticed me mulling over what I knew and suddenly looked intrigued. "Is this how you detect a murder, Nora?"

"I'm just thinking. I'm trying to imagine why Rush might have been killed. Somebody's usually upset over a family issue or money, according to Michael."

"Well, he would know."

I snapped my fingers. "Lately, Rush had started up his own company. Do you know anything about it?"

"Yes, it's a chain of pet stores and shampoo parlors."

"Laundro-Mutt," I said, remembering at last. "Has it been a success?"

"I haven't the faintest idea. I wash my dog with a hose in the driveway."

"Does Rushton have any partners? Anybody who might be involved in his business?"

"Just Gussie, I suppose. That is, if she loosened the family purse strings enough to invest in Rush's idea. I hear she's a tightwad like her father."

Family *and* money, I thought. Add passion, and I had a trifecta of murder motives.

Our waitress appeared beside the table then. "Is everything all right, ladies?"

"I'd like another beer," said Libby. "Do you have Guinness?"

The waitress painstakingly wrote down Libby's request. "There's someone who'd like to speak with you. I told him it's against our policy. We try to keep a serene atmosphere in the dining room, but—"

"Who is it?" I asked, but I had already guessed.

A young man in a black trenchcoat approached our table.

I cinched my pink robe tightly around my waist. Libby sat back in her chair, however, allowing her robe to fall gently open from her bosom. She put one hand to her throat in a classic Marilyn Monroe gesture. Even her hair was lasciviously mussed.

"Detective Bloom," I said. "Somehow I knew you'd turn up."

Libby looked completely relaxed, but I knew every molecule in her body had just vibrated to attention.

Benjamin Bloom stopped beside our table and proceeded to do a plausible imitation of a Little Leaguer accidentally barging into the wrong locker room.

"Hi, there," said Libby.

Bloom glanced between the two of us, scantily wrapped in pink robes, and he fought down a blush. The detective wore a neatly pressed coat over a sweater, wrinkle-free khakis and clean white sneakers. Sometimes I wondered if he still lived with his mother. He had liquid brown eyes in a narrow, trustworthy face. Unfortunately, I'd discovered he wasn't as trustworthy as he appeared, especially when he wanted information that might boost his career out of the sleepy suburbs and into a big-city homicide squad. When he wanted details on a crime, he could be as relentless as a jackhammer.

He had an interesting mouth and a lithe body, however, which Libby noticed right away. Surely she also noticed that he was considerably younger than herself, but that didn't seem to matter. She smiled, transparent as cellophane in her need to be desired by the only man in radar range. Plus, she looked as if she could actually cause a man with a breast fascination to collapse of a heart attack.

I wanted to kick her.

"Hi." Bloom avoided intense exposure to the searing rays of my sister's sexuality by looking straight into my eyes. "Feeling okay? I heard you fainted."

"I'm fine," I said briskly. "Do you remember my sister? Libby Kintswell. Libby, this is—"

"Yes, I know," she said. "We've met."

She slipped her hand in his, as if expecting him to kiss her fingertips.

He did not. Instead, Detective Bloom tried to shake her hand without actually looking at her. He had encountered my sister before, of course, during the investigation into Rory Pendergast's death just a few months earlier. Bloom looked as enthusiastic about renewing his acquaintance with Libby as he might with an amorous anaconda.

"Mrs. Kintswell, my superior would like to speak with you."

Libby's brows flew up. "Why?"

"You were nearby when Rushton Strawcutter's body was discovered, ma'am. We need to get information from you while it's still fresh in your mind."

"Where is your superior? Is he here?"

"She," Bloom corrected, "has asked me to take you to our office."

Libby suppressed her disappointment admirably. "Now?"

"As soon as you get dressed."

"Oh. Well, all right, but I'll need to pump first. If you'll excuse me?"

She departed in a flourish of naked skin glimpsed beneath her robe.

Detective Bloom frowned. "She lifts weights?"

"She's not pumping iron," I said. "She's— Well, you don't want to know."

"I hate to say it, but she scares me."

"You have good instincts." I checked my watch and calculated how soon the baby would need his next meal. I hoped the baby-sitter could convince him to take a bottle, but quickly lectured myself that Libby could handle her own child care without my intervention for once.

Bloom sat down in her vacated chair. "I just came from the hospital. Your sister Emma—"

"Is she all right?"

I must have looked frightened, because he put both hands up as if to stop a speeding car. "She's going to be okay. We'd like to talk to her, but a guy turned up who claims to be her lawyer. I gather you called him?"

"Yes."

"Well, you did her a favor. He's refusing to allow anyone but medical staff within ten feet of his client. In the meantime, I hope you can answer some questions."

I knew what was coming. This would not be the first time Detective Bloom had asked for my input in a murder investigation. He'd previously used my connections to a social circle that was foreign to him, and as a result he'd received two letters of merit in his official record.

"What can I do to help?"

He turned sideways in his chair. From that position he had a good view of my bare legs, which he tried not to inspect for more than five seconds. "You okay?" he asked. "Really?"

"I'm worried about my sister. And upset about Rush Strawcutter, of course."

Bloom opened his notebook but didn't need to refer to his scribbles. "Rushton Strawcutter was killed by at least three blows to the head from a blunt object."

Oddly enough, I didn't find death by blunt object nearly as horrifying as death by gunshot. Calmly, I asked, "Could he have been kicked by a horse?"

Bloom shook his head. "It was something small."

"Libby said you found a riding crop in the straw."

"Is that what it's called? It was a small whip. I was surprised that it had such a heavy handle. Like there's steel in it."

Years ago when I'd done a little riding myself, I had carried a crop—sometimes known as a riding stick—and knew it had a loaded grip on one end and a light tasseled whip at the other. "But surely it wasn't heavy enough to kill someone."

"Maybe not," he agreed. "The injuries were severe."

"Do you know when it happened?"

"Early this morning—probably between three and four A.M."

"Before the fox hunt began."

"Yes."

"Why didn't anybody see them earlier?"

"It was an empty stall, not used for a horse lately. Somebody went looking for extra straw after the hunt and found him."

"Have you started questioning everyone at the hunt breakfast?"

He nodded. "We took names and will be in touch with most everyone eventually."

"You didn't keep everyone at the club? When Rory Pendergast was killed, you didn't allow people to leave for hours."

"This situation is a little different."

I took a deep breath. "You believe Emma did it."

"Now, let's not start—"

"Please don't patronize me. She was found nearby and was covered with blood, I know. And that was her riding crop."

"We're doing everything according to procedure. Everything's going to the city forensics lab, and we've got a team going through the barn now. But suddenly looking for a needle in a haystack doesn't sound so funny." He hesitated. "I won't lie to you, Nora. It looks pretty bad for your sister."

I didn't realize I'd been weeping until he passed the handkerchief from his pocket. I pressed it to my eyes and tried to think sensibly.

At last, I said, "What about the envelope found with Rush's body?"

"How— Did you touch it?"

"No, Libby saw it."

He frowned. "Well, we're looking at it, of course."

"What was inside?"

He hesitated, then obviously decided not to answer my question. "Let's focus on what you know. What can you tell me about Strawcutter? How come he goes by that name?"

"His father-in-law insisted when Rushton married Gussie Strawcutter. It's not as uncommon in certain circles as you think, especially when a family line is going to die out. Gussie is an only child. There's a dynasty to consider."

"A dynasty, huh? How did Rushton feel about changing his name to join a dynasty?"

I pictured Rush in my mind. He had been tall and a little gawky, with floppy brown hair and a ready smile. "I didn't know him well, but Rush always seemed happy."

"Marrying into several hundred million dollars, who wouldn't be happy? Except his wife isn't exactly the prettiest girl on the block. Or the smartest."

"You're wrong. She's brilliant," I corrected. "Don't be fooled. Gussie has been her father's right hand for many years and can read a bottom line better than most thousand-dollar-an-hour tax attorneys, which I believe is what she studied in college. She's extremely smart, just not good with people."

"You have to be good with people to run a big company."

"Her father had social grace in spades. Now that his role in the company has diminished, I think Rush was starting to supply the people skills. He was sweet and even-tempered. He genuinely loved animals, and people respond to that—especially in their business."

"Maybe that's what drew him to his wife," Bloom said dryly.

"Are you calling her a dog, Detective?"

"Take it easy. Does your sister Emma know the Strawcutters as well as you do?"

I stiffened.

Emma and Rush were undoubtedly acquainted from the Tri-County Horse Club. Although Emma didn't have the kind of money it took to belong to the club, she was often an invited guest because of her horsemanship. She frequently coached people who wanted to improve their riding, especially new people just getting started riding to hounds. New people like Rush, perhaps.

I said, "I don't know if they knew each other at all."

"I hear Emma has relationships with a lot of guys."

"She likes the company of men," I said carefully. "Emma is young and single. She's allowed to have a social life."

"Does she tangle with married men a lot?"

"As far as I know, never."

Bloom gave me an assessing look. "You're not as informative as you've been in the past."

"Can you blame me?"

"It's okay," he said smoothly. "I don't think we're going to need you on this one, anyway."

I felt a zing of anger. "Because you think you've already got the killer? Look, if you think I'm going to stand around waiting for you to convict my sister when I know she certainly didn't kill anyone—"

"How do you know?"

"She just wouldn't, that's all."

"Even under the influence of alcohol?"

I took a deep breath.

"She's got a problem with booze," Bloom said.

"She's been drinking more than usual these last couple of months, yes, but she's still getting over the death of her husband."

"She was married to that football star, Jake Kendall, I hear. That must have been quite an experience. How long has it been since he died?"

"Two years," I said shortly. "Emma was in the car, too, and suffered severe injuries."

Combined with a recent broken arm just a few months earlier, Emma still hadn't worked her way back to riding at the top-notch level required of a Grand Prix competitor. The emotional and physical toll of the last two years had been very hard. In fact, I couldn't remember the last time I'd seen Emma entirely sober. The realization unnerved me.

"Emma's had a lot of problems," I admitted finally. "She's doing her best to get her life back on track."

"Jake was a pretty famous guy. I still see reruns of some of his great plays. Too bad he never made the Super Bowl. He had a lot of potential, even with all the drinking he did." Bloom continued to observe me. "Does your sister still go to football games, or has she just tried to forget?"

"You're trying to trick me into confiding more, Detective, and there's nothing to confide. Emma might be an emotional mess, but she's not a killer."

Bloom closed his notebook without writing down a single word. Softly, he said, "I hope you're right. But forgive me if I don't have much faith in your judgement."

I felt a lecture coming.

He said, "You have a history of trusting the wrong kind of people, Miss Blackbird."

"We're not talking about Emma now, are we?"

"I hear Abruzzo took a powder."

I should have guessed Bloom had more than just an open-and-shut murder investigation on his mind. He had obviously decided this case was going to be easy, and he was looking around for something more promising to work on. He had a lot of ambition, and dabbling in organized crime cases might attract the attention of his superiors.

More calmly than I felt, I said, "Michael is on a vacation."

"You're sure it's a vacation?"

"He hasn't run away from anything, if that's what you mean."

"When's he coming back?"

"I don't know."

Bloom and Michael shared a past that started in juvenile court and concluded with some jailhouse justice that left Michael serving a longer sentence and Bloom finally making his way into the police academy. Neither man had spoken of the details to me, and I had not asked to hear the story. I only knew there was no love lost between them.

Bloom said, "When he gets back, there'll be a lot of questions for him to answer. I hear there's some new evidence in a money-laundering scheme."

"I don't know anything about that."

Bloom shrugged. "Well, sounds like Emma isn't the only one who's in hot water right now."

Chapter 4

After Bloom left, Reed came over to the table, careful not to look at any of the other spa patrons as they lingered in their pink robes. "Phone call."

I thanked him and accepted his cell phone with shaking hands.

From across the Atlantic Ocean, Michael said, "Do you want me to come home?"

Yes, yes, *yes!*

But I said, "I'm coping reasonably well on my own at the moment, thank you. How did you hear?"

"I'm traveling with Josh, remember? My lawyer. He got a call from his partner, who's at Emma's bedside right now. Are you all right?"

"Just the usual stupid fainting spell, but somebody caught me when I fell."

"Anybody I ought to be jealous of?"

"I think it was Libby. But Detective Bloom was just here."

Michael laughed. "That chickenshit. He waited until I was a couple thousand miles away to make his move on you, didn't he?"

Michael had gone off on a fishing trip to broaden his horizons. Cheerfully admitting he was ignorant of the world beyond New Jersey, unless you counted the auction yards where he bought and sold muscle cars, he decided out of the blue he'd explore rural Scotland, of all places, with a handful of unlikely buddies. In addition to his lawyer, who may well have been billing the time, for all I knew, Michael traveled with a mysteriously wealthy cousin who baked bread, and a young man who wrote poetic articles for fishing magazines.

While listening to their plans, I thought they made their expedition sound like a grand adventure to an exotic land.

Michael said, "Bloom has stars in his eyes every time he looks at you. Come to think of it, so do I."

I smiled shakily and was glad he couldn't see how frightened I was. "Michael, Emma's in big trouble."

"Tell me the whole story."

I did so in a low voice, gathering my composure as he listened to the details.

When I was finished, he said, "So who killed the dog food king?"

"He wasn't the king. A prince, maybe. I don't know who killed him. I just know it wasn't Em."

"Think Detective Gloom and his pals are going to bother looking for anyone else?"

"I think they're going to try to prove Emma's guilt first, and when that doesn't work, they'll get around to looking for another suspect."

"When the evidence is cold."

"Yes."

"You've got to get involved again," he guessed. "In another murder investigation."

I knew he didn't like me snooping around in dangerous affairs. I didn't like it, either, but I had been forced to help friends and family before. This time, however, Michael wasn't available to watch my back.

Before he could object to my plan, I said, "I'll be careful this time."

"Who are you going to talk to?"

"I'm not sure yet. Rush Strawcutter was very easygoing. I'm having a hard time imagining who could have been angry enough to kill him."

"Maybe it wasn't anger."

Now and then I was uncomfortably reminded that Michael looked at crime from a different point of view than I did. "What do you think it could be?"

"The usual. Money. Sex. Revenge. Maybe a family thing. Or if he was such a prince, maybe self-defense, but that's rarely it. In my experience, a dead guy usually deserves getting smoked."

I closed my eyes and forced myself not to speculate about how many dead guys Michael had encountered in his life.

"Sorry," he said, guessing what my silence meant. "You can send a Jersey boy to Scotland, but he's not going to wear a kilt."

I laughed unsteadily. "Maybe it's a good thing you're there."

"Why?"

"I hear you're number one on the police hit parade again."

"Oh, that."

I wanted to ask more. Half the time I wanted to know everything about him because I knew firsthand what devastation too many secrets could wreak upon a relationship. I wanted to understand his efforts to remain estranged from his father and assorted ne'er-do-well half-brothers who were heavily involved in the Abruzzo crime family and seemed to take turns serving prison terms. But I counseled myself to trust Michael's judgement when it came to not sharing the parts of his life he believed might shock me. We were still wrestling with how much truth to share.

But I didn't want to address that now. Once again, the tug of needing him felt stronger than my fear that his business affairs might ruin both our lives.

So I said, "How is Scotland?"

"Beautiful. The fishing's like none I've ever done before. And they make some pretty good moonshine. We're staying in a castle—very swanky. You'd fit right in. It's no wonder Braveheart turned blue, though. It's freezing at night." After a pause, he said, "I think of you in bed."

I closed my eyes again and immediately imagined myself skin-to-skin with him under an eiderdown. Our relationship had not slipped into the bedroom yet, though there was plenty of sexual attraction going on. Okay, he wasn't handsome, exactly. In fact, his face sometimes scared people. But he had a quick laugh, an endearingly old-fashioned sense of protectiveness and an intuitive mind that appealed to me.

I might as well also admit he had astonishing shoulders, a supple stroll and a tight behind that any woman in her right mind would give up chocolate to get her hands on. He made me think of long, long nights between sweaty sheets, followed by mornings doing unmentionable things in the tub, against the bathroom sink, on the rug. . . .

And lately, I found myself wondering if being a good girl was overrated.

Emma had said, "Face it. You want to get laid, Sis."

No kidding. Even though I feared Michael Abruzzo wasn't as law-abiding as he could be, I found myself embarrassingly aroused by the man. Just his voice on the phone was aphrodisiac enough to cause impure thoughts and a warm flush that started deep inside me.

I swallowed hard. "I think of you, too."

"In your bed?"

I smiled. "Is this how phone sex starts?"

"Just tell me what you're wearing."

"A bathrobe, as a matter of fact. I think Libby is trying to book me a massage."

He groaned. "This is definitely phone sex now."

I laughed. "I'll get dressed. I'm going back to the hospital to see Emma."

"Am I ever going to get the chance to give you a massage myself? Or are you still living with Libby and the baby?"

"I'm moving out as soon as I can. But it's complicated."

"I'll be back by Friday. We'll uncomplicate it then."

Reluctantly, we said good-bye, and he disconnected. I listened to the overseas static for a moment.

Then, just to hear how it sounded, I said, "I love you."

*   *   *

The police did not arrest Emma, but they put a guard on the door to her hospital room and called it protective custody. They refused to allow Libby or me to see her.

"Why not?" I asked, standing in the hallway outside her hospital room.

"It's for her own safety," an officer assured me with a straight face.

Furious at being denied access to my sister, I asked Libby, "What did you tell Bloom's boss? Something that would incriminate Em?"

"No! Nothing. But I did suggest Captain Tucker try becoming a goddess. She has all the sacred potentials. She just needs to open herself to the cosmic possibilities."

"It's a wonder she didn't arrest you," I said.

"Hm." She was too distracted to be insulted. "Before we leave, I think I should find that nice Dr. Quartermaine to thank him for looking after you. Just wait here a minute."

As crazy as Libby could get, I decided her idea wasn't a bad one. Except I went looking to thank Tim Naftzinger.

Dr. Naftzinger was seeing patients on the pediatric floor, I was told, so I went upstairs to find him. While he consulted with a nurse in the corridor, I waited outside a room where a family of eight crowded around the bed of a pale little girl. The whole family was watching a *Mr. Rogers* rerun on `the television, their faces turned up to the set and reflecting the same peaceful expression.

Tim had always been quiet and controlled, and I wasn't surprised to see him just as sedate in his workplace as in his private life. He reminded me of a baseball pitcher—physically lanky, but mentally focused. Perhaps a pediatrician who faced life and death with small children needed to be even-keeled at all times. If he let his emotions roam up and down the scale, he'd be unable to prevent himself from flying off into the stratosphere in the wrong circumstances.

But watching him listen to the nurse, I suddenly remembered a day long ago when his wife had been driving the three of us around to various antique shops in New Hope. Rain pelted the windshield, and Caroline missed a stop sign. A teenager in a Porsche rammed us broadside. The impact wasn't hard—both cars had been traveling barely ten miles an hour—but we were all shaken up. The teenager got out of his car laughing. He was frightened, I know, but his reaction was giddy shock.

Tim had been furious. He leaped out of the car and

slammed the kid up against the Porsche to shout at him. I forced myself between them before fists flew.

Now, standing in the hospital corridor, I realized Caroline had probably been newly pregnant at the time. Tim had been protecting her.

The nurse stopped talking, and Tim began to write an order on the clipboard she held. She seemed respectful yet comfortable with Tim, and I thought he'd probably been nominated for Chief of Pediatrics because he was good at his profession and well-liked by the staff. He finished writing, then noticed me standing there and came over.

I noticed he needed a haircut. More accurately, he needed a wife to tell him he needed a haircut.

I said, "Thank you for looking after Emma this morning."

"I'm glad I was there." He put his pen into the breast pocket of his white lab coat. "I think she's going to be fine. I can't see her officially, but I have a friend in the emergency room and I put a bug in his ear. He's going to try to keep Emma here in the hospital as long as he can."

"Thank you, Tim. I appreciate your help."

"No problem." He hesitated. "Emma's been great to Merrie, you know, helping her with her jumping and . . . letting her talk." Slowly, he said, "Until now I've had a hard time connecting with Merrie. Emma's made it happen somehow. I'll do what I can to keep Emma here."

And out of jail. He didn't need to say the words, but he blanched just the same. I reached up and gave him a grateful kiss on the cheek. If I wasn't mistaken, he blushed.

I found Reed in the parking lot, holding Spike's

leash while the puppy attacked a discarded fast-food cup as if it were a rabid wolverine. He was a black, brown and white snarling blur on the asphalt, and the paper cup was already shredded. When he spotted me, Spike dropped the cup and joyously launched himself into the air. I caught him in my arms, and he lapped puppy kisses all over my face.

Reed's lock on cool was badly shaken. "Mrs. Kintswell was just here."

"Sorry, Reed. Did she hurt you?"

"No." Stung by my smile, he straightened. "She told me to tell you she was on her way home with her new friend."

"What friend?"

Reed shrugged. "A guy with a beard, wearing an earring and a stethoscope."

I sighed. "Did he look single?"

"What?"

"Never mind. Reed, can you take me to Boathouse Row?"

By way of an answer, he opened the car door and took my arm. I knew he was feeling sorry for me when he helped me into the backseat.

Rubbing Spike's tummy, I thought about who could have killed Rush Strawcutter. I couldn't imagine Rush having marital or family problems. He really had been an unthreatening, cheerful guy who made people smile when he turned up with his circus act of little dogs. Everybody seemed to like him. But another item on Michael's motives for murder was financial difficulty, and the best person to help me learn about the Strawcutter money situation was my friend Lexie Paine.

Richer than most of her megabuck clients, Lexie lived in the only privately owned boathouse on Philadelphia's famous Boathouse Row. The picturesque

Victorian houses stood on a magical curve of the Schuykill River and served as clubhouses for enthusiasts of various water sports, primarily rowing. Through her old family connections, a truckload of money and at least one semi-shady political deal, Lexie had been lucky enough to acquire one of the houses.

With gables, lancet windows and elaborate gingerbread trim, her home looked like a storybook house. The first floor was still a drafty boathouse, but her second-floor living quarters were home to one of the city's most valuable private collections of paintings. Lexie's interest in the art of making money was surpassed only by her appreciation of the fine arts. After her father's death, she became the principle partner in the brokerage house founded by her great-grandfather, and she counseled some of the city's most powerful families about their money matters. Her educated yet daring collection of paintings was the envy of many curators.

As Reed pulled into her driveway, his way was blocked by a parked white sports car, a postal truck and a minivan with the logo of a dressmaker painted on the side.

"Looks like Lexie's in high gear, Reed. This may take a while. I'll call your cell phone when I'm ready to leave. It will be an hour, at least."

"Okay." He sneaked a glance back at Spike, who was snoring on his back on the seat beside me, all four paws twitching in the air as he snarled dreamily. "You taking the animal with you?"

"He looks so peaceful. I hate to wake him. Puppies need their rest."

Reed glowered at me as I got out of the car.

Lexie Paine worked harder than a lumberjack, and I was lucky to find her at home on a weekend. Her assistant, the diminutive and quietly efficient Samir, let me into the house. He was holding a gigantic vase of lilies, which he'd obviously just arranged. Lexie came out of the bedroom wearing a black velvet ball gown. She was trailed by a stoop-shouldered seamstress with a mouthful of pins.

Lexie yelled, "Sweetie! Here I am dolled up like Cinderella, and you look like you just stepped off a Paris runway. See, Gabrielle, this is how I want to dress. Simply drop-dead gorgeous."

The seamstress eyed me coldly, and I realized I had interrupted a battle of wills between them. Lexie had firm ideas about her clothing, and her dressmaker was equally adamant. I was glad she had the pins in her mouth. She looked ready to scream.

"Thanks, Lex." I sidestepped a stack of shipping cartons in the foyer and kissed my friend. "Let's not use the drop-dead phrase today, all right?"

Lexie held my elbows and saw immediately that I was not myself. But with extra people in her home, she did not ask me to spill it all. Despite the ball gown, she hugged me hard, and the seamstress gave a squeak of panic.

"Come in and relax," she commanded, pulling me into a bedroom dominated by a Warhol life-sized portrait of Elvis in his gunslinger regalia. Samir placed the vase of lilies on a Stickley library table below the picture and gave the flowers a fluff before leaving.

Lexie climbed back onto the dressmaker's box and the seamstress grimly went down on her knees to attend to the gown's hem. Lexie looked svelte and gorgeous with her black hair skinned back in a ponytail and the subtle lines of the velvet gown giving her spare body a few gentling curves. "I'm just taking care of a few details today, but I'll be finished in two shakes."

Standing beside the box was a postal delivery man, complete with uniform and clipboard, looking delighted to find himself in the bedroom of a woman as glamorous as Lexie. He said, "Are you ready now, Miss Paine?"

"Oh, of course, sweetie, let me sign for those packages. I'm so sorry to keep you waiting. You've just done all my Christmas shopping, you know, and I'm very grateful."

The postman smiled as she dashed off her signature. "What did I buy everyone?" he asked.

"The DVD of *The Godfather*. You'd be surprised what a universal gift that is. All my clients get it, and my scads of nephews think I'm very cool. Thank you, sweetie, you've been blessedly patient with me." She shouted for her assistant. "Samir! Will you open one of those cartons and give this charming public servant a copy of *The Godfather*, please? I know he'll enjoy it."

"Hey, thanks, Miss Paine."

"Merry Christmas!"

Samir ushered the postman out, and Lexie said to me, "Nora, you know Claudine Paltron, don't you?"

Of course I did. Sitting on a slipper chair by the window and fingering an unlit cigarette was a tense blonde with lots of eyeliner, a swanlike neck and legs as long as those of a gazelle. Only a hermit wouldn't know Claudine, for ten years the principal dancer of the city ballet. Photos of her extraordinary leaps had graced magazine covers and the entertainment sections of newspapers nationwide. Even now, retired from the stage for a year, she radiated stardom.

"Hi."

I shook her cool hand. "I'm Nora Blackbird."

"Oh, sure," she said. "I remember you. You interviewed me for the paper once."

"I did, yes."

"Thanks. My agent said you didn't make me sound like an idiot."

"I enjoyed many of your performances. I hear the ballet is trying to woo you back to become the new artistic director."

She looked startled. "How do you know about that?"

"I'm sorry," I said at once. "I thought it was common knowledge."

Claudine waved her cigarette dismissively. "Maybe it is. I don't read the papers. Who does your clothes?"

I smiled. Because of my reduced financial circumstances, I had been forced to dive into my grandmother Blackbird's exquisite collection of couture clothing amassed over a lifetime of fashion safaris to Paris and Milan. Thank heaven most of the pieces fit me or I'd have nothing to wear to all the parties I attended. To Claudine, I said, "My grandmother."

"Oh, yeah? I like the boots especially. I wonder if they're my size."

Lexie gave me the eye and said, "Were you out with the gentry at the hunt breakfast this morning, Nora?"

"Yes."

"Oh." Claudine perked up. "Dougie Forsythe was there. Did you see him?"

"I— No, I didn't."

"Tell us who misbehaved, sweetie, that's always the interesting stuff."

The breakfast seemed weeks ago, but I forced myself to sound casual. "I bumped into Hadley Pinkham at first. He hasn't changed."

"Dear Hadley. What a posh sort of scoundrel he is. Did he crash the gate?"

"Of course. He could sneak into the Forbidden City, I think. And he always looks like a matinee idol."

Lexie laughed. "Oh, I hope he has a dark side. He'd be a cliché otherwise. Who else?"

"Tottie Boarman, looking furious."

"Of course he's furious! If you'd lost fifteen million dollars on Friday afternoon alone, you'd be out of sorts. I'm not telling tales—it will be front page of the *Wall Street Journal* on Monday."

"Good Lord."

Lexie waved her hand. "A drop in his bucket, sweetie. A mere drop."

Claudine said, "It's not a drop in my bucket. The bastard lost me a small fortune."

"You're on the path to wellness now," Lexie assured her. As Gabrielle finished pinning and sat back on her heels, Lexie turned on the box, studying herself in the mirror. "What do you think, girls? Will this do for the ballet Christmas gala on Friday? I'm making an appearance on behalf of the museum board as a show of cultural accord."

"It would do for a presentation to the Queen," I said. "It's stunning."

Lexie stepped down and patted Gabrielle's cheek. "Of course it is. Gabrielle is my secret weapon. Would you like a copy of *The Godfather,* my precious?"

"Sure," said Gabrielle, brightening.

"And let's get together soon for a talk about my spring clothes. I need at least two dresses at Easter.

Maybe one of them could look very Dolce, hm?" She put her slender arm around Gabrielle and guided her out of the bedroom. "I'm sure you've found some Merchant-Ivory fabrics. Just nothing with sequins. You know how I feel about sequins. The rest I leave up to you, of course. You're brilliant. A jewel."

Gabrielle was nodding. "I'll do some sketches and call you after the holidays."

"You're definitely my secret weapon, sweetie. Thanks for coming over. Now run along to get your DVD, and I'll have this ready for you in two shakes."

Lexie neatly handed Gabrielle over to Samir, who eased her away. Lexie closed the bedroom door behind them and began to strip off the gown.

"Honestly," she said, "I get so exasperated with divas."

I smiled.

Claudine said, "I don't know why you go through this, Lexie. You could run up to New York and buy whatever you like."

"I refuse to spend fifty thousand dollars on a dress created by an insufferable man who hates women and tells me to lose weight. Besides, I like to support the economy here in Philadelphia. I feel like Rosie the Riveter when I whip out my credit card."

"And Gabrielle is wonderful," I added.

"She is going to be huge some day," Lexie agreed, stripped down to her bra and panties. She threw the gown across her bed and grabbed a pair of jeans. Moments later, she was stepping into Ferragamo loafers and pulling on a sweater that looked like a woolly sheepdog and probably cost more than I was paid for a month's work.

The ever serene Samir came in with a tray of Waterford tumblers and small bottles of V8 juice. He set it on the hassock and gathered up the gown on his way out.

Lexie gratefully patted his cheek as he went by, then poured us a round of juice and flopped on her bed.

"I can't stay." Claudine sipped from the cut crystal. "This is too cold, anyway. I never drink anything chilled below seventy-eight degrees. I just wanted to thank you, Lexie, for all your help."

"Oh, stick around, sweetie. My chef was here yesterday and left enough food to feed the Sixth Fleet. And it's all very tasty, too, I promise. No wheatgrass. I put my foot down when it comes to wheatgrass."

"No, I have some real celebrating to do, and I want to get started."

"Of course," Lexie said.

Claudine turned to me. Her very long nose, pointed chin and heavy, arching brows made for an imperfect face that stage lighting transformed into beauty so astounding that audiences had been known to gasp when the curtain rose to reveal her. In person, though, she looked as though her features were made of stretched Silly Putty—longer, bigger, thinner than on stage.

She lowered her eyes in a stagey imitation of reticence. "I've just been through a terrible ordeal, and Lexie has been a godsend."

"Well," Lexie began.

"No, it's all right." To me Claudine said, "I was blackmailed."

Lexie sent me an apologetic glance. Now that the cat was out of the bag, I was required to be discreet.

Inadequately, I said, "I'm so sorry."

"Oh, I suppose I deserved it. Having an affair always has a price." She flashed her wedding and engagement rings, one with a diamond as big as a jelly bean and a blaze of smaller stones surrounding it. "My husband is a perfectly nice man who shouldn't have his name ruined because of my behavior. Especially now that he's raising all those millions for the ballet capital fund. It cost me a fortune to get the photos. Lexie had to help me organize the money."

Lexie said, "Against my will. I wish you'd gone to the police, Claudine."

"No way. Osgood would have found out for sure."

Years ago, Claudine had astonished the city by marrying Osgood Paltron, the sinfully wealthy inventor of an insect-repelling device for campers. In his younger days, he made shouting television commercials as the Zapper Czar, but eventually he retired with his millions and devoted himself to becoming a ballet aficionado. For years everyone had assumed he was gay. His marriage proved either he wasn't or he was prepared to pay Claudine's legendary credit card bills in exchange for a heterosexual reputation. The jury was still out.

Osgood's money and Claudine's fame combined to create pillow power that rivaled the most successful and bizarre husband-and-wife duos in show business or politics. As a team, they were nationally known. Separately, however, they were definitely second tier.

"Osgood still might find out," Lexie said. "Especially if you continue to see Dougie."

Claudine sighed. "Oh, I can't give up Dougie. He's completely stupid except in bed, and there he's Einstein and Man o' War rolled into one. And he's so jealous, which is always a turn-on."

Lexie and I dared not look at each other.

Claudine unconsciously stroked her own sinewy

arms. "I'm just relieved it's over now. The blackmail, I mean. It's been such a trial."

"Let me try just one more time," Lexie said quite seriously. "It's not too late, Claudine. You can still go to the authorities. Who knows if this person will come back to you later for more money? He's already dipped into your well three times."

"But I have the photos now. And the negatives."

"How can you be sure you have them all? You can't trust a blackmailer. And heaven knows he might try the same with other people—your friends. You'd be doing a public service by bringing him to justice."

"To hell with the public. I've given them enough already." Claudine stood up and suddenly looked every inch the exquisite, world-class ballerina—a tall willow with a core of steel. She cupped the lilies with one graceful hand and bent to inhale their fragrance in a gesture so feminine and beautiful that she had made grown men weep when she executed it during *Giselle*. She straightened just as gracefully. "I'm just glad I'm free at last. And I wanted to thank you, Lexie, for your help. You've been great. Enjoy the flowers. I've got to run now. I'm meeting Dougie this afternoon for a quickie, and then Osgood and I have a cocktail thing tonight. Nice to see you, Nora."

"If you change your mind," Lexie said, "I'll do anything I can to help."

"Don't worry. It's over now. Kiss, kiss. Oh, and can I have one of those *Godfather* DVDs?"

"Take two," Lexie urged as Claudine went out of the room.

When we were alone, Lexie said, "I'm so sorry about that, Nora. It's hell knowing other people's secrets."

"I won't say a word."

She slugged the rest of her tomato juice and stood with one fist braced on her slim hip. "I'm almost glad you know, actually. Have you heard of anyone else being blackmailed? Anyone among our friends?"

"No, but it's hardly the kind of trouble a person advertises."

"I know. It's trouble that's contagious, however. I've been seeing some very peculiar withdrawals lately, and I'm sure people aren't buying expensive Christmas gifts with the money." She glared at the flowers Claudine had brought for her. "God, I hate lilies!"

"They smell like funerals."

"Damn right." She carried the flowers outside and left them on her balcony. When she returned and closed the door again, she asked, "Do you suppose Claudine Paltron has read a single book in her life?"

"She's upset you."

"I swear, it doesn't pay to have small clients anymore. From now on, I'm only taking billionaires." Lexie pulled me to sit beside her on the edge of the bed. "Forget about me now. Tell me what's wrong, darling. You looked ghastly when you came in. What in the world has happened? Is it Michael? Has he been arrested? The whole money-laundering thing is true, after all?"

I shook my head. "The hunt breakfast."

I told her about Rush Strawcutter's death. Lexie was horrified.

"And Emma was in the same stall?" Lexie cried. "Oh, my God, what was she doing?"

"She was unconscious, Lex. She's been drinking lately, and I—we've—tried to talk to her about it, but—"

Lexie shook her head. "You can't control someone

else's addiction, Nora. You of all people, should know that by now."

"It's not the same as Todd," I said. "It really isn't. I should have helped her before now."

Lexie gave my shoulder a shake. "Do you hear yourself? This is exactly the kind of thing you were saying about Todd!"

"So sue me for not wanting to hear myself say the same thing if something happens to Emma!"

"Emma is an adult—"

"With problems and pressures we don't understand. She lost her husband, for God's sake, and a very high-profile life. Now she can't ride the way she wants to, which has to be—"

"You're making excuses for her."

"Dammit, Lexie!"

She hugged me hard and didn't let go. "Go ahead and get angry with me. I'm your friend, and I can take it. But you're tilting at the same old windmill."

"It's not a windmill," I insisted.

"Let's be constructive. Do you have a lawyer yet?" She held me away so that she could see my face.

"Yes, one of Michael's."

"Well, it doesn't get any better than that, I'm sure, so— Oh, sorry, sweetie. I didn't mean—"

"I know. Listen, Lex, I need to find out about Rush Strawcutter. If I can figure out what was going on in his life, maybe I can piece together what happened."

"Was Emma seeing him? I mean, were they lovers?"

"I don't know," I said honestly. "I'm trying not to think that way. I'm hoping to find out about Rush."

Lexie bit her lip. "Does client-broker privilege exist after death?"

"Is there such a thing?"

"Of course. Look, I can't give you dollar amounts, but I can tell you that Rush was not given free access to the Strawcutter fortune."

"What does that mean?"

"He received a small allowance. Very small. I'm not revealing any long-kept secrets if I say all the Straw-cutters are Scrooges. They have that huge, ugly house in Bryn Mawr, but it hasn't been redecorated since 1953, I swear. And Gussie has held the purse strings just as tightly as her forefathers. You know that old station wagon Rush drove?"

"He always said he used it so he could carry his dogs around."

"That was bullshit. It was all he could afford. I'm surprised he had enough money for gas. I'm telling you, Gussie hardly let the man have five dollars to buy his lunch every day. That's why he was starting that business of his."

"Laundro-Mutt."

Lexie smiled grimly. "Don't let the name fool you. He had a sound business plan. He thought he was inventing the Starbucks of the pet world."

"How did he get the start-up money for such a venture? Did Gussie help?"

"Lord, no. Their prenup forbade that kind of thing. He had to go elsewhere."

"A bank? Lex, please, I don't want you to betray a professional confidence, but—"

"Emma's in trouble. I know you'll be discreet, Nora. And I wouldn't say a word if Rush were still alive. Anyway, with accusations flying around the world of finance like confetti these last few days, I'm probably the last to start blabbing. Rush borrowed the money from Tottie Boarman."

Immediately, I remembered the furious expression

on Tottie's face as he'd dismounted his horse and stormed past me at the hunt breakfast.

"I know Tottie's already in the handbasket to hell, and the amount of dough he loaned to Rush is substantial—at least seven zeroes."

More than enough money to kill for, I thought.

"But listen, Nora. You can't just barge into offices all over town and start asking questions. These are very high stakes."

"My stakes are high, too."

"I know, I know how you feel about Emma. Just promise you'll be careful."

"Don't worry. I'll find a backdoor. In fact, I know just which latch to jiggle first."

Chapter 5

The best place to dig up juicy gossip about anyone was *The Philadelphia Intelligencer,* the city's sensational rag that printed equal amounts of news and innuendo. It was a far-from-hallowed institution that employed journalists either too young, too old, too encumbered with young children or too attached to their addiction of choice to work for a real newspaper, and the printed results were not the pinnacle of journalistic excellence.

It was, of course, the only paper that hired such unqualified amateurs as myself.

I'd been signed by the newspaper's owner to help cover the social beat with the understanding that I work under the experienced battle-ax who'd held most of Philadelphia's society hostage for years through her column and weekly social page. Using techniques that would make a master extortionist proud, Kitty Keough was the self-appointed high priestess of high society.

Kitty hated my guts for having been to the manor born while she'd grown up in a dilapidated Allentown double-wide that was foreclosed upon when her father ran off with the collected union dues of a steelworkers' local and later turned up dead on a railroad track. Which, I admit, were the facts I learned the day a chain-smoking coworker showed me how to work the *Intelligencer*'s computerized archive.

So Kitty hadn't grown up in a happy household where luxuries came easily. I, on the other hand, had been photographed for the *Intelligencer* when I was presented to society as a debutante, became engaged, married the son of an equally prominent family and was elected to office by my many pals in the Junior League.

For those events in my life, Kitty didn't just hate my guts. She wanted to cut them out with a rusty knife, roast them over fiery coals and throw the smoking remains in the Schuykill River to feed the carp.

I swallowed hard when Kitty belittled and abused me in full view of my colleagues. I could not risk being fired. With the tax man planning to acquire my two-hundred-year-old home any day now, I needed my job desperately.

Fortunately, my colleagues found Kitty's tirades entertaining. Most of the time.

"Oh-oh." My friend, Mary Jude, the quirky lead writer for the food section, saw me coming into the office late Saturday afternoon and shooed me off with a paperback cookbook. "Go home," she ordered. "We're too busy to call an ambulance for Kitty if she has a brain hemorrhage."

Mary Jude Yashurick wore a crooked set of reindeer antlers over her blond crew cut and a handknit sweater that depicted Rudolph, complete with a red light bulb for his nose, which flashed thanks to a battery pack hidden somewhere on her body. She was a Columbia School of Journalism grad, a single mom who could only work part-time, so she'd been hired by the *Intelligencer,* where her talents were exploited for a shamefully low salary. She favored short skirts with black tights to show off her lean legs and minimize her hips, which were large enough to give her the silhouette of a cello. Her mincemeat pie was the stuff of Christmas legend, and I looked forward to trying it for the first time at the upcoming office party. I understood I'd need a hockey stick to beat off the competition.

She tapped her computer screen. "I'm serious, Nora. I'm on deadline here so I can get home in time to take Trevor to a birthday party. I can't be distracted by the Kitty Show right now. I need all my concentration to analyze butter cookie recipes. Good Lord, what's that?"

"His name is Spike."

Mary Jude recoiled from my handbag. "Is he a dog, or a muskrat?"

Okay, Spike wasn't beauty-contest material, but I felt my defenses rise. "He's a Canadian bristle terrier. Be careful. He'll take your ear off faster than Mike Tyson."

"Here, let's keep him occupied with a cookie." She offered a tray of assorted treats, arranged and numbered on plastic plates. "See which one he likes best. I can't decide."

Spike took the proffered cookie like a shark snapping a minnow. He disappeared into my handbag with it. Only slightly more politely, I accepted a cookie, too.

"Delish," I said when it melted on my tongue.

"I never met a butter cookie that wasn't. Here, try another. Have you really come looking for Kitty?"

I nibbled my cookie and sat on the edge of her desk. "I need her permission to get into the archive. I don't have access."

Mary Jude grinned. "I do. Give me an opinion on these cookies, and I'll help you find anything you want."

"Deal."

She twisted her computer monitor around so I could see it. While Spike and I shared cookies, Mary Jude typed and clicked until we found half a dozen recent articles about Tottie Boarman's wheeling and dealing. We started in the business section, and I skimmed through long explanations of venture capitalists and how Tottie had allegedly made himself a bundle while taking his friends to the cleaners. He invested in start-ups, then demanded his money back as the business blossomed, usually forcing the owners to go public to raise money by issuing stock. Once the stock was issued, Tottie also bought the stock and sold it before cash-flow problems started, thanks to his original bail-out. He doubled his investment before the companies went bad.

"Nice guy," Mary Jude commented.

A basic biography told us that Tottie had never married and had no children. But I remembered hearing my father and his pals chuckling over brandy and cigars one night, making remarks about Tottie's "tarts." At the time, I remember wondering if he liked desserts.

We searched through other sections of the paper next. I was surprised to see several of Kitty Keough's social columns pop up in front of us.

"Look at this." Mary Jude stabbed the point of a cookie Christmas tree at the screen. "For a man who spends most of his time making money, this Boarman character sure gets a lot of space in Kitty's columns."

"He goes to a lot of charitable events."

"But only lately, see?"

I read the dates on the columns. "You're right. Now that I think of it, I haven't seen Tottie at many functions over the years. He must be trying to win back public approval by showing what a philanthropist he is."

"That's how it works, huh?"

"Oh, yes. Now and then somebody uses the social scene to score points. Remember Stewart Kane Archer? The canned-pea magnate who built the church in Germantown?"

"He was around in the twenties? Sure. My cousin was married at that church."

"Well, Archer was one of those few captains of industry who didn't lose his shirt during the crash of '29, and he managed to do it by ruining a lot of his friends—including a couple of great-uncles of mine. So he built the church to show what a nice guy he was. Except my grandfather started calling it Archer's Fire Escape. Archer eventually moved to New York to get away from the ridicule."

Mary Jude laughed. "Cute. I never heard that." She spun her chair sideways to look up at me critically. "You're perfect for this job, Nora. You don't even know what you know until you need it. Too bad we're stuck with Kitty. I can see why she's jealous of you."

"Kitty is loved by readers. I don't have the poison pen that sells papers."

"Hm. I see your point."

Spike reappeared and growled. Mary Jude tossed him another cookie, and he snapped it out of the air with raptorlike accuracy.

"Anyway, I try to mind my manners around Kitty," I said. "She's looking for any way possible to get me fired."

Mary Jude shrugged. "I think you're safe. Unless she's got a plan for her troll."

"Her troll?"

With a grin, Mary Jude jerked her head toward the

row of offices that lined the open area where all the reporters worked. "They're all in Stan's lair right now. Why don't you have a look? Just don't trip over the little guy."

Curiosity won over my distaste for Kitty. I gave Spike another cookie to keep him busy, and went across the features department floor to the office of Stan Rosenstatz, the department editor. Stan had stopped popping antacids and was slugging directly from a Maalox bottle when I tapped on his door. Kitty stood in front of him, decked out in a Mae West–style silver lamé dress with a boa draped around her shoulders. The feather kind. Her fur coat lay over a chair like a fleabitten bear that had passed out after too many cocktails.

Kitty was saying, "My assistant must come with me tonight, Stan. I need him to take my phone calls."

Stan put his Maalox in a desk drawer. "Nora is your assistant, Kitty. We're not paying anyone else to tag along with you."

"Andrew doesn't tag," Kitty said. "He's a vital cog in the wheel of my working machine. Plus he can take pictures, so I won't need a staff photographer."

"Staff photographers are on staff because we pay for their skilled services. We don't use amateur stuff."

I stepped into the office and nearly stumbled over a young man built like a tree stump. He didn't hear me coming because he had a cell phone in each hand, and the respective earpieces were fitted into his right and left ears. A large camera hung on a strap around his neck.

Stan looked startled. "Nora!"

Kitty turned and looked as if she wished she could open a trapdoor beneath my feet. "Sweet Knees," she said. "What are you doing here tonight?"

"Filing my story about the hunt breakfast." I put my hand down to the young man I had no trouble identifying as the troll Mary Jude had mentioned. He was wearing a badly fitted rental tuxedo with lapels as wide as duck wings. The pants puddled around his ankles. "Hello, I'm Nora Blackbird."

His face lit up behind Harry Potter–style glasses. "Oh, hi! I'm Andy Mooney. Hey, it's awesome to meet you! I've read about your family in the papers for years. You're real Philadelphia royalty, aren't you?"

"Shut up, Andrew."

"Sorry, Miss Keough. I've grooved on your column for so long, though, I feel like I've memorized all your good stuff. That piece you did on Mr. Charles Blackbird's funeral was really great."

I said, "My grandfather's funeral was fifteen years ago, Andy. How old were you then?

"Oh, my mother keeps a scrapbook. She read the clippings to me when I was little, and I got hooked. I still remember the way Miss Keough described the hundreds of people from all walks of life who went to the funeral to pay their respects to Charlie Blackbird. She said—"

Kitty interrupted. "Yeah, well, give people what they want, and they'll come out in droves."

I remembered my vow to behave with the utmost civility when in Kitty's presence. "It's lovely to meet you, Andy. Are you working with us now?"

"Oh, yeah, it's a major dream come true. I'm just an intern at the moment, but Miss Keough said I can work my way up to your job, Miss Blackbird."

"How do you like the sound of that, Sweet Knees?"

Kitty's silver dress was one I'd seen on her before, and she looked like a war horse strapped into its harness. She was headed for a fancy dress party, and I guessed it was the annual Children's Hospital Holiday Ball. I'd heard by way of a friend on the organizing committee that the guest host—a very popular television comedian who promoted children's charities when he wasn't playing the bumbling father of over-sexed teenagers—had doubled the ticket sales this year. I made a mental note to slip that information to Stan if Kitty didn't learn it at the ball. Stan could ease it into her column before it went to press, and Kitty would be none the wiser where the detail came from.

I said, "It's wonderful to have extra help during the holidays."

"Yeah, we're swamped," Kitty agreed, turning on Stan. "In fact, I want Sweet Knees to go to a few more parties. The invitations are coming in so fast, I can't keep up."

"That's exactly what Nora's for," Stan said. "To take up the slack for you, Kitty."

"Okay, then, she can go through the invitations, and Andrew can come along with me tonight."

Stan's patience was thin. "We don't have the money in the budget to pay your intern to—"

"Oh, I don't mind," Andy piped up. "I don't need to be paid to help Miss Keough."

"Great," Stan said quickly. "Then everybody's happy. Nora, you'll take a look at Kitty's invitations before you leave today?"

"Of course."

"And, Kitty, you're coming back in tonight to finish this week's column?"

She had already snatched up her ancient fur coat and was sailing out the door. "Don't worry about me, Stan."

Spike chose that moment to poke his head out of

my bag and issue a big puppy burp. Then he snarled at Andy. For once, he was picking on something his own size. With a startled expression, Andy skipped after Kitty.

"Hang on a minute, Nora." Stan waved me back into his office.

"Sorry about the dog, Stan. I won't bring him again."

"Don't worry about it. I love dogs." Then he did a double take. "Even one that ugly. Tell me what you saw at the hunt breakfast. The boys downstairs are working on the story now. I hear some young millionaire got himself killed."

I sat down in the chair opposite Stan's desk. I liked Stan. He worked hard and was loyal to the newspaper that paid him poorly for doing more than his fair share of work and taking a lot of abuse from maniacs like Kitty. He was an old-fashioned newsman who always met his deadlines at the expense of his tender stomach. At first I hadn't understood why he stayed with the *Intelligencer,* but after a few months I caught on to his unrequited affection for a certain fifty-something copy editor who thought he was invisible. For me, his smile was always tired, but it was genuine.

I told him what I knew about Rushton Strawcutter's death.

"And your sister," Stan prompted when I had finished without mentioning Emma's trip to the hospital and the police presence outside her room there. "Sorry, but I heard her name mentioned."

"My sister isn't involved in the murder," I said more calmly than I felt. "But the police are obligated to pursue all possible leads."

Stan smiled grimly. "You sound like a press release."

"Can you blame me?"

"No, but I hope you won't blame me for doing my job either. Mind if I call downstairs and ask if anyone wants to talk to you?"

I didn't want to talk to reporters, not even ones who were my friends. But it was naïve to hope the press was going to ignore Emma. I preferred to have some control over what was printed about her.

"Go ahead," I told Stan.

He reached for his phone to make arrangements.

A few minutes later, Mary Jude was pleased to see the team from the news department get off the elevator.

"Perfect," she said. "You guys can have these cookies if you tell me which ones you like best and why."

The three of them dug into Mary Jude's supply while asking me questions about what I had seen at the hunt breakfast. I tried to be honest but diplomatic, and I asked that I not be named as a source of their information. They agreed and quickly put the finishing touches on the story they'd spent the afternoon assembling.

Before they got up to leave, I asked if they were working on the story of Tottie Boarman's recent trouble.

"That's the business desk," Freddie told me, scratching his eyebrow with his pen. "Check with Marcy Edelstein. She's working that story. I just saw Boarman downstairs, though."

"Downstairs?" I repeated. "Tottie Boarman was here at the *Intelligencer*?"

"Well, only to pick up his date. His car came up to the curb when I went out for a smoke."

"His date?"

Freddie laughed. "Yeah, it was pretty funny, actually. Kitty went out with a kid on her heels, the both of them dressed like they were headed for a Mardi Gras party. When is she going to give that fur coat a decent burial? Boarman was pretty annoyed. I don't know if he was grossed out by their clothes or mad that Kitty had brought along a midget for a chaperone, but he was definitely peeved."

"Wait a minute," I said. "You mean Kitty got into Tottie's car?"

"Sure. And the kid climbed into the front seat with the driver."

Mary Jude laughed. "Well, that explains why Boarman's gotten so many inches in Kitty's social columns lately."

Kitty and Tottie? I couldn't have been more surprised if I'd heard Joan Rivers had started dating Alan Greenspan.

I said, "Surely they're not seeing each other."

"Weirder couples have happened," Freddie said, looking at me.

A short silence slipped past as the four journalists waited for me to say something about my own dating habits.

Before I found myself contributing to a news story about money laundering, Spike poked his head out and announced his low opinion of people who didn't share their cookies. I shoved him down into my bag and stood up. "I like the cookies with the green sprinkles best, Mary Jude. They're not so sweet that my teeth hurt, and they're thin enough that I can have a few and still fit into my dress this Friday night."

The others voted on their favorite cookie, too, and left Mary Jude to work on her story. I made my way through the labyrinth of reporters' desks until I found Kitty's. She had commandeered some portable walls to create a cubicle for herself, so I stepped into her improvised office. A mountain of invitations lay in piles on the surface of her desk. I sat down in her chair to go through the envelopes.

Balls, dinners, cocktail parties, teas. Christmas, Hanukkah, New Year's Eve. Kitty had already put aside the events she wanted me to attend. I flipped through a hundred invitations. No way could I attend them all. I sorted them by category. The host organizations ran from garden clubs and genuinely wonderful charitable organizations to the Sky Waiters, an earnest group of people who claimed they'd all been abducted and harassed by aliens. I wondered wryly who else was on their guest list. There was also a lovely card from an outdoorsman's club that liked to pretend it was not a front for the NRA. I was sure Kitty had given me at least half the invitations as a form of punishment.

Nearly all the cards required RSVP, which I would have to take care of quickly. I also realized I had been personally invited to more than half the events represented by Kitty's pile of invitations.

There was no way I could attend a fraction of those parties, of course. Certainly not now that Emma was in trouble.

I gathered up the stack of cards to take home and realized they wouldn't survive ten minutes in my bag with Spike. So I opened one of Kitty's desk drawers in search of something to carry all the invitations in.

There, on the top of a very cluttered drawer, lay a stack of oversized white envelopes. Eight-by-ten, just the size Libby had described seeing beside Rush Strawcutter's dead body.

I pulled out one of the envelopes and looked at it for a long time.

Spike squirmed his head out of my bag and nudged my arm.

"I don't know what this means," I said to the puppy.

I put the invitations into one of the white envelopes and took them all home. I needed time to think about what I'd learned, and I knew just the place to do that.

Chapter 6

I hadn't been home to Blackbird Farm in ages, and I got a ridiculous lump in my throat when Reed dropped me at the back door.

The lump evaporated when Spike dashed inside and promptly peed on the kitchen rug. The rug was already wet, thanks to a mysterious puddle of water that had appeared in the kitchen during my absence.

I sent Spike outside again to think about his transgression while I piled my mail on the kitchen table, threw the sopping rug into the scullery sink, swept the puddle out the door and turned up the thermostat. By the time Spike came tearing inside again, the house was warming up and my answering machine was spewing recorded phone messages.

One message was from Thomasina Silk, who assured me she had taken care of Mr. Twinkles, Emma's horse. He was stabled at Tri-County until Emma came to claim him. Boarding fees were $40 per day.

Hadley Pinkham said, "Kitten, I can't believe I missed you in all the ruckus today. Do call when you get a chance so we can rehash."

The last message was from Libby.

"You're not here, so I assume you stopped by your house. I just phoned the hospital—let's see, it's about seven o'clock—and the doctors say we can see Emma first thing in the morning. She's being a pain in the butt—no surprise. Want me to come pick you up? I'll be there around eight. No, make that nine. I might want to, uh, sleep a little late. I think I'll go to bed early, in fact, so don't call me. I need some time to regenerate my primal energy. The kids are fine, in case you were wondering. They assume you'll be back tomorrow. You will, won't you?"

I put the kettle on, gave Spike some puppy chow and telephoned the hospital myself. I was connected to the nursing station on the floor where Emma had been moved.

The nurse told me Emma was sleeping, and by her tone I gathered everyone was relieved that my sister was unconscious. I hung up feeling moderately relieved that Emma was okay.

The phone rang in my hand then, and I answered.

"Nora, honey!" shouted a female voice. "It's Delilah Fairweather! Can you hear me, or is the music too loud?"

I could hear the thump of a hip-hop beat behind her and immediately imagined my friend Delilah in her usual posture: dancing in the middle of a party with one long-nailed finger plugging her left ear while she clutched her cell phone to the other. The party girl with a Nokia; that was Delilah, who had given up a dull job as a computer programmer at age twenty-five to follow her dream. Since starting her own public relations firm, she was free to party at all hours of the day and night, and now she was in high demand as the city's hardest working publicist and event planner. Gorgeous, with butterscotchy skin and Tina Turner legs she showed off by wearing the shortest possible skirts, Delilah also had a contagious laugh and a legendary Rolodex to match her boundless energy—a combo that rocketed her to the top of her field.

"Hey, girlfriend," I called. "Where are you hanging tonight?"

"A new club on South Street. Come on down, honey, we're having a blast!"

"You could have a blast in a phone booth," I shot back.

"You got that right!" She howled, and I heard a chorus of voices howl with her. Then she said, "Down to business, babycakes. The fashion show for the Prom Fairy was a smash hit."

"Great!" I was pleased to hear that the organization recently created to collect fancy dresses to send to needy teenagers during prom season had gotten off to a good start. "Did you collect a lot of dresses?"

"Dozens—and real money, too. It was a hit fundraiser. My master stroke was mixing the vintage clothes with that new designer from Yardley—you'd love him, honey. So anyway, thanks for loaning me that gorgeous Mainbocher from your granny's closet. I put it out on a mannequin at the entrance, put a spotlight on it, and it really set the stage for the whole night. Very classy."

"Did the old thing survive?"

"Oh, honey, we took good care of your dress, and nobody dared wear it. It's too delicate."

"Grandmama Blackbird wore it a lot. It's just worn out, I'm afraid."

"But still amazing. Anyway, I have it all boxed up and ready to go home."

"Keep it handy," I said. "I'll be seeing you Tuesday night."

"Oh, you're coming to the thing? Perfect. I'll have it with me, then. It really was the hit of the fashion show, Nora. Oh, and somebody even wanted to buy it."

"Sorry, not for sale."

"I figured." The music changed behind her, and she said, "I hear you were at that nasty hunt breakfast yesterday. I knew I hated big animals for a reason."

"It wasn't the animals that made it horrible."

"So I hear. You okay, honey? Is your sister in a shitload of trouble?"

"Not for long, I hope."

"Poor Rush. I knew him way back when, y'know. Sweet guy."

"How did you meet him?"

"We took some college classes together. No Ivy League for us, of course, just state university on scholarships. Poor Rush was a washout. He had some kind of dyslexia, so I helped him study, and he helped me out when I needed an extra man for a party. Girl, I was party central! I liked doing the networking thing even then." She didn't need to explain that she probably knew more people in the city than the mayor did and threw much nicer parties. She added, "I introduced Rush to Claudine Paltron, in fact—which I'm still kicking myself about. It happened early in my career, before I knew how to handle misguided sexual attraction."

"Misguided? On whose side?"

"Claudine's, of course. I could tell you tales!"

I had forgotten that Delilah had counted Claudine among her clients when she first got started as a publicist. Claudine would have been a trial by fire for any PR person, but Delilah managed to control the self-centered dancer's public persona very well. Claudine's adoring fans stopped hearing about her many affairs and started reading about her charitable work on behalf of lupus and young dancers from underserved neighborhoods.

"And you introduced Claudine and Rush?"

"Long before he met Gussie, I swear. When I first got into the publicity gig, I snagged a lot of my college buddies as extra men. What can I say? You can never have too many handsome guys at events. And I dragged Claudine to a greyhound adoption rally he organized—a dud, actually, but it was his first attempt, and he really believed in the cause. I thought maybe Claudine would look good with a couple of grey-hounds by her side—kinda white-bread Josephine Baker, you know? Turned out she hated dogs. But she met Rush and that was a different story."

I hadn't remembered that Rush and Claudine had been seen together before Rush's marriage. "Fire-works?"

"More like a train wreck. You know how Claudine wants everything she sees? I swear it's because she had to starve herself all those years dancing."

"How long did it last between them?"

"I don't know. It sort of petered out gradually. He was good for her, but Claudine got tired of all those little mutts he had with him all the time. Anyway, it turned out okay. They broke up and he married nice, safe Gussie. Except who'da thought he'd die so young?"

Or so violently, I almost said.

"So, honey, am I going to see you at the ballet gala on Friday night?"

"I think so," I said. "If I can figure out something to wear."

"Nobody does vintage like you, Nora. You'll out-class us all."

Delilah's call waiting clicked, which was always the way conversation ended with her. Her business thrived because of her ability to field dozens of phone calls every hour.

"Gotta boogie, honey. See you at the gala!"

I thought about what Delilah had told me as I put a Lean Cuisine into the microwave. The rest of the kitchen was strictly ancient history. My parents had done few repairs and fewer upgrades to the estate, but when I moved to the farm more than a year ago, I'd brought a few essentials from my condo in the city. While my dinner hummed, I went through the stack of mail that had piled up during my stay with Libby and her family.

Spike leaped into my lap and helped by shredding a Williams-Sonoma catalog. I flipped the rest of the catalogs directly into the trash and created a pile of envelopes on the table. Mostly they were invitations and bills, plus a postcard from Kennedy Airport from Michael.

On the back he had written, "I miss you already."

Just looking at his handwriting sent my thoughts rushing into warm and fuzzy memories best suited for the sappiest pages of a romance novel—the way his stroll through my door made my knees quiver, his tantalizing touch lingering on my throat, his husky whisper good-bye when we last parted. Yes, I yearned for more—dark secrets as well as hot kisses shared late at night. But the sex part wasn't going to happen yet. Maybe not ever, but certainly not now. The sensible part of my brain cautioned that neither of us was ready to trust the other so unconditionally that lovemaking could be as natural—or as safe—as breathing the same air.

I hoped I would be able to recognize when we reached the right place. My life had been so shattered by Todd that even now I sometimes don't know which direction is up.

I propped Michael's postcard on the pepper mill in the middle of the table.

At the bottom of my heap of mail was a large white envelope, addressed to me in typewritten letters. The same kind of envelope in which I'd brought home Kitty's invitations.

I slit open the envelope with a knife. I shook out the contents, and a sheaf of three photographs spilled onto the kitchen table.

Photographs of me.

With Tim Naftzinger.

"Good Lord," I said.

Spike spat out the catalog and put his paws on the table. He studied the pictures with his head cocked and his lips drawn back in his usual snarl.

"This isn't what it looks like," I said to Spike.

It looked as if Tim Naftzinger and I were more than just friends.

I knew at once that the photos had been taken surreptitiously in the cloakroom of a hotel a month earlier. It had been at a party thrown to raise money for a safe house for abused children. I clearly remembered the evening. I had attended on behalf of the newspaper and had dinner with two other couples and Tim. He had come on behalf of the hospital, but was alone and therefore needed a seat at a table with an uneven number of guests. After the dinner, there had been dancing, but Tim and I both decided to leave early. He had helped me into my coat, I recalled.

But the photographs looked like something more than a gentleman assisting a friend in the cloakroom. My dress had revealed a lot of bare shoulders, and Tim had leaned closer than I remembered. He looked ready to nuzzle my throat, in fact, and in the next picture my innocent good-night kiss to his cheek appeared to be a flash of passion between two long-time lovers.

I dropped the photos on the table. As I did so, a note fell out.

Spike grabbed the note in his teeth. I wrestled with him and won.

The note read: *Ten thousand dollars by Wednesday or you are in big trooble.*

Trooble?

It took me a second to realize what the misspelled word meant, and then I couldn't get enough oxygen.

What followed were directions for placing a bag of hundred-dollar bills underneath a statue in Rittenhouse Square.

Suddenly, my hands were shaking so badly that I couldn't stuff the photographs back into their envelope.

Spike growled when I dumped him on the floor. I rushed to the telephone and picked it up, but couldn't imagine who to call for help.

Blackmail.

I dialed Michael's cell phone number with trembling fingers and prayed the call would reach Scotland.

It rang four times before he picked up, shouting hello from several time zones away.

"It's me," I said.

"Hang on," he bellowed. "I'll call you back from another phone."

I hung up and waited. For a man who assured me he had nothing to hide from the law, he spent a lot of time switching telephones. Thirty seconds later, my phone rang.

"Am I pulling you out of a trout stream?"

"Salmon," he said, in a normal tone of voice. "Scotland has salmon. But I'm—never mind. What's up?"

"I'm sorry. I don't mean to— What time is it there? Did I wake you?"

"It's okay. What's wrong? You sound scared. Is it Emma?"

"No, it's me, believe it or not. I just received a blackmail letter. A demand for ten thousand dollars. With photographs."

"Jesus Christ. Of us?"

My throat had a big, frightened lump lodged in it. "Nothing that easy. No, pictures of me with a friend in a hotel coatroom."

"Damn. How come I can't get cozy with you in a coatroom?"

"This is serious, Michael. I'm not kidding. The pictures show him just helping me with my coat, but they're very— They make us look intimate. Like an advertisement for perfume or diamond rings. Like we're in love with each other."

More lightly than I could have imagined, he said, "So are you going to pay?"

"You know I can't. And unless the blackmailer has just returned from Mars, he has to know I'm penniless, too." I could hardly breathe. "Why is this happening?"

"Take it easy. Maybe he thinks if I hear you're snuggling in the mink stoles with another man, I'll have the guy whacked?"

"That's not it. In fact, it's not even me I'm worried about. Well, I am, but— It's my friend I have to protect. He's a respected doctor, up for a big promotion at his hospital. He's got a wonderful daughter, and he's sticking by his wife, who's been in a coma since last January." I could feel my emotions building into the hot, awful lump just above my lungs. "He has so much to lose if something awful starts circulating, Michael. People will be shocked if they think he's having an affair while his wife is unconscious. And his daughter would be destroyed. It's horrible."

"Come on," he said. "Don't cry on the phone. I can't stand it."

"I'm not crying." Not exactly, anyway.

"You've got to get mad. And smart. Who the hell is doing this to your friend? Not to mention you?"

"I don't know. I'm too upset to think." I sat down at the table.

"Cool down and concentrate. He's counting on you panicking."

I tried to collect myself. "What should I do?"

"Just think for a while. What do you already know? What doesn't make sense?"

"None of it."

"Think."

"Well," I said slowly, "for one thing, there's a misspelled word in the note."

"A dumb crook. Now there's a surprise. What else?"

I almost smiled. "This afternoon I met someone else who's been blackmailed. She's a retired ballet dancer. But she has money, and I don't."

"Anything else?"

"I—I think the pictures came in the same kind of envelope that was found with Rush Strawcutter's body."

"Okay."

"And I found a stack of the same envelopes in Kitty Keough's desk drawer."

"I won't ask why you were digging through her

desk, but this is good stuff. Could the Keough lady be your blackmailer?"

"She's got the right personality." Hearing my tone of voice, Spike growled on the floor at my feet. I reached down and scratched his ears. The churning in my mind began to make sense. "And Kitty would love it if I suffered a misfortune."

"What's her connection to the ballet dancer?"

"I don't know. Except, well, there's a good chance she's dating Rush Strawcutter's business partner.

"Partners can be the death of anybody."

I picked up the envelope and carried it through the butler's pantry and the dining room. Spike followed in case I bumped into any dragons he could slay for me. I turned on the living room lights and curled up in my favorite chair with the phone pinned between my shoulder and my ear. Spike hopped onto my lap. "The partner, the man Kitty's dating, is in huge financial trouble right now." I started to tell Michael about Tottie Boarman's activities.

"I know about Boarman," Michael said. "I read the papers. He's one of those well-dressed felons. You know," he added, "crimes that happen at the same time tend to be connected."

"Do you think so?"

"I know so."

"Well," I said without asking how he had come by his insider knowledge, "Tottie Boarman made a big loan to Rush." I put my feet up on the arm of the chair and tried to put the puzzle pieces in place. "The common denominator in all this seems to be Rush, doesn't it?"

"Yep."

"Rush used to date the dancer, too. Did I mention that?"

"Yes, it all ties together somehow, doesn't it? Call your friend in law enforcement," Michael advised. "Maybe he can make the connection."

I cuddled Spike. "You, of all people, are suggesting I go to the police?"

"This is the kind of crime the police excel at. Blackmail attracts white-collar types, so the work of finding them in suburbia isn't dangerous. And unlike your garden-variety extortionist, blackmailers are emotional. They make mistakes. They're easy to catch because the shakedown requires them—"

"To show up in person to get the money?"

"Smart girl. Extortion, on the other hand, usually involves broken bones and nervous guys with big guns."

I shivered. "You know how I feel about guns."

"And justifiably so." His voice continued to soothe. "Give Detective Gloom a call. Believe me, I'm not happy to suggest he could help you, but he'll probably do something useful." In a different tone, he added, "Since this is an easy way for him to look like a hero, he'll probably jump at the chance."

"I'm afraid to talk to him. For fear he'll find a way to tie all this to Emma."

"Hm. Good point."

A moment passed while we considered the problem. I relaxed deeper into my chair and noted that Michael didn't sound perplexed. On the contrary, he seemed to enjoy the Machiavellian challenge of outsmarting a criminal. It allowed him to open a little-used valve in the back of his mind. For the moment, though, he asked, "How's Spike?"

"Not housebroken yet." I rubbed Spike's tummy, and he blinked innocently up at me before closing his eyes in bliss. "If I go to the police, I'll expose Tim to everything I'm trying to protect him from."

"Tim? That's the doctor?"

"He's a very nice person. He's— Well, his wife was hurt in a skiing accident. It's so sad. He stuck by her, visits her every day despite a full load at the hospital and being up for an important new job. Plus he's got a daughter to raise himself. She's sweet, too. You'd like them both."

"Think Spike would bite him for me?"

I smiled and reflected that Claudine's remark about jealousy wasn't totally off base. It did add a dash of spice to a relationship.

I flipped the envelope over in my hand to look for further clues. I looked closely at the postage sticker. "Michael, this was mailed a week ago!"

"What?"

Spike sat up in my lap.

"I've been staying at Libby's house! This envelope has been sitting in my mailbox for a week. I was supposed to pay the money last Wednesday! I missed the deadline!"

"Calm down."

"Oh, God, what does this mean?"

"A threat is meaningless unless you follow through immediately. Well," he said reasonably, "this takes the pressure off, doesn't it?"

I got to my feet. "I was supposed to hand over ten thousand dollars by now. Why haven't I heard from him?"

"This blackmailer has a relaxed timetable."

"But—" The thought hit me like a lightning strike. "Good Lord, do you suppose *Rush* was the blackmailer?"

Michael considered the theory. "Somebody decided to kill him instead of pay him?"

I wasn't sure whether to laugh or cry. A minute ago, I needed ten thousand dollars. Now, it seemed, I might be in the clear. "Do you think it's possible?"

"Did he need money?"

"Rush? Desperately."

"And he had an envelope on him when he died?"

"Yes. I wonder if he was trying to blackmail Emma? Wait, I'm making too many leaps."

"It's okay. Let yourself be creative. Theorize for a minute."

"The misspelled word," I said, reading the note again. "I just learned Rush Strawcutter was dyslexic." Suddenly, I wasn't as scared as I was excited. I headed back to the kitchen with Spike trotting behind me. "That's another clue that points to Rush."

"Maybe you don't need police assistance after all."

Behind me, the microwave dinged.

Michael heard it. "You're not eating plastic food again, are you?"

"I don't have time to shop or cook."

"When I get back, you're going to make time for a lot of things."

I tried to smile. "That sounds nice."

"Maybe I'll make you something with truffles."

"Truffles?"

"Yeah. Have you ever eaten them?"

"On special occasions. They're fabulous."

"Expensive as hell," he said. "But you just dig them out of the ground, you know. They're really rare."

"Yes, I know."

"We had such a great dinner last night that I started thinking about truffles."

"Are there truffles in Scotland?"

"Well—"

"You can't bring them into this country, you know."

"Not in your luggage," he agreed. "But they can be shipped. Restaurants pay a fortune for just a couple of ounces, did you know that?"

"Are you up to something?"

"I'm just thinking," he said, endeavoring to sound innocent. "Listen, I have to turn off the phone now. Don't panic about the blackmail, okay? If you haven't heard from the guy yet, you could be in the clear. Give it a few days. Now, tell me quick—how's Emma?"

"Sleeping at the hospital. I'll go see her in the morning."

"Give her a kiss for me."

"Fat chance."

He laughed and signed off.

Spike began to play on the kitchen floor in the puddle of water which had reappeared. In fact, it seemed to be growing larger.

I had found myself suddenly swimming in a lot of deep water. First a murder, and now blackmail. And nobody close enough to lend me a life preserver.

Except one person.

Chapter 7

Libby's minivan screamed up to my back door half an hour later than planned on Sunday morning.

She let herself in, wearing a white parka with a fur hood. The zipper was pulled low enough to challenge J. Lo's latest décolletage.

She said, "Do you think there's anything weird about these boots?"

From the scullery, I looked at her feet, which were encased in a pair of pointy-toed black boots with narrow heels and laces up the front. "Does your goddess enjoy sadomasochism?"

"Very funny."

"Why are you asking?"

"I respect your knowledge of fashion, that's all. You always look nice, and I only— Oh, never mind. What is all this water doing on the floor?"

Overnight, my kitchen puddle had become a pond, and frequent sweeping didn't seem to make any difference in the tide. "Whatever it is, it's going to be expensive. I don't want to know where it's coming from."

"Good thinking."

"But I called Mr. Ledbetter, anyway. He might as well give me an estimate."

"Maybe it's just condensation." Libby ignored my mention of the handyman who'd taken care of the house when my parents lived there. She had not liked Mr. Ledbetter ever since the day he'd caught her painting his portrait while he scraped paint off the parlor windowsills. Libby had painted him nude, drawing on her own adolescent fantasies to create a more romantic figure than Mr. Ledbetter cut in real life, and he—a good Christian—had not appreciated the results. She asked, "Do I have time for a cup of coffee?"

"I thought you'd given up caffeine while you're nursing. And where is the baby, by the way?"

"Safe with the teenage girl from next door. She's going to give him a bottle if I run late. I'm thinking of hiring someone on a more scheduled basis."

"Sounds sensible," I said cautiously.

"I mean, you seem to be too busy to help us now, so I might as well look for a stranger to share my heavy burden."

"Libby—" But I caught myself before letting her suck me into feeling guilty enough to move back into the zoo that was her household. "What about Rawlins? Isn't he old enough to baby-sit?"

"I haven't the faintest idea where Rawlins is these days." She sighed. "I know, don't lecture me. He went out with some of his high school friends again last night and hasn't come home yet. I'll be glad when he graduates."

If he graduates, I thought.

In motherly denial, she kept talking. "Did I tell you the twins have decided to use their new brother in their movie? He's going to play a defender of Santa Claus against an evil monster. I have a feeling I'm appearing in a cameo role as the monster. I need to be back in time for the baby's noon feeding, that's all, or I'll leak all over myself. Breast feeding is a wonderful experience, but some elements are downright embarrassing. Maybe I ought to stop now and let him discover the joys of the female breast when he's—"

"Coffee?" I asked desperately.

"Sure."

"There's some in the pot." While she found herself a cup, I debated about the best way to revisit the subject of her eldest son's deteriorating behavior.

"I hope this is decaf. What are you doing?"

At the scullery sink—which hadn't been used for dishes in decades and only served to clean garden pots and tools—I was elbow-deep in soapsuds, scrubbing the contents of my kitchen garbage pail out of Spike's rough coat. Spike happily snapped at the bubbles while I worked up a lather. "I assume that's a rhetorical question. Did you phone the hospital this morning? Have you spoken with Emma?"

"I couldn't get past the nurse's station." Libby poured herself a cup and spooned in enough sugar to sweeten a birthday cake. "They kept saying she was unavailable."

"I got the same message."

"Knowing Emma, she's cuddled up with a doctor or two."

I cast her a glance and noticed that Libby's complexion was pinker than usual. "You sound a tiny bit jealous. Or have you enjoyed the company of a doctor yourself in the last twenty-four hours?"

Libby fluffed the fur trim on her coat and sat down at the table. "I may have met a perfectly nice gentleman, yes."

"Did you play spin the bottle with Dr. Quartermaine last night?"

"Don't blow a gasket, please. I'm entitled to a sex life."

"Sex life? My God, you met this man yesterday and immediately took him home to your bed?"

"Of course not! Not with the children in the house. Good grief, what kind of mother do you think I am?"

"One who wants to try Tantric sex before menopause."

Serenely, she stirred her coffee. "I do, as a matter of fact. I'm not made of marble. But that has nothing to do with Melvin."

"Melvin? Why do I have a bad feeling about this?"

"I have no idea. He's interested in my goddess ambitions, and was extremely polite the whole time we were together. Not to mention generous. He bought me these boots when we left the hospital, so I invited him for dinner. Do you need help with that animal?"

From a safe distance, she watched me struggle Spike into a bath towel and wrap him up before he could fight himself out of captivity.

Buffing Spike while he attacked the towel, I said, "You have no willpower, Libby."

"We had a perfectly innocent evening! We discussed medical matters. For example, Melvin says it's important for me to maintain my weight while I'm nursing. He was firm about that, especially when he saw how much milk the baby requires and the quantity I'm donating to the milk bank."

My suspicions were instantly aroused. "Melvin watched you nurse the baby?"

"He's a doctor, for heaven's sake. He had dinner with us. Well, the kids had pizza in front of the television while Melvin and I had the dining room to ourselves. It felt very festive. I even lit candles. Bayberry scented."

"And then?"

"Nothing. Really. He stayed while I took care of

the baby, and we had a very pleasant discussion. Do you know how hard it is to find a man you'd actually spend more than half an hour with? Of course you do, if you ended up with— Well, we might see each other again. He was very forthcoming about medical subjects—things I'd never dreamed I should be thinking about."

"Such as?"

"Discipline, for one thing. He thinks I'm too permissive with the children, but he believes I can improve."

Anybody who thought he could inch Libby closer to becoming a more disciplined parent had my vote.

I put Spike on the floor. He headed straight for the pond and began to splash in the shallows. I pulled my envelopes and photos out of a kitchen drawer and put them on the table in front of Libby. "Take a look at these."

With astonishment, Libby stared at the photographs of Tim and me. "What's going on? Are you seeing Tim Naftzinger now? You make a nice couple, but— well, together, you're like the walking wounded or something."

"I'm not seeing Tim," I snapped. "Read this."

She scanned the blackmail letter. "Trooble? What's trooble?"

"Read it again."

Eventually, Libby caught on. After an explosion of *omigods,* I calmed her down by pointing out the past-due date on the letter and explaining my theory.

"I'm not the only person who received a threatening letter like this." Without mentioning Claudine's name, I told my sister about the other blackmail scam I'd heard about, as well as Lexie's suspicion that more blackmail was occurring in our social circle. Then I asked, "Are these envelopes like the one you saw with Rush's body?"

"Yes, they are. Except his had been folded in half." Libby struggled to absorb the deluge of information. "But Rush was such a nice man. He wouldn't misspell a simple word like *trouble.*"

"Unless he was dyslexic, which Delilah Fairweather says he was."

Libby smiled with pleasure. "How is dear Delilah? I haven't seen her in ages!"

"Focus, Libby. This is important. Do you see what it all means?"

Libby frowned at the photos again. "I get it. You think Rush was blackmailing people and somebody killed him for it!"

I showed her the extra white envelope. "That's my guess. Except I found a slew of these envelopes in Kitty Keough's desk drawer."

Libby looked confused. "What does Kitty have to do with anything?"

"I don't know yet."

We were prevented from discussing the matter further by the arrival of another car in my driveway. I told Libby to hide the evidence in a drawer, and I took Spike into the pantry to make sure he couldn't stage an ambush.

Detective Bloom was at the door when I came out of the pantry. Libby had greeted him with an offer of coffee, which he politely refused.

"Good morning," I said. "This is a surprise."

"I'm sorry to bother you at home." He glanced around the cavernous kitchen. "This is quite a place. I had no idea you lived like this."

Blackbird Farm had a way of astonishing first-time visitors. The massive house had been built by my an-

cestors two hundred years ago out of fieldstone dug
from the fertile farmland that stretched along the Delaware River. Twin oaks that had shaded William Penn
when he dropped by for a picnic still towered over
the front yard, and the split-rail fences ran more than
half a mile along the riverfront. The house itself had
eight bedrooms, two parlors, and a dining room where
John Adams had dined during the yellow fever out-
break of 1793 and Teddy Roosevelt wolfed a quick
dinner after buying a horse from my great-great-uncle
Blackie. There was also a rambling assortment of
added-on rooms—some of them still unheated—that
generations of Blackbirds had needed for purposes of
privacy, entertaining or subterfuge. There were no cel-
lars where runaway slaves were hidden, but my great-
great-grandfather had supposedly concealed a mistress
from his wife for four months in one of the attics.

The kitchen was adequate for preparing a banquet
for fifty, with a scullery, larder, laundry and a butler's
pantry large enough for storing several sets of china
and glassware in the glass-fronted cabinets. The kitch-
en's chandelier had come from France, and the Aga
was the size of a rhinoceros. The basic decorative
scheme was decrepit opulence, including fusty toile
curtains that depicted the ravishment of shepherdesses
by Frenchmen in powdered wigs.

Detective Bloom seemed surprised to find me in the
faded splendors of Blackbird Farm.

"Wow," he said. "Did George Washington sleep
here?"

"For all we know, he's still upstairs," I said.
"Come in."

"That's a lot of water."

The pond was now a lake that reached the middle

of the kitchen floor and seemed to be inching toward the butler's pantry.

"We're going to break out our bathing suits soon," I said.

Spike threw himself at the pantry door with a frenzy of barking, furious that he couldn't properly greet our guests.

Over the noise, Bloom said, "I'm glad you're both here. We need to talk."

Through the doorway behind him came two uniformed officers. I realized Bloom was not giving off his usual aura of a boy who wanted to invite me out to the playground to trade baseball cards.

"What's this about?"

"Your sister Emma."

Libby sat down at the table with a cry. "What's wrong? Is she—? What happened?"

"She's missing. She left the hospital sometime during the night."

"Oh, my God!"

"She left?" I repeated. "She had a police guard!"

"Yes."

"Did she leave, or was she kidnapped?"

"There are no signs of coercion. We believe she departed of her own free will."

Libby said, "You were watching her! The police had her surrounded in that hospital room. You had armed guards making sure she didn't go anywhere."

Bloom visibly controlled an urge to respond to the accusation. "She isn't in our custody, and we'd like to know where she is. For her own safety."

"She isn't here," I said.

Libby said, "She could be in danger!"

Bloom continued to look at me. "We'd like to look

around your house, if we may. To make sure Emma is all right."

"You think I'm harboring a fugitive?"

"It will only take a few minutes."

"Do you have a search warrant?"

"I felt sure you wouldn't want us to wait for a warrant. We're as concerned about her as you are."

"Bullshit," said Libby. "You're going to arrest her."

Suddenly, I couldn't breathe. Emma was missing. Detective Bloom guided me to a chair, and I sat down hard. He pushed my head between my knees.

I heard Libby arguing with him. "You can't barge in here without a warrant. I watch *Law and Order*. You need a judge's permission to come in here with your storm troopers. Look what you've done to my sister! Nora? Nora, are you all right?"

"Go look around," I said from between my knees. "Look anywhere you want. She isn't here."

"Don't let them, Nora. You should never let the police in your house."

"Emma's gone, Libby. We need to find her. The sooner they figure out she's not here, the sooner they'll go looking in the right places."

"Why don't you go upstairs with the officers, Mrs. Kintswell? You can supervise their movements. I'll take care of Miss Blackbird."

He went to the sink and ran some tap water into a drinking glass. Libby led the other two officers out of the kitchen, warning them to keep their boots off the carpets. Spike stopped barking and began to dig. I could hear his claws scratching at the stone floor inside the pantry. I hated being such an emotional idiot.

Bloom came back and pushed the glass into my hands. He sat down at the table and watched me take a tentative sip.

When I could speak, I said, "When did she escape?"

Bloom's tone was much less formal without Libby or his colleagues listening. "Between one and two in the morning. She must have walked out when the nurses were busy with another patient."

"Where was the guard?"

"The officer on duty received a phone call that his car was being vandalized in the parking lot. Which turned out to be false."

With my head still spinning, I squinted at Bloom, trying to make sense of what he'd just said. "A phone call about his car caused him to leave his post? That sounds suspicious."

Bloom shrugged. "We're a small police force. We hire moonlighters for duty like this. It was his private vehicle, and he felt it necessary to check."

"Who phoned him?"

"We don't know."

From Bloom's grim expression, I gathered one moonlighter was out of a job. I said, "Did Emma leave alone? Or did somebody help her?"

"I thought you might have information on that subject."

"I was here last night."

"Can you prove it?"

"I was on the telephone for a while. You could— No, I guess not."

Bloom watched my face intently, and I saw that he had managed to combine two high-profile cases into one illegal search of my house. The detective said, "He's still out of the country?"

"If you mean Michael, yes."

"And you talked to him last night? Do you know where he is? Or what he's doing?"

With a quick flame of anger suddenly warm inside

me, I said, "I know he wasn't at the hospital helping Emma tie bedsheets together so they could climb out a third-story window, if that's what you're asking."

"Do you have any idea who might have helped her?"

"If Emma wanted to get out of that room, she could have done it all by herself, Detective."

"So where is she now?"

"Her apartment?"

He shook his head.

I said, "Maybe she just wanted . . ."

"A drink?"

"Some fresh air."

He continued to look grim. "Nora, this is a serious situation. We didn't arrest Emma earlier because she was hurt. But her escape combined with some other evidence is enough."

He took a sheet of paper from his coat pocket and unfolded it. On the page were three photocopied pictures.

I didn't want to look.

But Emma's image drew me at once. She had always been the beautiful sister, the one whose face was truly arresting when captured on camera. Her smoky blue eyes had a soft, sensual flicker in them as she put her arms around a man's shoulders.

Rush Strawcutter's shoulders.

Rush, looking more handsome than in real life, smiled awkwardly down at my sister, who sent a quiet, sexual message back up at him. By the angle of the photograph, it was difficult to be sure, but she appeared to be naked.

The second and third pictures were equally unclear about her lack of clothing. But the aesthetics were the same as the first. They were romantic pictures. Soft focus, with a greeting card quality.

The same photographer had captured me with Tim Naftzinger.

"Where did you find these?" I asked.

"Three separate photographs were in Rush Strawcutter's coat pocket when we went through his clothes. We're keeping the originals for evidence, of course."

"Who took the pictures?" I asked.

"I hoped you would know."

I turned the photocopy facedown on the table. "They're very pretty."

For a moment, I contemplated showing Bloom the photographs that had been taken of Tim Naftzinger and me. But I knew Bloom would use the photographs to delve into my life—ostensibly to help find the person who was blackmailing me. He'd use that excuse to dig into the people around me, including Michael Abruzzo and, by extension, his family.

I decided to play dumb. "What do the pictures mean?"

"I don't know yet. But I have an idea. I hear your sister is having trouble making ends meet."

"The economy has been tough for everyone."

"She rides horses for a guy who uses her sporadically. I understand she teaches riding lessons to teenage girls sometimes, too, and coaches other people. But that's hardly enough income to live on."

"What does this have to do with her disappearance?"

Gently, he said, "Her landlord says she's a couple months behind in her rent."

Suddenly, I knew where he was headed. "If Emma needs money, she has property she could sell," I said.

"We all received something when our parents left the country. I got this house, Libby got all the family furniture, and Emma received the collection of paintings the family accumulated. She could sell one and pay her rent for the next ten years."

"Why doesn't she?"

"We have trouble parting with anything that comes from the family," I admitted. "It's stupid, maybe, but it's true. I could afford to fix up this house if I sold it, but you see the catch-22. I don't want to lose the house. Emma doesn't want to break up the art collection either. It's worth more than money to us."

He glanced around the kitchen, which could have passed for the cavern of an epicurean vampire. "So you're all broke."

"Essentially, yes."

"So maybe Emma has a few leaks to fix, too." He gestured at the water pooling on the floor. "If she doesn't want to sell anything, maybe she's looking for another source of income."

I tried to summon up some indignation. "What are you suggesting?"

"Just that your sister could have hired a photographer, might have tried to make some money off her rich boyfriend."

"My sister is not a blackmailer."

"Are you sure?" Bloom reached for the paper and turned it over so I could see the photographs again. "I think she found an easy way to shake down a guy for a few bucks."

Coldly, I said, "I hate to ruin your theory, Detective, but Rush Strawcutter was even more broke than Emma. It's common knowledge that he hardly carried enough pocket money to buy himself a cup of coffee.

Besides, if Emma were blackmailing him, it makes no sense for her to kill him. So which crime do you think she committed?"

For the first time since his arrival, Bloom looked uncertain. Spike gave up digging at the floor and began to claw at the pantry door, growling as if possessed.

"Okay," Bloom said finally. "So maybe it was the other way around."

"What do you mean?"

"If Strawcutter was the one who needed money, maybe he hired a photographer. Maybe he was blackmailing her."

"He would have been smarter to pick somebody who actually had some cash."

"He could have been pressuring her to sell off a painting. And she didn't want to sell, so she did what she had to do to avoid paying him."

I wanted to encourage the detective to investigate Rush. Whereas I couldn't gather enough evidence to prove my theory about him, the police had the resources to learn if Rush had been blackmailing his friends or not. But Bloom had already made the leap I didn't want him to make: that Emma might have been Rush's latest target.

"So Emma killed him?" I asked lightly. "You're back to that theory? You've got to choose one, Detective."

He sighed. Then he picked up the photocopy and folded it in half. He tucked it into his pocket, avoiding my gaze. "Don't be mad at me. We're running around in circles, and I thought you might know something that could help."

"I don't like your tactics."

He shrugged.

"You're still going to hunt down my sister, aren't you?"

"We don't have any other leads at this point. Emma's the key to this, no matter which way you look at it. We need to talk to her."

"We'd all like to talk to her."

Bloom still didn't meet my eye, but suddenly he put his hand over mine on the table and pinned me there. "Nora," he said. "I'm really not the bad guy here. I can help."

"You and your merry band upstairs?" I asked. "What kind of mental anguish are they inflicting on Libby?"

He glanced up and actually smiled. "I'm not worried about her," he said. "She'd survive a nuclear blast."

"Don't pretend you're worried about me."

"I am." His hand stayed where it was, but the pressure changed to something more gentle. "You're upset about your sister. And I don't think you understand the seriousness of the situation Abruzzo's got himself into this time, either."

"I don't think he's done anything wrong."

"Everybody in his family has. Gambling may be the least of it. He's got to be mixed up in some of it, too. But he's smarter than the rest and stays under the radar. The big fish swim deep, you know."

I tried to pull away, but his touch tightened again.

"Nora," he said. "You've already had one big tragedy in your life. Don't let yourself get dragged into another one. Abruzzo is not a domesticated animal. Let me help you."

He radiated all the good virtues a policeman ought to have. Soft-spoken and gentle, yet with an underlying strength that felt bulletproof. Maybe he was a paragon among men, the kind good girls ran away from home to be with. I felt something stir inside me, but I couldn't decide what it was.

The phone rang.

I disengaged my hand and got up to answer it, half fearing it might be Michael calling again just when Detective Bloom was here to take credit for tracking down America's Most Wanted.

But in my ear, Emma said, "It's me."

"Oh." I turned away so Bloom couldn't see my face. "Hi, Rawlins. How are you?"

"What?" Then she said, "Oh, shit. The cops are there."

"You're right." I hoped my tone sounded unsuspicious. "Where are you?"

"I can't say. And they're telling me I can't talk long or this call could be traced. I'm fine, okay?" her voice quavered and she laughed without amusement. "I'm not fine, but don't worry about me."

"We are, though."

"I know. And I—I appreciate anything you can do to help. Please, I just need to know if I did something stupid. I can't stand it if—" She caught a gasp, and I knew she was choking back tears. "Never mind. I'll explain everything when things settle down."

"I'll do what I can, you know."

"Thanks. I— Thanks, Sis. I'm okay, that's all I wanted you to know. Don't worry, really. I'll call again when I can. I gotta go. I'll be in touch."

"Okay," I said. "I'll tell your mom you're fine."

"Yeah, right," she said, and hung up.

I couldn't believe I'd heard her voice. My hands were shaking when I disconnected the call.

Bloom looked up at me and said, "It was her, wasn't it?"

Chapter 8

Libby came downstairs, and using the full force of her goddess-given obnoxiousness, she managed to send the police packing.

"Emma's safe," I told Libby when we were alone again and Spike was running around the kitchen peeing wherever he could smell the footprints of strangers.

"We need to find her!"

"No, we need to make things safe so she can come home by herself." I picked up Spike and tried to think logically. "If we find her, the police will, too. For the moment, the best thing we can do is prove she's innocent of murder as well as blackmail."

"How do we do that?"

"I have some ideas. I just hope I don't make things worse by asking the wrong people the wrong questions."

"Things can't get any worse for Emma."

I thought Libby was wrong about that, but forcing her to see the light wouldn't help the situation.

I set my plan in motion by phoning Reed, and he came in the town car. Libby reluctantly went home to stand guard at her house in case the police showed up with a warrant to search there. Spike let himself be hastily stuffed into my handbag, and we set off on my mission.

My first stop was Rittenhouse Towers, the condo-
minium where Claudine Paltron lived with her husband Osgood, the Zapper Czar. Their doorman
informed me that the Paltrons were out. Osgood had
gone jogging—information the doorman managed to
deliver without laughing. I knew better. No doubt Osgood had wandered up the street to find a Sunday
brunch that served bourbon.

Claudine, reported the doorman, had probably gone
to the rehearsal hall. She had been carrying her work-
out bag when she left. I needed to speak to Claudine
about her blackmail experience. Most of all, I hoped
she could guess who took the pictures. If Rush had
been the blackmailer, surely he hadn't taken the pictures himself—at least not the photographs in which
he appeared. For my theory to work, he must have
had an accomplice. And maybe Claudine knew who.

Reed drove over to Broad Street and past the Academy of Music to the cultural district and a double
town house that had been expensively refurbished into
a no-frills rehearsal hall for the ballet company and
two city dance troupes. To my surprise, the stage door
was unguarded and unlocked on a Sunday morning. I
slipped inside and found myself in an echoing stair-
well. Above, I could hear the music of a rehearsal
piano, so I went up the stairs.

In the second-floor rehearsal hall, a perspiring and
stormy-faced young man and an ethereal girl in a
performance-quality tutu were pounding through the
steps of a pas de deux with JoJo Welch, the ballet
company's longtime director. The pianist appeared to
be reading a newspaper while the explosive JoJo
shouted a tirade at the dancers. I did not disturb
their work.

The stairs had not been swept in years. I was struck

by how sordid rehearsal spaces could yield such incredible beauty onstage.

On the third floor, the staircase opened into a loungelike area with faded sofas and ragged overstuffed chairs for dancers to use between sessions. Three smaller rehearsal halls opened onto the lounge, but their lights were turned off.

On one of the sofas lay an amazingly handsome young man. With one arm thrown over his head and his face turned toward the light slanting from the window, he appeared to be sleeping. He was dressed in expensive black trousers and a black turtleneck sweater with the sleeves pulled up. His Prada shoes hung over the edge of the sofa.

He heard my steps and sat up.

"Oh." I said. "Hello, Dougie."

I was fleetingly sorry that I hadn't found Claudine right away. But Dougie was almost as good. Maybe better.

Douglas Forsythe sat up on one elbow, ran one manly hand through his shining hair and assumed a pantherlike pose right off the glossy pages of a men's fashion magazine. He'd been a model in his youth. Now over thirty, he had been forced to seek other employment and occasionally found work as a personal trainer, I'd heard. He hoped to be "discovered," went the rumor, and find himself wildly successful as a movie actor. Mostly, however, Dougie managed to survive without a formal job.

"I'll bet a thousand dollars," Hadley Pinkham had once predicted, "that Dougie Forsythe ends up getting shot by somebody's husband."

I should have taken the bet. Instead of being shot, Dougie became best known around town for being stabbed by the fifty-something socialite DaisyAnn

Hicks when she discovered he'd given her one of the less dire sexually transmitted diseases. There was an immediate run on antibiotics among some ladies who regularly lunched at the Four Seasons, and DaisyAnn went to jail. During the trial coverage, Dougie took a liking to being a celebrity. He quickly ascended through the ranks of attention-starved rich women until he reached Claudine, whose fame satisfied his ambition.

Personally, I didn't see the attraction. Dougie's smiling face was as handsome and empty as that of a game show host.

"Hey," he said. "Aren't you the newspaper lady?"

"Yes," I replied patiently, having introduced myself to Dougie at least half a dozen times since taking my newspaper job. "I'm Nora Blackbird."

He snapped his fingers and got up with a photogenic smile. "Yeah, right. Howya doin'?"

"I'm looking for Claudine, actually. Have you seen her?"

"She's upstairs. Talking to some guy in his office. Secret negotiations."

Not so secret anymore. I decided Dougie must need jumper cables to start his brain every morning.

Dougie sighed. "She said she'd be done in time to get some lunch, though. You want to wait?"

"Thank you." I wondered how tricky it might be to get him to talk about Claudine's blackmail. "I hope I'm not disturbing you."

"Nope." He took a pack of Nicorette gum from his trousers pocket and popped a piece into his mouth. "You doing a story on Claudine for the paper?"

"Just some fact-finding." I sat on the edge of one of the chairs, a safe distance away. "How is she enjoying retirement?"

"Oh, you know. She's antsy. Needs something to do, she says. I told her I could keep her plenty busy, but you know how women are." He strolled closer and tried his smile on me again.

I managed not to fall at his feet and tear my clothes off. "She's been under a lot of strain, I understand."

"Yeah, a lot."

"She's lucky to have you for a friend."

Another grin, less attractive this time. I realized he was trying to get a read on my personality. "Sure, I'm good at relieving strain."

"She must have been very upset when the ordeal started."

"Oh, yeah." He caught my drift and began to nod. "I'm not supposed to say anything about it, but when the first envelope came, she ran yelling and screaming over to my place like I had something to do with it. But I got her calmed down."

"You saw the envelope?"

He winked. "I saw everything."

"A white envelope?"

"And some very hot pictures, if you know what I mean." Dougie preened at the memory. "We looked *good*."

I said, "Did Claudine guess who was behind the photographs? Who took them, I mean?"

"Nope, we didn't have any idea."

"You are a model, though. You must know dozens of photographers."

"Sure. Even a few of the guys who do art stuff. But I have no clue who did those pics of me and Claudine."

"Do you know when they were taken?"

"At a party we went to at some guy's house. Claudine and me ended up in a bedroom with all the coats, you know?" Dougie tried to look shy about his participation in the tryst. "We had a little fun, see, and I guess somebody saw us and snapped the pictures. I'd like to know who it was, actually. I'd take some copies. You know, for my portfolio."

"Do you remember who attended the party? Any of your photographer friends?"

He shrugged. "Loads of people were there. A lot of dancers because it was after her final performance. I talked to a few of the girls while I waited around for Claudine to get rid of her husband."

"Do you remember anyone else? Was Kitty Keough at the party?"

"Who?"

I could check Kitty's schedule on the newspaper computer to find out where she'd been the night of Claudine's final curtain. "It doesn't matter. Anyone else there? Besides people from the ballet? What about some donors?"

"Sure, some of the usual people. Mostly old ladies."

"What about Rush Strawcutter? Do you know him?"

"The guy who got killed at the foxhunt thing? No, I don't remember him being there." Dougie began to comb his fingers through his hair again. He knew he didn't like my questions, but he wasn't sure why.

"Did you know Rush well?"

"A little, maybe."

"I understand he and Claudine used to be close."

"That was a long time ago," he snapped.

Pushing Dougie's buttons seemed to be working, so I said, "Rush was a nice guy. I imagine that he remained friends with Claudine after they broke up as a couple."

"They were never a couple. Not really." Dougie's

brow began to glow with perspiration. "Claudine says they only talked."

"But Claudine is a sensual woman. I'm sure she and Rush—"

"He wasn't the full package. I'm the one who's got everything she wants. If she wants somebody to talk to, she can talk to me now." Dougie's voice rose to an agitated whine. He stood very tall over me. "I'm the man. I'm the one she wants."

"I'm sure you are," I said, rising to my feet. I wanted to put more space between us in case his temper flared. I didn't know him well enough to guess his reaction if I really pressured him. I'd try again sometime when we weren't alone. I checked my watch. I needed to phone Libby to learn if Emma had shown up yet, anyway.

Besides, I felt as if just talking to Dougie was causing my brain cells to atrophy. "Well, thanks, Dougie. I appreciate your help."

He frowned. "You're not going to wait for Claudine?"

"I'll catch her another time."

"Listen," he said, stepping closer. "I hope you don't tell her about what I said. I think I was supposed to keep quiet about that stuff."

"Don't worry. I won't tell anyone."

Suddenly, he was looming and seemed taller than before. Lower voiced, he said, "I mean it. She'd be upset."

"Really, Dougie, I won't say a word."

Upon close inspection, I realized his eyes had a mean pinch at their corners. He said, "I'd do anything for her. So let's just forget we had this little talk."

I felt instinctively that Dougie's performance was

just that: a performance. But I wondered uneasily how far he'd take the role.

I said good-bye and hurried down the steps, wondering exactly what qualified as the "anything" he'd do for Claudine.

Out on the street, a little flurry of snow was drifting in the cold afternoon air, transforming the city into a pretty snowglobe. I glanced both ways, then crossed the street to the curb where Reed had parked the town car.

But just as I reached the car, another vehicle sped up to me and stopped in the middle of the street. A soprano horn beeped twice in a friendly greeting. I turned to look.

"Hey, kitten." Hadley had rolled down the window of his vintage MG convertible and leaned out attractively. "Want to have a hot buttered rum with me somewhere?"

"Hadley, I didn't think you got out of bed before five on Sunday afternoons."

"I just came from worshipping at my favorite religious institution, but Lord and Taylor didn't have my shirt size today, can you imagine? Come on. Let's go for a spin. I want to hear everything you've heard about Rush Strawcutter's demise."

I hesitated. I wanted to call Libby, but somehow I knew Hadley would be a good source of information. I put up one finger to ask for a moment, then I spoke to Reed, thanking him through the open car window and telling him to go home for the night.

Reed looked across the street at Hadley. "Who's the guy?"

"An old friend."

"I'm not supposed to leave you with anybody suspicious," he reminded me.

"Your *jefe* is on another continent," I said, meaning Michael. "I've known Hadley since we were kids."

Reed looked unconvinced. "You call if you need me."

When he reluctantly agreed to go, I took Spike with me and crossed the street again.

Half a minute later, I was sitting beside Hadley in his low two-seater sports car, cozy beneath the canvas roof. Spike popped out of my bag and braced his paws on the dashboard to look out the windscreen. His stumpy tail vibrated madly. Hadley rattled the gear shift, and we roared off down the street with the wind whipping snow through the badly fitted windows. Spike barked with excitement.

In equally high spirits, Hadley was wearing a tan leather-collared field coat over wool trousers and a jaunty sort of cap that an English country gentleman might keep by his back door. Over the roar of the engine, he said, "This car is so old it doesn't even have seat belts, so hang on for dear life. And it's freezing, know. There's a lap blanket on the floor, if you need it. Or is that animal of yours enough to keep you warm?"

"I'm fine."

He grinned attractively at the sight I made sitting with Spike in my lap. "You're not one of those women who gets a dog just to see if she can stand to have children, are you?"

"Think I could keep a baby in my handbag?"

"You could, but he'd turn out more twisted than am. Hold on!"

I grabbed Spike and clutched the dashboard as we rounded the next corner, going too fast. In the next instant, the latch on the glove box gave way, and the door fell open. A snowstorm of little yellow papers fell into my lap. Spike forgot about the view and began to tear into the pile.

"What's all this?" I wrestled paper out of Spike's jaws. "Hadley, these are parking tickets!"

"Just stuff them back where they came from, kitten. I never met a parking ticket I felt like paying, but I love to see my collection grow. Oh, now and then I pay one, but I write someone else's name on my check. I love playing with their heads."

"Wait—these are all unpaid?"

He nonchalantly waved one hand, exquisitely clad in a buff leather driving glove. "Who has time to take care of details? What are you doing in town this morning, for heaven's sake? Or have you been out all night, you little devil?"

"I tried to see Claudine Paltron."

"The dead swan? What on earth are you seeing her about? Did she take the artistic director's job or not? Honestly, by the time she accepts, that story will be such musty news nobody will care. She has no sense of timing. Never did. Did you see her?"

"No, she was busy. Dougie was there."

"Ah, the Incredible Hulk. He belongs in a recliner with a Pabst in one hand and a television remote in the other. And he probably measures his penis when nobody's looking."

I heard the anger beneath his mocking tone. "Why do you dislike him so much?"

"Do I? I suppose I do. Because he's nothing but an accessory. Claudine doesn't need a pink poodle on a rhinestone leash when she's got Dougie on her arm. The man is useless." Hadley gave a short laugh. "Besides, he looks better in clothes than I do, which I cannot forgive."

"So that's the truth of the matter. You envy his clothes."

"Which Claudine buys, for the most part. And I envy his youth. He'll still be Adonis when I start looking like Liberace in Sansabelt pants. Did he astound you with his clever banter?"

"He tried to threaten me, I think. I'm not sure, though. It's been a very trying morning for me, Hadley, so be nice, please."

He was instantly sorry and reached over to touch my hand. Spike gave him a warning snarl, so he pulled back. "My dear kitten, tell me your troubles. Shall we go find a drink somewhere secluded and confess our sins to each other? Do you belong to any clubs we could invade? Some place posh, I hope."

"I don't belong to anything that costs money. I'm broke, remember? And getting more threadbare by the minute."

He shot me a look of arch dismay. "You can't be broke as long as you hold the deed to Rancho del Blackbird. Hasn't a shopping tycoon offered you millions for the old homestead yet?"

"I can't sell the place, Hadley."

"Oh, don't let sentimentality ruin your fun." He glanced at me more shrewdly. "How despondent you look. Is it Emma? How is she feeling?"

"I can't even guess because she's disappeared, Hadley." I threw caution to the wind and said, "She walked out of the hospital, and I don't know where she's gone. Neither do the police."

"Were they planning to put her in a lineup?"

"Yes. She flew the coop instead, and now it's up to me to prove she's innocent before they catch her again."

"Courage, kitten." Hadley sounded genuinely sympathetic. "Let's cozy up for an hour and I'll spoil you

a bit. Do you mind rubbing elbows with the unwashed masses?"

Without waiting for an answer, he pulled into a
parking lot across from the Reading Terminal Market
and hopped out of the old car to assist me. He ducked
the lot attendant with casual expertise, and in a few
minutes we were across the street and making our
way through the crowd of tourists and neighborhood
people who had flocked into the old railroad building
that now housed a noisy food bazaar. I shoved Spike
deep into hiding so we wouldn't be arrested by the
sanitation squad.

Behind me and with his hands on my hips, Hadley
guided me past the counter-service restaurants and the
line that had formed for cheesesteak sandwiches and
French fries. We wound our way past the Amish
women who were shyly selling baked goods like shoo-
fly pie and homemade biscuits. The noise deafened
me, but the heavenly smells made me suddenly raven-
ous. Spike whined from captivity.

"Next stop, coffee," Hadley said in my ear.

He pushed me onto a stool and raised two fingers
at the unshaven man who ground coffee beans on the
other side of the stainless steel counter. "Nothing
fancy, barkeep. Two javas, no additives."

Then Hadley slipped onto the stool beside me. He
tugged off his gloves and neatly tucked them into his
pocket. "Tell me why the police think Emma was the
one to put Strawcutter in cold storage."

"You mean besides finding her near his body, covered in blood and unable to explain herself?"

"She wasn't holding a dagger and moaning about
hand washing, was she?"

"Not quite. But her riding crop was there, also bloody."

"Are they doing DNA testing?"

"Yes. Meanwhile, the police have something almost as damning." With Hadley gazing at me with such empathy, I felt a rush of warmth for my old friend. "Can I trust you, Hadley?"

"With your life and chastity, cross my heart."

I took a chance and told him about the white envelope and blackmail photographs that had been on Rush's body. And the letter I had received after Rush's death. I was careful not to mention Tim Naftzinger's name. I allowed Hadley to assume the blackmailer had photographed me with Michael.

Hadley wasn't surprised by my news. He took the revelation calmly. "I've heard rumors," he said. "About several fat cats getting blackmail letters."

"Really? Anyone I know?"

He put one finger to his lips. "Sworn to secrecy, kitten. Let's just say they are people of influence, not to mention big bucks."

"Have you seen any of the photographs?"

"Sorry, no."

"I thought you might be able to tell me something about them. The pictures have a unique flavor."

"You know I'm a complete ninny with cameras. I'm all thumbs with any kind of mechanical gadget, actually. I never took to the family trade."

Our coffees arrived, fragrant and steaming. I waited while Hadley pulled a silver flask from his pocket and poured a little nip into each cup. Calvados, was my guess by the scent. I took a sip and found the drink tasty and stimulating.

"The photos look pretty," I said finally. "Not the kind of grainy, unpleasant pictures you imagine coming from a criminal. They're actually good—almost character studies."

"So the blackmailer isn't just some amateur with an empty wallet?"

"No, he's got talent. Do you think Rush was a photographer?"

"He hardly seemed the type."

"No. And he couldn't very well take his own picture with Emma, either, I suppose. Unless he had an accomplice."

"On the other hand," said Hadley, "it would make sense, considering how barefoot Gussie kept him."

"I know." I drank my coffee and looked longingly at the blueberry muffins on display. But dressing for the Christmas gala loomed before me, so I asked, "What do you remember about the hunt breakfast? You were there early, right? Did you see anything happen?"

Hadley drank and looked thoughtful. "I arrived earlier than most of the horseless guests, but I didn't see much except crimes of fashion. Including ding-a-ling Dougie Forsythe."

"What was he doing there?"

"Looking for a photo op, I presume. Or a girlfriend more connected than Claudine, if that's possible. I hate a blatant gigolo. Later, of course, we both saw Tottie acting like a Cape buffalo."

"Right. This whole murder thing would make more sense if Tottie were the dead man, wouldn't it?"

"Yes. He's got more enemies than a city councilman." Hadley poured more liquor into his cup.

"I understand Tottie and Rush were compatriots in a business scheme."

"I heard that, too. On Friday night I spent the cocktail hour with a couple of financial boy geniuses celebrating the end of the work week. Once they partook of some little white lines of high spirits, they revealed all kinds of gossip."

"Such as?"

Hadley shrugged. "Tottie has a girlfriend. I suppose if silverback gorillas can have a tryst in the mist now and then, so can he, but it comes as a shock to imagine him cuddling up to anything but a mutual fund."

"You'd be surprised."

Hadley raised his brows. "You have insider information?"

"I believe Tottie had a full dance card, that's all. But listen, do you think Tottie and Rush could have had a falling out?"

"Tottie murdered Rush? Before going off on the foxhunt? My goodness, kitten, I never thought you had such a devious imagination!"

I smiled grimly. "Necessity. I need to find someone who rode in the hunt, someone who remembers seeing Tottie before it started."

"You know Tim Naftzinger, right? He was there. You could ask him."

"Yes," I said, carefully noncommittal.

"Or we could ask some of Tottie's chums. In his newfound quest for sainthood, Tottie's throwing a party this afternoon. I thought you might be going."

"I haven't been invited."

"It's not that kind of party. It's Koats for Kids. Tottie's the new sponsor, and they're having a mad tea party for children. It's bound to be a gas. I'm hoping Tottie puts on a Santa suit."

"You're going?"

"Of course. You know how I love irony. Want to come along? There's bound to be food. Cookies for the kiddies and tidbits and cheap chardonnay for the rest of us, I suppose. You might get a chance to do some detective work."

It was a chance to see Tottie again, too. "I'm in," I said.

Chapter 9

Before setting off with Hadley, I phoned Libby. She had had no word from Emma, and was ready to launch into another meltdown, so I signed off quickly.

The Pressley, a stately hotel with gas lamps out front and crystal chandeliers in the marble lobby, had been knocked down and replaced by an extremely generic glass-and-steel chain hotel that catered to large families of tourists who came to see the Liberty Bell and eat cheesesteak sandwiches. In the off-season, the new hotel tried to stay in black ink by renting out its ballrooms for conventions. It was known around town as a good place to get a party room and so-so food on a budget.

Hadley and I rode the escalator up to the mezzanine, drawn by tinny Christmas music and Mylar balloons. At the top of the stairs, I saw my friend Delilah Fairweather issuing commands into her cell phone. We crossed to her. She snapped her phone shut and hugged us both.

"A total disaster," she said, as if we'd arrived in midconversation. "Why did I take this job? It's a total disaster. I should know better. Never take a party at the last minute. And never take a job somebody else started and screwed up."

"What's the catastrophe? Everything looks fine."

Delilah wore a red minidress with a beaded bolero

jacket and white boots. Her hair was cornrowed tight against her skull, then exploded into a top knot of braids at the crown of her head, decorated with a twist of tiny silver stars. The taut hairstyle made her almond eyes seem more slanted than usual, but they were sparkling with anger. "Tottie Boarman's people coordinated this party with the hotel, but they realized nobody was going to come, so they asked me to step in to round up the usual suspects. I had a day free, so why not? The pay's astronomical. Just goes to show I should never take a job for the money. These people are idiots!"

"What people?"

"Tottie's crew! They know nothing about event planning."

"What do you expect?" I asked. "Tottie probably never threw a Christmas party in his life."

"If it weren't for such a good cause, I'd walk out right now. But Koats For Kids—ever hear of it? It used to be a charity that gave away coats and mittens to underserved families every Christmas. But it fell apart last year when the organizers retired. Tottie stepped in this week and donated a big chunk of change to the organization. He wanted a party complete with the Cratchit children singing carols, but his people dropped the ball. I hate having my name attached to a bomb." She checked her watch. "I'm waiting for the kid chorus now. They're late."

Hadley said, "If Tottie shows up with a sack of gifts, I'm going to puke in the sleigh."

"Yeah, reeks of Christmas spirit, doesn't it? He's buying goodwill, but what else is new?"

"Can you get us in, Delilah?"

She waved us toward the open ballroom doors. "Of course. The crowd is going to be thin because there's a *Monsters on Ice* show this afternoon. Anybody who's here has been bought and paid for by Tottie's people, who wanted a mob for the sake of photographers. Any extra bodies will be more than welcome."

"Count on us." Hadley took my arm. "Let's go."

The ballroom had been set up with a small stage with a piano at one end, no doubt for the children's chorus that hadn't yet shown up. An artificial tree, decorated with childish drawings pasted on lace doilies, stood in the center of the room, looking too small and slightly crooked. A few children in expensive holiday clothes wandered listlessly around tables that had been set up with games. Three college girls in elf costumes tried to entice the children into tossing rings over bottles and dimes into goldfish bowls. I figured the kids were the children of Tottie's staff members. The adults stood around in Christmas finery trying to make the best of the enforced festivities while keeping their offspring under control.

One little boy, dressed in a brass-buttoned vest, tartan pants and red bow tie, hung on his father's hand and whined that he wanted to go home to his Xbox. A little girl in layers of tulle bawled brokenheartedly while her mother knelt and whispered in the child's ear soothing promises of treats to come. Two more boys were batting each other with spoons stolen from the refreshment table, making light-saber noises.

Spike woke up and poked his head out of my handbag. He peered with predatory interest at the children.

Hadley plucked a sugar cookie from the buffet and sniffed it suspiciously. "Think I could get a real drink from someone?"

I pointed at the punch bowl. "Fruit juice."

He shuddered. "What a waste of perfectly good

maraschino cherries. Why put them in anything but a Manhattan?" He tossed the cookie back onto the buffet and went in search of alcohol.

Across the room I saw Tim Naftzinger, of all people, standing awkwardly by himself with an empty punch cup in one hand. I went over to him.

"Hi, Tim."

"Nora." He was surprised to see me.

"Is Merrie here with you?"

"No, she's at home. I— The hospital asked me to stop in. The staff is giving a donation, and they wanted me to present the gift."

"That's wonderful."

"It's all part of the promotion process." He looked sheepish. "I think this is a test to see if I'd make appearances as Chief of Pediatrics."

Of course, I wanted to ask Tim all kinds of questions. There was a chance he knew something about the blackmail photos I had received. But it would have been heartless. He looked overwhelmed already.

"Do you really want the new job?"

He started to sip from his punch cup and seemed puzzled to find it empty. "I don't know. I enjoy working with patients, but the top job would mean more administrative duties, with hours I could control. I'd get to spend more time with Merrie."

"That sounds like plenty of incentive."

He tried to smile, but it looked forced. "I hoped to make a quick appearance and go home to her, but I understand all the donors have to wait for Tottie Boarman to show up." With more feeling, he said, "I hate being on parade like this."

"I'm sure the organization will accept your check even if you leave early."

He perked up. "Think so? I hate to spend any extra weekend time away from Merrie. I see so little of her during the week."

His schedule was brutal, I was sure.

But he lingered for another moment. "I heard Emma left the hospital without being discharged. Is she all right?"

"Actually, she gave her police guard the slip and took off," I confided. "I'm going to keelhaul her if she ever turns up."

Tim's face went slack. "You haven't heard from her?"

"She's fine," I assured him. "I appreciate what you did to help her."

"I wish I could have— I'm just glad she's all right. I hope she— I mean, Merrie is very fond of her."

"Emma has that effect on people." I smiled at Tim. "She's a natural instigator, and kids respond to that."

Quite seriously, Tim said, "It's more than that. She's got a lot of heart, I think. She tries to hide it, but she has something to offer other people."

He caught himself, but I found myself watching Tim's face. For an instant, I had seen honest emotion there. Did he care differently about Emma than I'd first thought? But his fleeting expression was gone.

"Well," I said, "I hope this mess blows over soon. I know the police think she's mixed up in Rush Strawcutter's death somehow, but that's ridiculous. She'll be cleared soon. And then—well, Emma needs a chance to get her life back on track."

Tim considered saying something, but stopped himself.

He looked very vulnerable standing there, out of his element and longing to be at home with his daughter. Looking at him, I knew for certain I could never tell

Tim about the photographs I'd received in the mail.
Tim didn't need another burden to carry.

But should I warn him? Was his family in danger
because I couldn't pay the blackmailer?

We were interrupted before I could speak. The late-
arriving chorus trooped into the ballroom, led by a
very short, stout woman in a stiff black cape and a
fur toque set at a jaunty angle over her stern face.
She carried a folder of sheet music under her arm and
marched straight for the stage, followed by two dozen
children all wearing neat white shirts, black pants and
Santa hats. The last boy in line—perhaps ten years
old and less than pleased to find himself paraded into
the room looking silly–had snatched off his hat and
hidden it behind his back. The conductor directed her
singers into place and plopped the boy's hat on his
head when he passed by. He rolled his eyes.

Spike wriggled in my bag, keenly absorbed by the
puffy white balls on the Santa hats.

"I think I'll take your advice and go home," Tim
said beside me.

"Okay," I said. "Merry Christmas, Tim."

I moved to kiss him on the cheek, but he flinched
away. Without another word, he walked rapidly for
the door.

Hadley strolled over again. "No booze at all," he
reported. "How can we have holiday spirits without
holiday spirits?"

I was about to answer him when I noticed Kitty's
new assistant, Andy Mooney, lurking nearby. He was
so short that he blended in with the kids, but he
snapped a picture, and his camera's flash caught my
attention.

"My God," Hadley cried with delight. "A real elf!
No, perhaps more of a gnome."

"Andy," I called. "Come meet a friend of mine."

Andy came over with a big smile. He still had a cell phone earpiece, but only in one ear this time. "Miss Blackbird! Awesome to see you again."

He desperately needed a breath mint. I introduced Andy to Hadley, who looked amused when Andy pinpointed the Pinkham bloodline right away.

"Oh, I've admired the Pinkham photographs for years," Andy gushed. "I'm a bit of a shutterbug myself."

"A shutterbug," Hadley crooned. "How awesome. Don't you think, Nora? Do you have a portfolio, Mr. Mooney?"

"Oh, nothing that formal. I just snap for my own pleasure. And for Miss Keough now, too, of course."

I said, "Andy has been accompanying Kitty Keough to social events. I think Andy aspires to be a social reporter himself someday."

"Oh, it's my calling," Andy assured me seriously. "It's my wildest dream."

"Is Kitty here, Andy?"

"Yes. She stepped out to freshen up."

Hadley was undeterred from his line of questioning. "What do you do with all your snaps, Andy? Do you keep them in an album?"

"Not all of them. I have so many!"

"What do you do with the rest?" Hadley asked. "The ones that don't go into albums? Do you destroy them?"

"Oh, no, just store them in envelopes."

"What kind of envelopes?"

Andy raised his camera lens to his eye to frame a picture of the children assembling on the stage. "Just standard photographer envelopes."

"The white, laminated kind, you mean?"

"Yeah, those. Do you think I should try getting some shots of the kids? You know, just in case Miss Keough wants to add some warmth to her column this week?"

"I'm sure she'll add a little warmth," I said. "It's almost Christmas, after all."

"Okay, I'll be right back."

"Interesting," Hadley said. "Don't you think so?"

"I take back all the rude things I ever said to you, Hadley. You're brilliant."

"Oh, look, there's Pixie Northram, the cosmetic surgery addict. Do you think it's safe for her to stand so close to a radiator? She's going to melt."

While the chorus finished organizing itself, a cherubic little girl in blond pigtails saw Spike and ran over to us. Her velvet sash had come untied, and both ruffled socks had worked their way down into her patent leather shoes. Her face was sticky with pink goo. She pulled her thumb out of her mouth to ask, "What kind of dog is that?"

"A Moravian possum terrier," Hadley volunteered.

"He's ugly. Can I pet him?"

"I don't think that's a good idea," I said gently. "He's not very friendly."

Spike, trembling with the extreme effort of staying calm in such close proximity to very tempting prey, growled deep in his throat.

The little girl frowned at me. "If you don't let me pet him, I'll tell my daddy to fire you."

"Well, I don't actually work for your daddy, so I think I'm safe."

Hadley said pleasantly, "Buzz off, brat."

She glared up at Hadley. "You're prissy."

"You're odious."

"You're stinky."

"That's practically a synonym, you little gremlin. It doesn't count."

"I hate you!"

"Double for me."

"Hadley—"

"See here, you little urchin, we've got more important things to do besides listen to your adenoidal fussing, so take a powder before I kick your butt from here to Christmas Eve."

She opened her mouth for a comeback, then decided she was beaten. With a wail, she ran off, trailing her velvet sash on the floor behind her.

"I love children," Hadley said. "Usually with hollandaise."

Just as the chorus hummed to the quaver of a pitch pipe, Tottie Boarman made his entrance. First came an honor guard of assistants armed with the latest electronic gadgetry, plus one carrying a briefcase. Then Tottie marched in, looking more like a general setting foot on a battleground than a host emceeing a children's Christmas party. He had a hard expression on his face, every inch a man who was making an appearance against his will.

Hadley and I happened to be the first guests in his path.

"Pinkham," Tottie said. "Isn't it illegal for you to be in a room with impressionable little boys?"

"Well, if it isn't Ebenezer," Hadley replied. "Happy Holidays to you, too, Tottie."

"Don't give me that Christmas crap." Squinting at me, Tottie said, "You're Charlie Blackbird's granddaughter?"

"Yes, I am. I'm Nora."

"Your idiot father borrowed a thousand bucks from

me before he ran off to Brazil or wherever the hell he's hiding."

"I think he's in Argentina at the moment."

"Having a wonderful time, no doubt. On my dime."

Fortunately, I was saved from responding.

Delilah Fairweather hurried up to us, pasting Christmas cheer on her face. "Mr. Boarman?"

Tottie swung on her and immediately pegged Delilah as someone on his payroll. "Yeah, that's me. Let's get this show on the road. Am I supposed to light a tree or a menorah or something?" He looked at his watch.

"Yes, the tree lighting will take place after the choral performance, so if you'll just—"

"The tree lighting takes place right now," Tottie ordered. "And then I'm getting the hell out of here. I have an appointment."

"But—"

The little girl with the sticky face ran past us and threw cookie crumbs at Hadley before dashing away with a squealing laugh.

The sight of a fleeing victim was too much for Spike. With a murderous bark, he suddenly burst out of my handbag like a fighter jet launched from the deck of an aircraft carrier. He landed with an explosion of trumpeting flatulence and tore off in hot pursuit of the little girl, snapping ferociously at her sash. Over her shoulder, she took one look at Spike's flashing teeth and screamed.

"Jesus Christ," said Tottie.

Children scattered in terror. Waiters dove for safety. Parents shrieked for police protection. The chorus began singing "God Rest Ye Merry Gentlemen."

Hadley said, "You could pretend he's not yours."

I ran after Spike with a desperate hope that he wouldn't actually hurt anybody.

Destruction was another matter. Already Spike had clamped his teeth down on the tail of the little girl's velvet sash. He tried to dig his paws into the carpet to hang on while the child raced in a screaming circle, but her momentum sent him as airborne as a kite in a typhoon. He crashed into the legs of a busboy's stand, and I saw a tray of dirty dishes teeter precariously. I made a dive to save it, but too late. The whole thing crashed to the floor. Dishes and glassware scattered in all directions.

A foolhardy waiter made a flying leap to grab Spike, but slammed into one of Tottie's assistants instead, and the two hit the floor just as the chorus began singing about being saved from Satan's power.

I skittered through the debris to try to catch Spike on their next lap around the buffet, but the little girl raced into a crowd of cowering parents and children, who shrieked and scattered like bowling pins. In the melee, Spike finally managed to tear the sash off the girl's dress. He galloped around the Christmas tree with glee, waving the sash overhead like a victory flag and breaking wind with every joyous leap.

Andy Mooney swung his camera case at Spike. The puppy immediately dropped the sash and latched on to Andy's trouser leg. Andy yelped and began to dance. Spike hung on, growling like a homicidal mongoose.

Hadley lurched up beside me, breathing hard. "Here's a Christmas cookie. Lure him under the buffet table, and I'll make a diversion so you can get him out of here."

"No more cookies!" I cried. "How do you think he got into this condition?"

Spike ripped off a hunk of Andy's trouser leg, revealing an argyle sock beneath. He made a pouncing dive to attack the sock, but Andy kicked his leg into the air with more gusto than a frenzied Rockette.

Spike immediately lost interest in Andy and decided to attack the bunting on the buffet table. Again, the crowd surged back from his furious assault. With the linen in his teeth, he braced himself and proceeded to yank, yank, yank until the punch bowl teetered on the edge of the table. Two waiters bravely leaped into the fray. One snatched up the bowl in a Herculean clean jerk, but the slosh of red punch washed over his tuxedo shirt and splashed him in the face. He sputtered, bobbled the bowl and dropped it. Glass and ice exploded on the floor in a tidal wave of faux fruit juice. The second waiter slipped in the sugary lake and executed a belly flop into a tray of macaroons.

Spike snatched up the little girl's sash again and made another noisy victory lap around the quaking Christmas tree. Then, triumphant that he'd ruined every aspect of the party, he quit the battlefield and bolted under the table with his trophy.

The chorus switched to "Winter Wonderland," but the singing was hardly audible over the weeping of children and parents.

I crawled under the buffet table.

Delighted to see me on my hands and knees, Spike ran over and began licking my face.

"That's it," I told him. "I'm never having kids."

He wriggled into my handbag and gave a delighted sigh.

I peeked out from under the table in time to hear a fresh wave of shrieks as the decorated tree gave one last precarious wobble and began to keel over. Hadley darted over to the buffet table and motioned me to make my escape, obviously ready to sacrifice himself so I could make a clean getaway. Clutching my handbag closed, I crawled out from under the table and inched to the nearest exit—a fortuitously close service door.

In an instant, I was safely out of the ballroom and leaning against the service corridor wall and panting in exhausted humiliation.

Two men from the hotel security team rushed up. "Are you all right, miss? We heard there's a rat in the ballroom."

"A rat? Yes, right there." I pointed a shaky finger toward the door I'd just come through.

They dashed past me.

I looked around to decide which way I could make my quickest escape and saw Tottie Boarman hotfooting it away from the party. Alone, he darted down the service hallway, heading for the back of the hotel. He was carrying a briefcase.

To Spike, I said, "Where in the world is he going?"

With a throaty growl, Spike suggested we follow.

Outside, it was getting dark. The slight snowfall had increased to a thick flurry that looked picturesque and would soon have the city engulfed in several inches of traffic-stopping white stuff. I gave Tottie a head start, and he walked quickly across the street, glancing over his shoulder only once to make sure he wasn't being followed. I turned my back and pretended to be waiting for a cab. When I turned back, he had flipped up the collar of his suit around his ears and gathered the lapels with one hand to stave off the cold. Or to become a man who wouldn't be recognized. Then he set off walking down the sidewalk in the opposite direction from where his car ought to have been parked.

More curious than ever, I followed him.

We went about three blocks, then cut one block east, then two more. I noticed his gait gradually slowed down and looked more pained as we walked. In ten minutes, we were in the park at Rittenhouse Square. The fast-falling snow had driven most neighborhood people indoors to their apartments in the surrounding high-rise buildings. I kept a screen of trees between Tottie and myself so he wouldn't see that he'd been followed.

He stopped at one corner and glanced around. I had just enough time to sit on a snow-covered park bench and duck my head. When I looked up a moment later, Tottie was crossing the square and heading for the tables where people often played outdoor chess in the summer. Now, however, the tables were empty.

He came to a hobbling stop beside the chess tables and glanced toward a Barnes and Noble bookstore where two customers were lingering on the sidewalk and chatting as the afternoon light faded into evening. Tottie seemed troubled by their presence and glared in their direction for a long time. I used the moment to find a secluded spot behind a lamppost and some overhanging tree branches.

"Nora?"

I gasped and spun around.

Hadley caught my elbow and eased me back into the shadow of the lamppost. "Steady, kitten. What in the world are you doing?"

"My God, you scared me. I'm following Tottie. Look."

Hadley peered across the park. "What's he doing?"

"Certainly not acting like a man who's giving a Christmas party right now."

"What's in the briefcase?"

"I doubt it's old issues of the *Fortune* magazine."

We tried to determine what Tottie was doing, but he appeared to simply stand beside the tables, watching the bookstore customers.

"Is the party a disaster?" I asked.

"I left before the police showed up. Look. Tottie's on the move again."

We peeked around the lamp. The bookstore customers had parted ways. As they left, Tottie suddenly walked away, too.

I said, "He forgot the briefcase."

Empty-handed, Tottie began heading diagonally across the park. Hadley and I edged around our lamppost to avoid being spotted.

"Hold the phone," Hadley whispered. "Check out that car."

An aged white Mercedes eased to a stop along the curb opposite the side of the square where Tottie was headed. The driver killed the headlights, but left the engine running. The driver's side door opened and a woman got out of the car. She wore a heavy fur coat, which I recognized.

The woman left her car and headed into the park. "That's Kitty Keough."

"What's *she* doing?"

All the puzzle pieces suddenly made sense. "She's picking up Tottie's briefcase."

"Well, hitch me to a sled and call me Rudolph! She's the blackmailer?"

With my heart beating in little jerks, I watched Kitty make her way through the snow to the chess tables. Her molting mink coat was unmistakable, but the darkness had begun to gather quickly around us, and the lamps had not yet flickered on. It was difficult to see what she was doing. She lingered only a moment at the chess tables, then rushed back to her car, slipping precariously on the sidewalk.

"Does she have the briefcase?" I asked.

"I can't see. I've got an idea," Hadley said. "We have to split up. You go after Tottie, and I'll follow Kitty. My car's parked just around the corner. Call me tonight, and we'll compare notes."

I turned and looked up into his handsome face. His eyes were alight, and I felt a rush of grateful thanks. "Hadley, this isn't your problem."

"Nonsense, kitten, I'm having more fun than Mrs. Claus when Santa leaves her alone with all those elves. All we need is decoder rings, and we'll be independent crime stoppers!"

"Hadley, thank you. You're a real friend."

"Just don't call me Watson. I'm too young for the role. I'll phone you later. Now go."

He gave me a shove in Tottie's direction. I glanced back to see him dashing off toward his car in high spirits.

I hitched my handbag more securely on my shoulder and tailed Tottie across the square. My boots slipped in the icy snow, and I found myself breathing hard as I peered ahead and tried to catch up. Tottie paused at the corner to allow a limousine to leave the Rittenhouse Hotel and pass by. The headlights caught him square in the eyes. And he turned his head to avoid the glare. Then the limousine's headlights raked me, too, silhouetting me perfectly against the dark backdrop of the park. Tottie saw me.

He panicked and ran across the street. The limousine swerved to miss him. Another car had just rounded the corner and cut sharply aside, just ahead of a following city bus. Tottie leaped out of its way. The car slammed glancingly against the curb anyway, and the bus slew sideways in the slush to avoid ramming it. Horns blew.

When the oncoming car straightened, it was headed straight for me.

I threw myself out of its path, but my feet slipped out from under me and in the next instant I was somersaulting over some shrubbery. I twisted in midair, trying to avoid crushing Spike in my bag. Then the snow rushed up and smacked me in the face.

Silence.

A door slammed and someone came crunching through the snow. A tall figure in black leather and jeans. Above me, he said, "The women in Scotland didn't throw themselves at my feet. What a nice welcome home."

Chapter 10

Even alone, Michael always seemed like a man who had an entourage. He just naturally exuded the presence of a Mafia prince.

He helped me to my feet and I tottered over to the side of one of his ridiculous muscle cars, which should have made any red-blooded gangster blush with shame. It was red and low-slung except for the rear wheels, which had been hoisted up to accommodate tires that looked as if they'd been pumped up by giants. The car looked ready to take a load of television hillbillies on a joyride.

Michael leaned me gently against the passengers door and smoothed my hair away from my damp face. "You okay?"

"My dignity is beyond repair."

Then I forgot about hillbillies and noticed that the snow was suddenly looking very pretty and romantic. Michael's dark hair was windblown and flecked with flakes, and the curving planes of his face looked both dangerous and amused. The sapphire blue of his eyes still took me by surprise, especially when they reflected a daunting amount of sexual arousal. His hands cupped my elbows, and he eased his knee warmly between my thighs.

Smiling, he said, "I missed you."

"If you kiss me right now, I'll bite you."

He laughed. "Have I done something?"

"You almost ran me down!"

"I saved you from being run over by a bus." He pulled his knee back from where it had felt really good. "What the hell were you doing, anyway? You don't usually run out in traffic."

Spike fought his way out of my handbag and interrupted my response by leaping onto Michael's chest. With excited piglike squeals, the puppy wriggled his whole body and licked Michael's chin.

I suppressed the urge to do the same thing.

Michael grabbed Spike by the scruff of his neck and detached him. Spike burrowed his head inside Michael's half-open jacket and continued to make adoring noises. With a grin for me, Michael said, "Don't you want to kiss me, too?"

"I'm too busy thinking you're supposed to be in Scotland."

"I just got back."

I put two and two together. "It was you, wasn't it? You helped Emma get out of the hospital."

He shrugged modestly. "Not me personally, no."

"But you made it happen. I should have known."

"Emma's fine, if you were wondering."

Relief rushed through me so fast that my head went light. "Where is she? Can I see her?"

"Don't worry. She's fine. We're moving her around a little, just to dazzle the competition."

"Michael," I said at last, "I am so pathetically glad to see you."

I kissed him then. He tucked Spike under his arm and ran one of his hands through my hair to the back of my neck to pull me hard against him. I collided with the powerful length of his body and heard myself make a carnal sound in the back of my throat. I slid my hands up his back and hung on for dear life while my insides felt as if they were taking a trip on a roller coaster.

Part of me wanted more than anything to take that last flying, gravity-defying plunge somewhere wonderful with him. But not yet.

A few heart-pounding minutes later I mastered myself again, and he smiled as if he knew better and bundled me into the car. He got in beside me and turned up the heater. Spike stayed in my lap but didn't take his worshipful gaze from Michael.

I regained my voice and said lightly, "Wasn't this car in a TV show once? Only with a Confederate flag on the top? And a girl with hardly any clothes?"

"You have no respect for automotive excellence. Maybe I should take you on an educational field trip to Detroit. I bet we could find a romantic hotel and still get you a tour of the hall of fame. I'd take you to the Auto Show, but I can't wait that long."

"I don't think the Detroit Ramada is going to do it for me," I said, although at that moment just holding his hand was doing plenty.

"I suppose Daytona is out of the question? Or Indianapolis?"

"I was thinking of Venice."

He deliberately misunderstood. "Vegas? We could catch an Elvis impersonator there to get us in the proper romantic mood. I love Elvis."

"Somehow that doesn't surprise me."

He turned sideways in the seat. "Are we really going to go away together? It's cruel if you're just teasing."

Maybe I'd fallen in love with him. Against my better judgement, I had certainly fallen in lust, and for some women that would be enough. For me, however, after suffering through years of Todd's addiction and the hell of his final months, I needed some assurance that life wasn't going to blow up in my face again. Taking up with a convicted criminal, no matter how straight the line he claimed to be walking these days, seemed as sensible as signing on for the *Titanic*'s second voyage.

But, boy, was I tempted. My lips still tingled, and the rest of me longed for his slow attention.

I clamped my knees together to suppress any involuntary physical response. "Tell me about Emma. Is she really okay?"

He put the car in gear and pulled away from the park. "You mean is she drinking? No, she isn't."

Sometimes he was more observant than I gave him credit for. "Michael, did you ask her about Rushton's murder?"

"A little. She doesn't remember much. She needs to know what happened, Nora. She's scared." He added, "It's been rough on her."

"Of course it has. The doctors were very concerned—"

"No, I mean there was something between her and the dead guy."

Startled, I said, "Oh, no, I was afraid of this. Was she having an affair with Rush?"

"An affair? That word sounds like old movies. I can't tell if Emma actually sleeps with all the guys she dates or just ties them to her bedpost and tortures them. She cared about this one, that's all I know. Does that make an affair or just better-than-usual sex?"

I remember the photograph I'd seen, with Emma looking up at Rush with something more than a sexual come-on in her eyes.

Michael said, "Emma didn't whack the guy. But she's afraid she contributed somehow, and it's killing her. Whatever she had going with him, she's broken up now."

"Did she cry on your shoulder?"

"A little," he said.

While I processed that information, he reached across and patted my knee.

I took his hand in mine again to ease the harshness of what I was about to say. "You shouldn't have helped her, Michael."

"What?"

"When Emma left the hospital, she just made herself look guilty."

"She already looked guilty. I only helped her buy some time."

"When the police find out you were involved, you'll be in worse trouble than before."

"Who's going to tell them? You?"

I let him withdraw his hand. "According to my sources, you're not considered the most upstanding citizen at the moment. I'm worried, and not just for Emma. I don't want your own trouble getting blown out of proportion by a connection with a murder."

"Stop," he said.

"I mean it."

"I do, too. Stop."

Spike had been looking between us as if we were smacking a tennis ball back and forth. He gave a nervous whine.

I said, "The police think you left the country to avoid prosecution for money laundering."

"I came back, didn't I?"

"Do they know that yet?"

"I didn't set off any alarms at the airport, if that's what you mean. What's got you more upset? Emma accused of murder or me looking like a goodfella?"

"Are we going to argue about this again?"

"I'm game if you are."

I didn't respond, but my heart was beating very fast. Spike gave a long tremble, and I smoothed the bristly hair on his back.

A moment later, Michael said more gently, "Tell me what you were doing in the park."

"Talking a walk."

He shook his head. "You're a terrible liar. Reed called me to say you were acting suspicious, so I came over. It looked like you were tailing a guy. Who was he?"

"Tottie Boarman."

"The financier who lost all the money?" Michael sounded surprised. "What's he doing that needs you to watch?"

"I suspect he was leaving a briefcase for the blackmailer."

Michael drove too abruptly around a corner and overcompensated, making Spike lurch in my lap. "I thought the blackmailer was dead. Jesus, what the hell are you doing? Getting hit by a car wasn't the most dangerous thing that could have happened to you tonight. Did you see who picked up the case?"

"Yes. Kitty Keough."

He frowned. "How does that make sense?"

"It doesn't. My friend Hadley Pinkham followed her to see what happens, and I was supposed to stick with Tottie."

"Who's Hadley Pinkham?"

"And old friend. You'll hate him on sight, I'm afraid. He's a completely useless person, but a lot of

fun. Anyway, we split up. Hadley followed Kitty, and
I went after Tottie."

"Why?"

"Well, why not? To learn something, of course."

"And your friend is going to watch what Miss Kitty
does with the briefcase?"

"I presume she'll take it home and start counting
the cash."

"In that case, she's really stupid."

"Startled, I said, "Why?"

"What blackmailer goes to the drop in person?" He
shook his head in derision. "A rookie move like that
should have had the cops getting their promotions
long ago."

I considered the logic of his theory. When it came
to crime, Michael was rarely wrong. "So maybe Kitty
was picking up the briefcase for someone else?"

"If she wasn't, your criminal is an idiot."

My imagination went into overdrive. I thought
about what I knew. Kitty had access to Andy Mooney,
a photographer who labored at her beck and call. She
also possessed the white envelopes and knew people
who had pots of money. And she had the egocentric
chutzpah to believe she was more entitled to the
money than the current owner.

But if Kitty was the blackmailer, why was Rush
Strawcutter dead?

I had finally become aware of our surroundings and
didn't recognize the neighborhood. We had left Rittenhouse Square far behind and were thumping
through potholes and passing places of business I had
never patronized.

"Where are we going?"

Michael said, "I don't like doing this with you in
the car, but it'll only take a minute, I promise. Then

we'll get some food. I know a great pizza place near here."

"Good heavens, you eat something as pedestrian as pizza?"

"Sure. It's my sister's place."

The possibility that I might meet an actual member of the Abruzzo family struck me dumb. I knew he had a great affection for his sister and her two young daughters, but he had never before suggested we meet.

He drove into a dark alley, past a line of trash cans that stood drunkenly against a crumbling brick wall. The snow had tapered to light, lacy flakes. Michael eased the car into a parking space alongside a large dark automobile with a sagging tailpipe. Then he shut off the engine and said, "Hop out."

With Spike in my arms, I climbed out of the car and met him at the trunk. He unlocked it, and in the dim light I saw two duffel-style suitcases and a long, tubular case for carrying fishing rods. He handed me the rod case and shouldered the larger of the two suitcases before picking up the other in one hand. Then he closed the trunk and led the way to the other car, carrying his gear.

He said, "You'll like my sister. Vanessa's my half-sister, of course, but she's smarter than my brothers. She makes a great pizza, if you can stand the advice that always goes with it."

With another set of keys, he unlocked the trunk of the other car. It opened, and a light went on inside. He said, "Hey, Em. Warm enough?"

My sister Emma sat up in the trunk and threw a tire iron at him. It missed.

She snapped, "I have to pee, you son of a bitch. Another ten seconds, and I was going to do it right here in your goddamn car. I was supposed to be here just five minutes!"

"I ran into somebody." Michael picked up the tire iron and reached to help Emma out of the car. She smacked his hand away.

"Oh, Em," I said.

She climbed out of the car and allowed me to hug her, but she was still angry. Then Spike squirmed and tired to climb onto her. She pulled him out of my arms and gruffly said to me, "Oh, damn, you're not going to faint, are you?"

I leaned weakly against the tail fin of the car. "I'm just glad to see you in one piece."

"No thanks to Studmuffin here. What was I supposed to do for half an hour?" she demanded of him. "Hold a séance in there?"

"Scared of the dark?"

My little sister, stiff and pale, said, "I thought I was hiding from the police, not entering some kind of bladder competition. What were you and Rawlins arguing about after you locked me in there? Oh, never mind. My molars are floating and I'm going to burst if I don't find a place to pee real soon."

Michael seemed very pleased with himself as he loaded his luggage into the open trunk and slammed it shut. With the smaller duffel in hand, he said, "C'mon. Through that door."

The three of us trooped through an unlocked, windowless steel door. Last in line, I found we had entered the unsavory back hall of a restaurant. Kitchen steam blew at us from a blindingly bright room on our right. We heard pots banging and voices shouting. Across the narrow hall was a wooden door labeled with a grimy silhouette of a Victorian lady. Emma handed Spike to me and pushed inside.

Michael said, "Give me a minute to do some business."

And he disappeared down the hall, duffel in hand.

I followed Emma. The bathroom was a two-seater with a rusty sink and a towel dispenser that hung crookedly on the wall. The floor was so scuzzy I didn't dare put Spike down. Emma went into the first stall.

She'd been cursing under her breath since we left the alley.

I interrupted her to say through the door, "I'm glad you're safe, you know. The police came looking for you at the farm this morning."

"I gathered. Did you tell them anything?"

"Did I know anything?" I asked. "Except you're probably an idiot for staging an escape from a hospital."

"I knew the cops were going to arrest me in the morning. When Mick's co-conspirators showed up, it seemed like an opportune time to leave."

"Co-conspirators?" Things were getting more complicated every minute.

"Oh, yes, delightful chaps. Do you know those guys he hangs out with?"

"Not by name."

"Good thinking. I've never seen so many tattoos in one place at the same time outside a circus tent. With the exception of Rawlins."

"Rawlins?"

She flushed and came out of the stall, zipping up a perfectly new pair of blue jeans. So new they still had the tags attached to the hip pocket. While she washed her hands and face in the sink, I tore the tags off and presented them to her when she had dried her hands with a wad of paper towels.

"Yes, our nephew was front and center." She tossed

the towels and tags into the overflowing trash can.
Spike attempted to lunge after them, but I held him
fast. "Afterward, Mick's posse encouraged Rawlins to
have a motherly tribute permanently imprinted on
his butt."

"As a comment on his upbringing?"

"Something like that. He refrained, though."

I had mixed feelings about Rawlins hanging out
with Mick's motley crew of misfits, but I had to admit
my nephew was showing more signs of responsibility
now than he had when he'd associated exclusively with
his high school pals. Still, it seemed unwise to encourage a young kid to spend his evenings with men who
had done hard time and looked like they could cause
serious trouble for the Hell's Angels.

Emma stared at herself in the mirror. She was very
pale, and her short, unwashed hair stuck out in a
primo bed head. She had a shiner under her left eye
that I hadn't noticed before. Her lower lip was swollen
and chapped, and I thought her hands were shaking.

But, dammit, there was nobody who could wear a
hospital scrubs shirt tucked into a pair of blue jeans
along with her own still-muddy riding boots and manage to look as if she just stepped off a flight from
Paris. The meager overhead light caught the sharp cut
of her cheekbones, and her feathery dark lashes cast
delicate shadows beneath her eyes.

I opened my bag and handed her a lipstick. "You
okay, really?"

"I refuse to get back into that trunk again. I don't
care if the police haul me off to a chain gang, I'm not
getting in the trunk again." She applied the lipstick
gingerly.

"You can come back to the farm with me." I took
the lipstick back when she was finished.

She rubbed her temples and managed a rueful smile. "No, I'm on the lam now, right? Sounds like an adventure I shouldn't miss."

"But, Em, if you have nothing to hide, why not go to the police and tell them everything?"

She looked balefully at me in the mirror. "Because I can't remember."

"What?"

"I was drunk." She put both hands on the edge of the sink and leaned there, head down. "Maybe I passed out, or maybe it was some kind of blackout. I don't remember much about that night."

"Do you remember going to the hunt club?"

She nodded. "I drove the trailer over there around two in the morning. I was going to sleep in the truck, but I had a bottle."

"So you drank in the truck?" Alone, I thought with a twist of sympathy.

"Next thing I know, Rush is knocking on my window. I let him into the truck and we had a few laughs, I guess. I don't remember much."

To me, she looked as if she hadn't laughed in weeks. "Do you remember going to the barn?"

She turned away from the sink and leaned against the wall, hugging herself, face still turned away from me. "Yeah, I guess so. Rush and I left the truck and . . ."

Her voice quavered, and I said, "Em, I'm sorry."

I saw her summon up the strength to hold back tears, but a single fat one spilled out of her left eye and traced a salty line down her cheek before trembling on the edge of her jaw. She said, "He was a good guy."

I felt my own heart crack and whispered, "I'm so sorry."

She nodded, and a terrible moment ticked by. At

last, she said, "Gussie turned up when we went over to the barn. It was early in the morning—before dawn. Rush hadn't expected her, and she caught us together." She frowned. "There were some pictures. Rush was showing them to me and she came in. I remember she got hysterical." Her hand strayed to the bruise under her eye and her frown deepened, as though she was trying to remember how she had come by her bruise.

"What do you remember about the pictures?"

"Nothing. Just— Nothing. But they were both upset about them."

"Did Gussie hit you?"

"I think so. Or maybe it was Rush. He was upset about the pictures. I can't put the pieces together." She ran her hand through her short hair. "There were other people, too, I think."

"Like who?"

She squinted at me. "Tottie Boarman. Does that make sense? And other people from the hunt club. Mostly, I heard voices. I think I was passed out."

"Like who?"

"Tim Naftzinger?" she guessed.

I nodded. "Tim was there with Merrie that morning."

Emma swiped her hands down her face slowly, thinking. "Merrie's a good kid, but I don't remember her being there. I know this is weird, but I think that really stupid guy came in, too. That peckerwood ex-model."

"Dougie Forsythe."

She tried to grin but failed. "I must have dreamed that one, right?"

"Not necessarily. Did you see Rush argue with anyone else besides Gussie?"

Before he was killed. But I didn't say the words.

Emma sighed. "I don't know."

"What about your riding crop? Do you remember what you did with it that morning?"

"Did I have it with me? I don't know. Jesus, I just don't know anything! It's driving me nuts, Nora. I was too drunk. Maybe I did something wrong. Maybe I—"

"No. You didn't kill Rush."

"But I must have done something. It's got to be my fault that he—that Rush—"

Emma cried then. She clenched her fists against her eyes, but she couldn't stop the tears. Tough, strong Emma suddenly looked lost and scared and bereft. I hugged her, crying, too, while Spike whined and struggled between us.

Emma pulled away first. I wiped my eyes and watched her try to make sense of the jumbled images in her head. But abruptly Emma gave up. She stopped weeping, shoved her hair off her forehead and blew an irritated sigh. "This is all par for the course, though, right?" she said with a bitter laugh. "We Blackbirds always pick the wrong men."

"I'm so sorry he's gone, Emma. I hadn't realized Rush truly meant something to you."

"I know better than to fool around with a married man. I almost fell for the old I'm-going-to-leave-my-wife line. Funny, isn't it? You'd think I'd be smarter than that."

I hated seeing her heartbroken and hopeless again. I knew if I didn't figure out what had happened, she was going to tear herself apart with grief and guilt. I'd seen her do it before, and I wondered if she'd survive it this time.

She couldn't help herself. Not yet. She needed to get healthy first.

"Let's go get something to eat," I suggested, putting

my arm around her again. Spike licked her face. "You look like you could use a meal and a good night's rest."

She leaned against me for the briefest moment and let Spike erase the salty line from her cheek. "What I need is a drink."

Michael knocked on the door then, and I opened it.

"Ready to go?" he asked.

"Emma's not getting into the trunk again."

He grinned. "Whatever she wants."

I noticed he wasn't carrying the duffel anymore. He took Spike from me.

By the time we reached the alley again, another car was pulling up beside the parked vehicles. Michael turned, Spike in his arm, and recognized the car. He waved it into a parking space.

I didn't know the man who got out of the car, but Michael missed a step at the sight of him.

Michael said, "What the hell are you doing here?"

"Aldo sent me. He couldn't make it."

"He couldn't make it? What'd he do, break a nail?"

The new guy grinned. He was younger and not as tall as Michael, but he had a swagger and a hard body under a leather jacket and jeans. He'd make a daunting adversary in a brawl, I found myself thinking. He wasn't bad-looking despite having slicked his black hair into a ponytail. He said, "Hey, she sent the Shakespeare kid home early, and Aldo's getting his sister out of custody tonight, so here I am."

Michael sighed.

Emma went over and said, "Who's this? Another one of your minions?"

"Nothing minimal about me, baby."

Michael said, "This is Danny Pescara."

"Mick's cousin," Danny supplied. "Kind of, anyway. Who are you, baby?"

"Cut it out," said Michael.

"You don't need to fight my battles for me." Emma sized up Danny Pescara with a practiced glance. "I can take care of an asshole with one hand tied behind my back."

Danny smiled and fingered the toothpick in his mouth. "We could do a few more things with your hands tied. What are you wearing, anyway?" He looked at her boots. "That's some fashion statement you got going."

"Know anything about horses?"

"I been to the track a few times."

"I don't like this," I said to Michael.

"You and me both. Look, Danny, let's just forget about this thing."

"Don't change your plans on my account." Emma was looking at Danny as if he might make a good punching bag. "I want to see if this idiot can keep the romance alive for more than three minutes."

"First we gotta find out if you can interest me that long, baby."

"Wake up and smell the inadequacy, big boy."

"Oh, Jesus," said Michael. "What's it going to be with you two? Machine guns at dawn?"

"He won't live that long," Emma predicted.

Danny laughed and strutted over to the hillbilly car Michael had just vacated. He opened the driver's side door and bowed to Emma. "You coming?"

She looked at Michael and managed to keep her cool. "Where am I going?"

He saw through her act and softened his tone. "We're just going to keep you out of the limelight for a few days. You'll be someplace safe. At least," he added with a meaningful glance at his cousin, "you better be, or I'll have a smaller family by morning."

Danny shrugged. "You want safe, call an ambulance."

Emma lightly punched Michael's arm. "It's okay, Mick. I'll go with this moron if he promises to buy me a steak."

"Before or after?" Danny asked.

"Just make sure you're not followed," Michael commanded. "And you call me every hour, got that?"

Danny raised his eyebrows at me. "You want to be interrupted every hour, that's no skin off my nose."

To me, Emma said, "Don't worry, Sis. You and the love machine have a nice night. I'll see you tomorrow."

"Be careful, Em."

But I knew I might as well have tossed those cautionary words off the edge of a cliff. Emma went around the car and got into the passenger's side. Michael reluctantly threw the keys at Danny, who winked and slid behind the wheel. A minute later, they were gone, Danny accelerating so the car's rear wheels skittered sideways in the snow before catching some traction and speeding off down the alley.

Michael put me into the other car and got in beside me. He sat for a moment, looking thoughtfully into the rearview mirror.

"Is he really your cousin?" I asked.

"My stepmother's sister's kid," he said absently, still frowning at the disappearing car. "You think Emma can handle him?"

"Emma," I said, "can handle starving alligators on speed. You forget she was married to Jake Kendall."

Michael stopped frowning at the mirror and stared at me. "Jake Kendall? The football player? Why didn't I know that?"

"I don't—"

"Emma's husband was Jake Kendall?"

"Didn't I mention his last name? I assumed you knew that."

"Oh, shit," he said. "Oh, shit. I don't believe this."

He started the car and whipped it around to follow Danny and Emma. But we reached the end of the alley and they were gone. Michael got out of the car, swearing until Spike began to bark.

Michael stood in the snow and punched buttons on his cell phone. Whoever he called didn't answer, and he started cursing again.

At last, he got back into the car and said, "I think I just made a big mistake."

Chapter 11

After a minute, he said, "I better take care of this tonight. You mind if I take you home?"

"No pizza?"

"Sorry."

"Are you going to tell me what's wrong with your cousin?"

"No," he said.

Once again I got the message that I was better off not knowing anything that I might have to discuss on a witness stand. But this time the safety of my own flesh and blood was at stake. So I said, "What branch of the family business is Danny in? He isn't your accountant, is he?"

"He probably has to take his shoes off to count higher than ten. No, he's not my accountant." Michael seemed to understand I needed more reassurance. "He might run a few football pools, and sometimes he gets creative with that and there's trouble."

"Michael—"

"Don't ask," he said. "Not yet. Some things happened long ago, and I was never completely sure how Danny was involved."

"Football things? Was Jake mixed up in it?"

"Really," he said. "Don't ask. Let me handle it."

Jake Kendall had been a golden boy, a talented athlete with a big personality, a hot temper and a lot of other larger-than-life qualities that Emma reflected back to him. Despite his wild ways on and off the field, he'd been a straight arrow behind the bad boy persona. Or at least the world thought so. I didn't want to hear now, years after his sudden death, that things weren't as they had appeared.

Michael said, "Tell me what Emma said about Strawcutter's death."

I told him what I knew, which was that in the early morning hours before the hunt, Emma and Rush had encountered Gussie, Tottie, Dougie and even Tim Naftzinger at the stable. Michael must have heard the frustration in my voice.

"Maybe she'll remember more detail as time passes," he suggested.

"I hope so. Meanwhile, I have to keep asking questions. I'm worried about her, Michael."

"I know. She's tough, but she's scared she killed him, isn't she?"

"She's confused and upset. She feels guilty."

"I'm glad to see her get a little emotional with you, though. I was seriously thinking of taking her back to the hospital. She was ready to crack, and not in a good way."

"Watch her carefully, will you?"

Michael reached across and touched my face. "Don't worry too much."

An impossible request.

Michael took me home, and he wasn't happy to see an unfamiliar truck parked in the rear driveway. "Who's this?"

I went inside to speak with Mr. Ledbetter, the man who had done his best to look after Blackbird Farm during my parents' occupation. He still possessed a key, and he was standing in the kitchen wearing the same overalls I remembered from my childhood, along with an orange-and-blue parka that advertised the furnace company he used to own.

He rubbed the stubble on his face with an elderly baseball cap and began shaking his head. "This is very bad, young lady. Very, very bad."

I introduced Michael, and they shook hands solemnly. Mr. Ledbetter continued to wag his head.

"What's the prognosis?" I asked. "Why do I have a swimming pool starting in my kitchen?

"It's the roof." He looked grim. "You gotta leak up there like Niagara Falls. The water's running down between the walls and ends up here 'cause there's no place else for it to go, unless you want me to put in a drain right here." He tapped his steel-toed boot on the tile floor. "But you'll never fix the trouble until you fix the roof, same as always. Pretty soon, the walls will start to buckle and the whole place will come down. That dang roof is always the trouble."

"Yes, I know, and it's too expensive to fix properly."

"Well, we can patch it up with some of those slates out in the barn, but they're old and brittle, too, y'know, and won't last. New ones aren't going to match the old ones, plus you could put a whole new roof of composite shingles on for the same price it's gonna take to patch just one of the big holes up there with slate. But I know what you're gonna say about that."

"The house was meant to have a slate roof," I said on cue.

"Well, putting slate on the whole roof is gonna cost more than you got, young lady, so my advice, which you're not gonna take, is for you to sell this old mansion before it's a pile of rubble."

"What can we do in the meantime?" I asked with as much schoolgirl charm as I could muster, having grown up observing my mother shamelessly flattering Mr. Ledbetter for his expertise.

He sighed mournfully. "I guess I could put up a tarp tomorrow. It won't fix anything, mind you, and it's going to look like Hades."

"But it will hold back Niagara Falls for a little while?"

"It won't hold it back, but it'll make it so's there's no standing water in your kitchen or eating away at your walls, which isn't safe, y'know."

"All right," I said. "If you could bring a tarp out here tomorrow, I'd be very grateful. Do you have somebody who can help you? Or do you want me to—"

"You're not climbing out on no roof," Mr. Ledbetter said. "I'll bring my boys out, and we'll see what we can do. I won't promise nothing."

"Thank you." I showed him to the door. "Thank you very much. How is Mrs. Ledbetter?"

He pointed at the table. "She sent you some of her pierogies. Fresh-made today. All's they need is some butter in a frying pan. You're a real favorite with her, y'know."

Quite honestly, I said, "She's a real favorite with me, too."

He lingered in the doorway. "You ready to go, young man?"

Michael smiled. "I think I'll stick around for a little longer."

"Not too long." Mr. Ledbetter gave him a steely stare, his face flushing. "This young lady is so pretty because she gets her beauty rest, you know what I mean?"

"Yes, sir," said Michael.

I waved good-bye, and a red-faced Mr. Ledbetter clomped off into the night.

"Stay for some food," I said to Michael, who suddenly looked as if he'd just flown across the Atlantic under his own power. "You'll catch up with Emma and your cousin eventually."

Michael sat down at the table and peeled back the foil on a plate of Mrs. Ledbetter's pierogies. Spike was hungry, too, and didn't bother chasing Mr. Ledbetter to his truck.

I took off my coat, put a sauté pan on the stove and lit the gas flame. While it heated, I poured a portion of puppy chow into Spike's dish and gave it to him, then retrieved a bottle of chardonnay from the refrigerator and placed it on the table in front of Michael. While Spike ate and Michael opened the wine, I got a broom out of the pantry and tried to sweep the worst of the water out the back door.

Michael took his time removing the cork from the bottle. By the minute, he looked more interested in sleep than anything else. "Ledbetter seems like a regular around here."

"He took care of the house for years. My father likes puttering with a croquet mallet, not a hammer, and my mother suffers from household hysterical blindness. Mr. Ledbetter has kept this place from falling into ruin."

Michael poured wine into two glasses. "It's as close to a ruin as a house can get and still not be condemned, Nora."

"I know." I swept harder.

"You want a loan?" he asked.

"No, thank you."

"I earned it," he said. "It's legal."

I put the broom away and let Spike out the back door. Then I slid the pierogies into the sauté pan. I found a bag of prepared salad in the fridge, and freshened it up in a bowl. While the food warmed on the stove, I mixed a quick dressing in a cruet. In three more minutes, I had the salad on the table and the pierogies on two china plates.

I slid one plate in front of Michael. "Give me your coat."

He shrugged out of it and put it on the corner of the table. He took an experimental bite of Mrs. Ledbetter's famous pierogies. "Not bad," he said around a mouthful.

Definitely jet lag, I decided. He would never had eaten anything as mundane as Mrs. Ledbetter's bland food if he weren't exhausted. He hadn't shaved in more than a day, and there was a decided drop in his usual energy. He almost looked vulnerable.

"How long have you been awake?"

He frowned and swallowed before saying, "A couple of days, maybe."

I leaned down and kissed his rough cheek. "Thank you for coming to the rescue."

His smile was tired, but still flickered with a certain alchemy that warmed my insides.

Until that moment, I hadn't been sure he ever needed sleep. When I'd first met him, I had visions of him tossing and turning with a guilty conscience over his life of crime. Or maybe he'd spent so much time resting in jail in his youth that he didn't need sleep anymore. But I'd come to see how much he preferred wakefulness—the better to indulge his many appetites.

As my touch lingered on his cheek, I wondered if it might be wise to choose a night when he wasn't up to full strength to invite him to bed. I wanted to take him by the hand and slip upstairs with him. We could spend the night snug in the bedroom, shutting out the world for a little while and learning new things about each other. It was a tantalizing idea.

He seemed to absorb that thought, too, and his gaze sharpened with interest.

He reached for me with heat flickering in his eyes.

"Eat your dinner," I said, easing his hand away reluctantly but firmly. "It's not truffles, but it will keep your strength up."

He sighed. "Venice sure feels far away right now."

"Want to see my blackmail letter instead?"

"Is that a trick question?"

I found the envelopes and photos in the drawer where Libby had stuffed them. Michael ate one-handed and shifted through the paper until he came to the photographs, which he lingered over. I stood behind him, looking down at the pictures, too.

"This is the doctor?" he asked, looking at the shot of Tim inhaling my perfume.

"Tim Naftzinger, yes."

"How long have you known him?"

"Years. He was a classmate of my husband's. We used to be a foursome, doing things together."

"What kind of things?"

"Boating, mostly. Weekend antiquing."

"Looks like you know each other very well."

"That's the creepy element about this," I said. "The photographer caught something that isn't really there. The pictures look dreamy, don't they?"

"Dreamy?"

I put my hands on his shoulders. "Thing is, I am beginning to wonder if Tim has a yen for Emma. Of course, every man alive goes for Emma—"

"Hey, now."

"—so maybe I'm just imagining it, but I wonder if Tim— Well, his wife will never recover from her injuries. He's been grieving for her for a year, but he can't say good-bye, can he? Not while she's alive. So he spent time with Emma, and you know what kind of effect Emma has."

"Doesn't look like he's got Emma on his mind here."

"That just proves what a good photographer this person is. Tim can barely speak to me."

"Why not?"

"Because of our past, I guess. He felt he could have helped my husband when things went haywire. And he failed. We both failed. We don't want to talk about it, but it's there between us."

Michael flipped the photograph over. "Your photographer develops his own pictures, I see."

"No marks from a developing lab, I know."

Michael put the photos back into their envelope. Then he read the blackmailer's typewritten letter. "You still think this came from the dead guy?"

"That theory doesn't make sense anymore. I jumped to too many conclusions. Except if Rush didn't send this letter to me, why haven't I heard about missing the deadline? Nobody contacted me again."

"Maybe he or she is following through on the threat to make trouble for your doctor friend."

"Wouldn't I have heard that by now? You said yourself punishment should be swift or the threat meaningless."

We had reached a stalemate. I patted his shoulder, and he began to eat again.

I went to sit down at the table with Michael, but his coat lay in my way. I picked it up with the plan of putting it over one of the chairs. As I did so, something heavy in one of the pockets clunked against the table. Immediately, Michael glanced at it. I saw him stiffen.

Of course I looked into the pocket.

And a pistol fell out of his coat into my hand. Heavy, lethal, very ugly.

I dropped it at once. It hit my plate with a crack. The plate broke, and the gun skittered across the table and came to rest against the pepper mill.

Michael was on his feet before it stopped moving. "Nora—"

I backed away until I collided with the stove. A gun. A gun much like the one the police showed me the night my husband died.

"It's not what you think," Michael said.

"You brought a gun into my house."

He caught my arm. "Sit down before you faint."

I yanked out of his grasp. "How long have you had that thing? Have you always carried it?"

"It's not mine."

"If you're lugging it around, it's yours! Do you know how much I hate those things?"

"Yes, I do—"

"Get it out of here. Get it out."

"Will you please—"

"I want it gone now. Right now."

"Nora—"

I picked up the weapon myself and ran to the back door. I opened it, and Spike dashed happily into the kitchen. I threw the gun out into the darkness, and Spike tried to double back and go after it, as if it were a toy he could retrieve. I stopped him with my foot and slammed the door.

"You can't do that!" Michael went past me and yanked the door open. "You can't just throw it out where anybody could pick it up. It's dangerous."

He went outside into the cold air.

I slammed the door after him and considered locking it. Instead, I snatched up Spike and hugged him.

Michael came back a minute later, looking angrier than I'd ever seen him. "I put it in the car. You can relax."

I faced him from across the kitchen and struggled to control the hysteria that churned inside me. "I can relax? I just found out you're carrying a loaded gun."

"It isn't loaded. You think I'm crazy?"

"I don't know what to think! You've got a handgun, Michael. The sole purpose of a handgun is to shoot people."

"It's not mine."

"It's in your possession!" I felt the room wobble, and I couldn't catch my breath.

He crossed the kitchen and caught my arms. He eased me into a chair.

"I'm not fainting."

"Put your head down," he said from miles away.

"Don't touch me."

He crouched beside my chair, one arm behind my back. "Nora—"

I sat up, dizzy and nauseated. "What was in that suitcase tonight?"

"What suitcase?"

"The one you got out of your trunk and took into the restaurant. Was it cash? Are you laundering money, like the papers say? Is that why you need to carry a gun? To protect yourself? Or to threaten people?"

"The suitcase did not have money in it."

"Was it something legal?"

He didn't answer.

"It wasn't," I said when saw his face. "Michael, I know you're not an angel, but one thing I thought I could count on was that you didn't carry a gun."

"You can count on more than that, and you know it."

"Can I? You've lied to me."

"Never."

"About this you have. It was in your pocket!"

He got up. "What is this? Suddenly you believe everything you ever heard about me? Suddenly I'm Tony Soprano? Well, let me make an observation, sweetheart. You *like* that I'm dangerous. It lets you justify keeping me out of your bed."

"What?"

He grabbed his coat. "You pretend I'm a bad-ass, a guy you can't possibly let into your clean, perfect life. Okay, now you can pretend that's my gun. Use it to throw me out again. But let's understand what's really going on, Nora. The bottom line is that you don't trust me."

"That's not true."

"Bullshit. I've looked after your sisters. I've kept you safe. But you still don't trust the decisions I make. You're still afraid of me."

"You don't understand."

"The hell I don't. You thought you could trust the guy you married—the guy with the good family and nice manners and the rest of the bullshit, but he still turned out to be a fuckup who got himself killed."

"How can you call him names after you've come in here with—"

"Nora, I want you to love me the way you loved him. No, I want more than that. A lot more. But we have to trust each other first."

"Leaving your weapon at home would have been a good start."

He cursed shortly and put on his coat.

"Okay, I don't trust you!" I cried. "I admit it. I've seen what happens to people who think they can play by their own rules."

"News flash. I'm not your precious Todd."

"But—"

He reached the door. "When I was a kid, I almost blew my life, Nora. But now I can absolutely guarantee I'm not going to shoot drugs or whack anybody or otherwise jeopardize what's probably my last chance for something good. When you figure out how I can prove it, let me know."

"And if I can't do that?"

His face shut down, smoothed emotionless by years of hard lessons. Coldly, he said, "I'll get over it."

He left then. Spike dashed over to the door and scratched it.

I couldn't stand up. I told myself I was angry. But it felt more like shame. It streamed hot through my veins like an overpowering narcotic, setting me on fire, burning me from the inside.

The phone rang. I couldn't get up to answer it, but I heard Hadley's voice on the answering machine.

"Kitten? Hope you made it home without running afoul of Tottie. I followed Kitty, but I'm afraid I lost her in traffic. What a bore, right? Give me a buzz and we'll plot our next move. Night, night!"

*   *   *

I tried to make my heart stop pounding, but a storm of feelings kept me awake most of the night.

In the morning, I telephoned Libby.

"What's wrong? You sound awful."

"Nothing's wrong. I have an idea that might help Emma."

"Count me in."

"Can you pick me up this morning?"

"Sure. Want me to bring some Valium when I come?"

"Just get here as soon as you can."

When she arrived and I climbed into her minivan, she said, "My God, what's gotten into you? You sounded terrible on the phone, and you look like hell."

"Thanks a heap." I slammed the door and balanced Spike on my lap.

"What's wrong?"

"Nothing," I snapped.

She shot me a cut-the-crap look. "Did you try to make whoopie with the gangster last night? And it was a bust? I knew it! Men who look divine on the outside always turn out to be the pits in bed. I knew a yoga instructor once who—"

"Can we spend ten minutes together without discussing your sex life?"

"Probably not. I'm not driving you anywhere until you tell me. Is it Emma?"

"No."

"The gangster."

"Libby—"

"Aha—it is him! What happened? Did you break up again?"

"Permanently," I said, barely holding back tears. "It's over."

"You," said Libby with her clearest diction, "are an idiot."

I stared at her. "You are the one who keeps telling me he's all wrong! That he's dangerous! That he's—"

"Well, that doesn't mean you can't enjoy his company! Look at me. I've had a string of bad men. But does that deter me? Certainly not! For heaven's sake, Nora, nobody needs to get in touch with her inner goddess more than you. Do you ever let yourself have fun anymore? I'll bet you've never even seen him with his clothes off. Now, that's the kind of missed opportunity you can't take to your grave, so—"

"You're insane. Certifiably insane."

"No, I'm just a sensually adventurous woman who—"

"I'm going to scream."

"Go ahead. It will do you good. I suppose that means you don't want to hear about my problems."

"No, I don't."

I had spent the night in an emotional turmoil and had hoped that for once my sister would back me up. No such luck. Here she was extolling the virtues of free love at the moment when what I really needed was some support for my decision to end things with Michael.

Instead, Libby allowed ten seconds to tick by before saying, "Can we talk about my problems now?"

I sighed. "Are there any problems left for you to have, Libby?"

She burst out, "I just don't think I've made any kind of parental impression on my children!"

"I don't think I have the strength for this discussion right now."

"Well, I think my offspring are a little more important than your lack of a sex life." She drove down my driveway and needed no encouragement to continue. "Rawlins is completely out of control, and the twins are right on the edge, Nora. At light speed, they're traveling beyond my power to contain them. I dote on them when they're babies, feed them from my tender breasts, and look what happens. They grow up and leave me!"

"Maybe boys aren't meant to be civilized."

"Do you think so? Melvin thinks I could be a natural disciplinarian if I'd just try a few simple techniques, but somehow Placida's goals seem to be taking me in a different direction."

"You saw Melvin again?"

She swept on. "I can't get a truthful word out of Rawlins anymore, and he's always sulking or angry. I have no idea where he went these last two nights. Do you think that's normal?"

"Emma says he was with Michael yesterday."

"I'm afraid he goes to see Mr. Abruzzo when he— Wait a minute. When did Emma say that?"

"I saw her last night. Sorry. I should have mentioned that. She's okay." Unless she had run off somewhere with Danny Pescara. I decided not to mention Michael's cousin to Libby, but I told her all about Emma's escape and current situation.

I had decided to focus my attention on helping Emma. First of all, I needed to figure out why Rush Strawcutter had been murdered. If I could channel all my energy into solving that mystery, I didn't have to think about the mess the rest of my life had become.

At my request, Libby drove me to the King of Prussia Laundro-Mutt, a massive building located in a park of similar big box stores, all surrounded by asphalt parking lots full of SUV's. The enormous vehicles looked like a herd of elephants standing with military precision, ready to accept large quantities of paper towels, groceries and home-improvement supplies

from the tiny suburban women who seemed to be
their predominant drivers. Libby whipped her red
minivan into a parking spot beside a Land Rover. Its
rear bumper was decorated with stickers proclaiming
a love of Pomeranians, pride in an elementary school
honor student and the vacationing virtues of the
Outer Banks.

I carried Spike, wrapped in a towel, through
Laundro-Mutt's automatic doors. My right hand had
a death grip on his collar. I wound his leash around
my wrist while my hand simultaneously supported his
bottom and clamped his hind legs together to thwart
his escape.

Spike looked around Laundro-Mutt and announced
he was ready to rip the place to shreds.

Libby followed me inside, stuffing her keys into her
shoulder bag. "You think it's wise to let somebody groom
him here? I mean, do they carry enough insurance?"

"You're hilarious. This way."

The clerk at the grooming station greeted me with
an innocent smile. She looked as if she'd reached vot-
ing age, but just barely. "Hi, I'm Kelly. Welcome to
Laundro-Mutt, where your pet is our problem."

Libby muttered, "You don't know how true that
slogan is about to become, Kelly."

"Hi, Kelly. This is Spike."

Kelly had pigtails pulled up with orange ribbons to
match her Laundro-Mutt smock. The Laundro-Mutt
logo depicted profiles of an orange poodle and an orange kitten poised to kiss each other on the backseat
of an automobile that was about to enter the yawning
maw of a car wash.

Behind the counter, an annoyed Pomeranian stood
in surly silence inside a dog crate while a blow dryer
fluffed her already very poofy coat.

Kelly looked as sweet as the cartoon animals on her shirt. She picked up an orange pen with a pom-pom on the tip. In a baby voice, she said, "Hey, there, Spikey. How are you doing today, little guy?"

Spike's growl indicated he did not appreciate being called "little guy."

"He's nervous," I said. "He's never been here before, and it takes him a while to warm up to new places and new people."

"Either that," Libby muttered, "or he's channeling Satan."

"Is that so? Well, don't worry." Kelly waved her pen tantalizingly in front of Spike's nose, oblivious to his fierce glare at its pom-pom. "We'll take good care of him. Today's special is the deluxe grooming, which includes a bath, nail trim and— What's that smell?"

I plunked Spike, towel and all, on the counter. "We had a little problem this morning. Spike dug his way into the paddock where my sister keeps her horse. It was only a minute before I got there, but—"

Kelly began to look less perky. "He sure stinks."

Libby said, "That's actually his normal smell, just slightly intensified today."

"If you'd give him a bath, that would be great. Should we wait in the store while you do it?"

Kelly had finally become aware of Spike's steady snarl, too. "That might be a good idea."

"Great." I handed over his leash. "How long will it take?"

"I'll call you over the PA system when we're finished."

"Perfect!" I tried to exude confidence. "I'm sure you two will have fun together."

I grabbed Libby's arm and dragged her away from the grooming station.

Libby said, "It'll be on your conscience if that poor child is maimed."

"She's a professional. I'm sure she'll be able to handle a ten-pound puppy."

"Ten pounds of dynamite. Okay, now what?"

We stopped beside a display of litter boxes. I said, "This is the store where Rush Strawcutter had his office. See those steps over there? His office is upstairs."

"You don't plan on breaking and entering in broad daylight?"

A peek into Rush's office might answer a lot of questions. I particularly wanted to know if he had a camera or a darkroom on the premises. But reluctantly, I said, "I just thought we could ask around a little."

"In the store?"

"Right, among the people who worked with him every day. Somebody might have useful information. Get a shopping cart. We'll browse around and see who turns up."

"And maybe you'll have an opportunity to go upstairs? I get it. You brought me here to distract people."

I tried to ignore the steady, furious barking over in the grooming area, but it sounded as if Spike was disagreeing with the Pomeranian. Libby grabbed a shopping cart and we ambled around the huge store. The only clerk on duty was helping another customer sort through a daunting display of leashes and collars.

Finally, Libby's impatience got the best of her. She marched up to the leash display and said, "Oh, look at these rhinestone collars, Nora. What do you think?"

The store clerk finished with the other customer and turned to us. She was a large woman, and the color of her hair matched the orange of her store smock.

Her badge said, LAKEETA, MANAGER. She said, "I have a large inventory of rhinestone collars. What size do you need, honey?"

"Small," I said.

"Medium," Libby corrected. She found a black one she liked. "What do you think?"

"It's huge," I said. "It'll never fit Spike."

"Never mind Spike How does it look on me?" She held the flashy collar up to her own throat. "See? Wouldn't Placida approve?"

LaKeeta said, "Placida is your dog?"

I closed my eyes.

"No, Placida is my goddess within," Libby explained. "The goddess of tranquility, sexual adventure and weight loss. I worship her daily, and she rewards me with her gifts."

"No kidding." LaKeeta put one hand on her ample hip. "How's she doing with the sexual adventure part?"

"Well . . ." Libby slid her eyes at me. "The results have been mixed so far."

"What do you mean?" I asked.

"Yeah, what do you mean?" LaKeeta asked. "Who is this Placida chick? She gonna try leading me into temptation? 'Cause I can usually find that all by myself."

"Placida is my personal goddess," Libby assured her. "You might choose someone totally different, depending upon your needs and inner resources. Would you be interested in a goddess support group?"

"Hell, yes, if it gets me some sexual adventure."

"Libby," I said, easing away, "I think I'll go look around a little."

"Sure," Libby said. Then, to LaKeeta: "She needs a goddess, too, but she's a little unfocused right now."

I moseyed away from the two of them, ignoring another spate of barking over in the grooming department, followed by a crash and a human yelp.

I spotted the stairs and tried to stroll casually in that direction. When I reached a display of flavored pigs' ears, the front door of the store whooshed open, and Gussie Strawcutter walked into the store.

"Gussie!"

She hesitated, then recognized me. "Oh. It's you."

She was dressed for business in a plain navy pantsuit, and she carried a battered black briefcase that thumped against her knee.

"I'm so sorry about Rush," I said to her, unsure what the rules of etiquette dictated in such a situation. Her husband was dead, and my sister was primary suspect in his murder. But I couldn't walk away, so I said, "He was a kind and very sweet man, Gussie."

She peered into my face as if I were speaking a language she didn't understand. "Why do you say that?"

"I always respected his involvement with humane-society work."

"And his involvement with your sister?" Gussie began to glare at me. Her frizzy hair was almost tamed by a thick black headband, but her face was blotchy and her eyes looked as if they'd been tenderized.

"I'm sorry," I said. "Until this weekend, I had no idea they even knew each other."

She swallowed that information with no change of expression. But her voice went hard and accusatory. "Did she give him money?"

"Money? Emma is barely making ends meet right now, and I can't imagine—"

"I found sixty dollars in his sock drawer. In quarters and dollar bills, mostly. Sixty dollars."

Gussie let go of the briefcase, and it hit the floor at her feet. She groped for the counter and sagged against it. I realized she was ill and quickly grasped her arm. "Let's go sit down," I said. "You'll be all right in a minute."

"Not here." She began to weep. "Help me out of here. I'll go to my car. Anything—just don't let me make a scene in a place of business."

I picked up her briefcase and held her arm firmly. She leaned against me and we staggered out of the store.

Chapter 12

Outside, she took gasping breaths of cool air. "I haven't eaten anything. Not for ages. I should have had some breakfast."

"There's a restaurant across the parking lot."

"No, that place is too expensive. There's a bagel shop . . ."

I saw the bagel shop only two doors down in the strip mall. In three minutes we were inside, and I eased Gussie into a booth across from the display counter. I spoke to a young man behind the cash register, and he brought me two cups of coffee right away. I ordered a toasted bagel for Gussie, and he went to prepare it.

She accepted the coffee without thanks. When I slid into the seat across from her, she was reaching for a paper napkin from the table dispenser. "I'm sorry," she said, dabbing her cheeks. "I haven't been myself lately."

"Gussie, you should be at home," I said gently. "With everything that's happened, you need to take care of yourself."

"I have a company to run. There's too much to do. The annual report, the shareholders—"

"For a few days, you can trust your employees to manage things."

She took off her glasses and wiped her eyes with a

napkin. "My father always says it's vital to know what's happening with the company at all times."

Her father had been a controlling egomaniac, I'd once heard my mother declare, who drove his wife to an early grave with his obsession for making money. Here was Gussie, similarly driven.

Did she have a life? I couldn't remember seeing her attending any social events, and I couldn't recall hearing any people call her their friend. Now she was struggling alone to cope with one of life's most devastating blows. She obviously felt betrayed and abandoned. I recognized her state of mind.

"Take a few days, Gussie," I soothed. "You'll be able to think more clearly."

She stared at the cup I'd placed in front of her but didn't reach for it. "It's been horrible. Everybody's talking. All the questions, the police. I just want it to be over."

"I'm sure you miss Rush, too."

Tears flooded her eyes again. She hiccoughed and grabbed another napkin. She pressed the paper to her mouth and couldn't speak.

"I know it's hard," I said. "He was in your thoughts a hundred times a day, and now he's gone. Maybe it doesn't feel real yet, but it hits you every few minutes, doesn't it?"

Gussie heard me, but suddenly her stare intensified as if I'd sprouted horns and a tail. When she could speak, her voice was a rasp. "What do you want?"

"I don't want anything."

"Everybody wants something."

"Okay, I want my sister exonerated," I admitted.

"She was chasing my husband," Gussie said flatly. "You Blackbirds are always looking for somebody to mooch from."

I felt my face warm at her assessment of my family.
"Emma isn't like that."

"I caught them together Saturday morning."

That was why Gussie had been crying when Hadley
and I saw her at the hunt breakfast; she'd surprised
Rush and Emma together in the stables.

I said, "I'm sure Emma and Rush were only
friends."

"You're wrong. I saw them together. And I saw
the pictures."

My pulse quickened. "The pictures?"

"She was giving Rush some photographs. I grabbed
them and saw. They were lovers. She was going to use
those pictures to get money from Rush. But my husband didn't have any money of his own."

I wasn't going to get any useful information if Gussie persisted in accusing Emma, so I asked, "If he
didn't have any money of his own, how did Rush start
Laundro-Mutt?"

The question didn't offend her. "He borrowed it. I
told Rush that was a poor business plan, but he had
to do it, he said."

"So he borrowed from Tottie Boarman."

"That was a mistake, too." Gussie said flatly. "Mr.
Boarman was a very bad choice."

"I'm surprised Rush asked Tottie to be his partner."

"They weren't partners. Mr. Boarman only loaned
the start-up money. Then he wanted a return on his
investment sooner than expected. He pressured Rush
to go public and issue stock. But Rush told him the
groundwork wasn't ready."

"Did you agree?"

"I had nothing to do with Laundro-Mutt." She
picked at a ragged tear beside one fingernail.

I must have looked as bewildered as I felt. "But

surely an investment from you would have prevented Rush from going to Tottie in the first place."

"Rush understood that all Strawcutter money has to stay where it is. He knew that before we were married. My father and I made Rush aware of our family policy from the start, to avoid misunderstandings. It was the only way to be sure Rush wasn't marrying me because—well, for the Strawcutter fortune." She flushed.

I felt a surge of pity for gruff, unattractive, badly dressed Gussie. "I see."

The bagel I had ordered for Gussie appeared. I wondered if Rush, like all newly married spouses, assumed he could break down the barriers imposed by a prenuptial agreement. After a few happy years of marriage, most prenups bit the dust. Had Rush gone to Tottie after finally realizing there was no hope of easing even a few dollars out of the Strawcutter coffers?

Had he further resorted to blackmail to raise the money denied to him at home?

Gussie picked up half of the bagel and took a bite. She only barely managed to choke it down. She sipped more coffee and seemed to calm herself. "I told Rush not to borrow any money, but he went looking for investors, anyway, and came up with Mr. Boarman. Debt is a bad way to start a business, my father always said."

"What should Rush have done instead?"

"Saved enough to start Laundro-Mutt himself."

"But a start-up like Laundro-Mutt must have taken millions."

"You can't have everything right away," Gussie said. "You have to work for good things."

Poor Rush. Saving the change from his lunch money

couldn't have raised ten thousand dollars in a decade. I did not point out that Gussie had been given one of the country's most profitable businesses on a silver platter. But looking at her, sitting in that bagel shop, I realized she was miserable. All the money in her family fortune did not make her happy.

Gussie leaned across the table. "You've been spared a great burden, you know. When your silly parents took off, they did you a favor, Nora."

"I guess that's one way of looking at it."

"No," she said earnestly. "You should be glad they spent all the money. A family fortune can be a terrible weight, an awful responsibility. It's better to have nothing than hundreds of millions of dollars."

"You could give it away if you hate it so much. So many charities are desperate for—"

Horrified, she said, "I can't give it away!"

She couldn't spend it either, I thought. Clearly, she didn't buy clothes or extravagant meals or expensive treatments at spas. She just watched her bank account grow.

Gussie snatched more napkins from the dispenser and blew her nose.

Almost everyone dreamed of winning the lottery someday. But I had friends who inherited vast fortunes, and their reactions to receiving sometimes unimaginable wealth were not as simple as rushing out to buy a new car. People who had enough money to make the wildest dreams come true sometimes didn't have the capacity to dream at all. The emotional legacy that came with inherited wealth could be crippling—a laughable quandary according to the average Joe, perhaps, but very real nonetheless.

Looking at Gussie, I remembered a childhood friend who was given fifty million dollars when he turned eighteen. He spent a year staring at the numbers on paper, paralyzed by the opportunities for success and failure the money represented. He'd never have to work a day in his life, and he could have spent every penny pleasing himself. But within a year, he shot himself. His younger brother, in his turn, became a profligate playboy who ruined one expensive sailboat after another, ate and drank like Henry VIII and had recently been arrested, I'd heard, for drugging young girls for the purpose of having sex with their unconscious bodies. I'd seen his bloated face plastered on supermarket tabloids for weeks. He was barely twenty-five years old.

Different rules applied to the very rich. But the rules had to be self-created, and that task proved too difficult for many.

For Gussie the rule was that she had to keep the Strawcutter fortune inviolate. It was her way of coping with the guilt of great wealth, the mistrust of people who tried to reach her emotionally and the paralysis of purpose that had come with all her millions. I felt dreadfully sorry for her.

I said, "What will become of Laundro-Mutt now? Will you take over?"

"Oh, no. I'll shut it down as soon as possible."

"Shut it down?"

"The real estate will be worth something. But the sooner I can stop the payroll, the better."

I thought of LaKeeta and Kelly, doing their darnedest to cheerfully sell silly collars and bathe obnoxious pets like Spike. Did they know they'd soon be out of their jobs?

I said, "Will Tottie get his investment back when you close Laundro-Mutt?"

"There's nothing left to share with Mr. Boarman.

Rush used the initial input of cash to build the business, and he overexpanded. This morning, I was on my way to Rush's office to start liquidation procedures."

Just like that. I'd heard of coldhearted CEOs, but Gussie was an iceberg.

The clerk interrupted us by putting the bill on our table. I reached for it automatically.

Around her mouthful, Gussie said, "What's my share?"

I picked up the slip of paper. "I'll buy."

"No, I want to pay my share," she insisted. "How much do I owe?"

I showed her the bill and watched her do the simple math very carefully.

She nodded. "Okay, I'll pay for my coffee and the bagel. We don't need to leave a fifteen percent tip, do you think? After all, he didn't really wait on us. Maybe eight percent is sufficient."

"Whatever you think."

She opened a thin change purse and counted out the exact amount. She placed coins on the table for the tip. Then she wrapped the remaining half bagel in a napkin and put it into her handbag. That done, she stood up and looked at me with those red-rimmed eyes devoid of emotion. She said, "I hope your slutty sister rots in jail for what she did to Rush. People who steal ought to be locked up until they die."

I stood up, too. "Gussie—"

But she cut me off calmly. "If you tell anybody Rush was screwing around, I'll sue you. I'll punch you in the face. I'll run you over with my car. I'll do it, I really will. Nobody can ever know he didn't love me."

Her face was very red, and her hands were shaking as she turned to go.

I reached for her. "Gussie, wait. My husband was

killed, too, you know. I didn't understand right away, but I'm finally figuring out what happened to us. It wasn't at all what I thought it was at the time. Rush did love you. I'm sure he did. I'm a good listener. Call me if you need a friend. Maybe I can help."

She snatched her hand away. "Don't bother."

"One more thing," I said desperately. "Just one. Can you tell me if Rush had a camera? Did he do any photography?"

Gussie looked at me as if I were crazy. "No, of course not. What a waste of money."

She left the shop, and I sat down slowly, shaken by how bizarre Gussie had been. Did she realize how her penurious ways affected her husband and her marriage?

An even more jolting thought hit me. Was Gussie so consumed by jealousy and humiliation that she might have killed Rush herself?

I had to find out if Rush Strawcutter's business affairs were as strange as his marriage had been. I headed for the parking lot.

Chapter 13

Libby was standing beside her minivan, holding the end of Spike's leash while he rolled in a muddy puddle.

I left the bagel shop and crossed the parking lot to them. "You couldn't have kept him clean for five minutes?"

She handed me the leash and a twenty-dollar bill. "Here. They want to pay you to never bring him back again. And they offered me a special deal on one of those electronic shock collars. Poor Kelly was going to quit her job. I had to tell her about Placida to calm her down."

I sent Libby back inside to return the money, and I did my best to clean Spike up with the old towel. He was very pleased with himself. Libby kindly dropped me at the nearest train station and even agreed to take Spike home, although she hoped he could behave himself while she went into her bank to open a checking account for her new goddess support group.

I rode the train into Philadelphia and hiked over to Lexie Paine's office.

Lexie's firm—once her late father's along with several influential partners' but now nearly Lexie's outright—commanded three floors of a downtown landmark. The corner office on the top floor, with views of the Schuylkill on one side and the spire of Old City Hall on the other, was Lexie's command post. She had decorated it with some family furniture—an exquisitely delicate French desk with ivory and gold inlays, and a collection of armchairs from the pieces her mother left behind when she ran off with a polo player. The coffee table was fashioned from the top of a Steinway that had been destroyed in the fire set by one of her crazy Tuxedo Park cousins. On it stood a rosewood humidor, a jokey gift from a senator Lexie helped finance. Laid diagonally across the floor, a Tibetan rug glowed in light cast by the gas logs in the fireplace, a cozy touch as snow blew outside the tinted windows.

Over the mantel hung a half-complete oil study painted by a Dutch master of a serene girl spinning wool. Because of the painting, a security guard kept a vigil outside Lexie's door.

I looked at the painting and tried to absorb some of the subject's tranquility. When Lexie got off the phone, I said, "Shouldn't that be in a museum?"

"I suppose, but I like having it around." She gave me a kiss. "She makes me think if the stock market crashes, I could have an alternative career in textiles."

"Sorry to bother you this way. I thought I might lure you out to lunch. But looks like you're busy."

"I'd love to have lunch, but I can't get away until the Asian markets open." She returned to her desk to glance at one of her three computer screens. "Prices are insane today, and the museum board is in an uproar, too. We had some unpleasant business over the weekend, and we're not sure how it's going to play in the press. We had to kick somebody off the board."

"Somebody influential?"

"Yes, and the family's been attached to the museum

with grappling hooks for generations, so it's going to look like a crisis of faith when he leaves, but actually he's simply going broke."

"There's a lot of that going around these days."

"Well, it's very ugly, with bad feelings on both sides. Normally, we'd carry him for a while longer, but a cultural board can't afford to keep dead weight hanging around indefinitely, and he just hasn't lived up to his promises, so it's the boot. And it's awful. What can I do for you?"

"I just came from a weird discussion with Gussie Strawcutter."

"No wonder you're so pale."

Lexie looked perfect in very spare Armani, her business attire of choice. Her earrings, double diamonds that seemed small and therefore tasteful on a bad stock market day, flashed blue in the reflected light of her computer screens. Her black hair was pulled back with a simple Gucci leather clip. Even in a financial crisis, Lexie looked as serene as her wool-spinning Dutch girl.

I sat on one of the armchairs while my friend grabbed two chilled water bottles from the silver tray on her credenza. She passed one to me and sat behind her desk. She twisted the cap off her bottle. "Tell me about Emma first. Is she all right? Have you heard from her?"

"I believe she's okay," I said carefully. "The police are looking for her."

"So I've heard." She sipped water and watched me. "Dare I ask if Michael is back in the country?"

"He is."

"Are the police hounding him on that money-laundering thing?"

"I don't know. I'm staying out of it."

"Good thinking. Ignorance is bliss—and it will keep you from being indicted."

I wanted to ask Lexie if she thought Michael had gone to Scotland to trade in dirty currency, but I didn't have the courage to hear her answer. For an instant, I was overwhelmed by emotion.

Lexie saw my expression and came out from behind her desk. "I'm so sorry, sweetie. You must be in hell. Forget I brought it up. It was out of line, anyway."

"It wasn't out of line," I said, regaining myself. "You're my friend."

"I am indeed." She perched on her desk in front of me. "As long as Emma's safe for the moment and Michael's not in the pokey, I guess all's right with the world. Now, what did you learn from Gussie?"

I was suddenly relieved not to be discussing Michael. "I learned Gussie has more troubles than a murdered husband. She's bizarre. I watched her count out an eight percent tip for breakfast."

"All that dough and can't spend a nickel?" Lexie folded her arms across her chest and nodded knowingly. "Yeah, remember her mother? Wore the same three dresses for years, and I swear they all came from a thrift shop. Do you think Gussie is one of those who feels guilty for being born rich?"

"Yes, guilty and a few other things. She doesn't trust anyone—including her husband."

"Trust is a tricky animal, isn't it? I remember a rumor about their prenup. Gussie wanted a lock on the sugar bowl. Poor Rush. He was such a mensch, but a babe in the woods, really. Or do you think he hoped to charm Gussie out of her bank account?"

"I didn't know him well enough. But Gussie has strong feelings about her family and their stupid money—the money has become who she is, in a way."

"So you're wondering if Gussie was capable of whacking Rush over the family fortune?"

"To protect it," I guessed. "It would be like self-defense, in her mind." I saw Lexie's skeptical expression and smiled. "Okay, it's far-fetched."

"Did Gussie keep Rush so broke that he might have resorted to other forms of income?" Lexie asked.

"The blackmail? Yes, it's quite possible Rush resorted to extortion. I just don't know where the photos came from."

"But he borrowed a fortune from Tottie Boarman. Why would he need more?"

"Tottie wanted a return on his investment."

"Aha. With all his financial problems, he needed some cash back from Rush, of course."

"Lex, now that Rush is dead, is there any way Tottie can profit?"

Lexie didn't have to think for longer than a second. "Insurance. I'm sure Rush's life was insured to protect Laundro-Mutt in the event of his death. It's common practice with companies owned and managed by one dynamic person. Martha Stewart is a prime example. And yes, investors might receive hefty payouts when the leader dies. Are you thinking Tottie might have— Oh, my God. Tottie? Tottie killed Rush?" She looked as if she'd swallowed her water bottle whole.

The intercom on Lexie's desk interrupted us. "Lex?"

Shaken, she hit the button on her intercom. "Yes, Carly?"

"Claudine Paltron is here to see you."

Lexie and I exchanged surprised glances. Lexie shrugged. "This is turning out to be one crazy day. Send her in, Carly."

"Kiss, kiss!" cried Claudine, already sailing through

the door with long-legged strides. "How unlike me to be anywhere this early in the morning, but here I am. It must really be a crisis, don't you think? Hello, Nora. Good morning, Lexie." She gave Lexie a double kiss without touching.

"What brings you here?" Lexie asked, more bluntly than usual.

"Business, of course, but I don't mind a bit if Nora stays. What a nice jacket. *J'adore!* Where did you get it?"

"I don't remember," I said, startled by Claudine's manic good cheer.

"I'd like one, so if you remember, let me know. Now, look, the two of you can't gang up on me. Even together, you can't talk me out of this."

For once, Claudine's stage-friendly good looks seemed to have aged. Her face was tight behind her wide smile. Her eyes were huge pools of turbulent waters, and her famously fluid body seemed to be controlled by an angry puppeteer today. She plopped unattractively into the armchair I'd just vacated.

"What's going on?" Lexie asked.

Claudine pulled a cigarette case from her handbag to stall. "Look at me—I've taken up smoking again. I found this old case in my bedroom the other day, and now I'm using it again. What a stupid habit, especially if I don't have to fit into costumes anymore. Oh, hell, I suppose I'd better just come out with it. Another blackmail letter, I'm afraid. It came this morning, slipped to my doorman by a taxi driver, if you can imagine."

"Again!" Lexie cried.

"Another one?" I asked. "Now?"

"Oh, God." Lexie sat down behind her desk.

"It's just too horrible," Claudine said.

"The taxi company could trace the envelope," I said at once. "The police could find out where the envelope came from."

"No police." Claudine tapped her cigarette on the top of the case, still playing the role of the gallant victim. "Absolutely not. I just need twenty thousand dollars, and this will all go away."

"Forget it," Lexie said. "I won't be a part of this anymore."

"Claudine," I began.

"Please don't give me all those arguments again. I've made up my mind. What's money for, if not for emergencies like this?"

"For your retirement," Lexie said. "You're not going to enjoy life on Social Security, Claudine. You've already dipped far too deeply into your investments, and there's no end in sight. This must stop!"

"Of course there's an end in sight. He promised this time. It's absolutely the last request." Claudine broke the cigarette she'd been tapping, and her cool facade began to crack. Tears of frustration trembled in her eyes.

"No bawling," Lexie snapped. "It unnerves my staff."

I tried to be gentler and sat down beside her. "Claudine, have you any idea who might be sending these letters? Or who took the pictures?"

She used the backs of her fingertips to wipe the tears away before they ruined her makeup. "No, of course not."

"What about Dougie?" Lexie asked.

"Dougie?" Claudine blinked in surprise. "Dougie isn't blackmailing me. He can hardly spell his name, let alone write an entire letter."

I had to agree. Between Claudine and Dougie it

was a toss-up which one ought to be wearing the I'M WITH STUPID T-shirt right now.

"What Lexie means is whether or not Dougie has any idea who the blackmailer might be."

"Why would he?" Claudine groped for another cigarette.

"Did he know Rush Strawcutter?"

Claudine swallowed convulsively. "Why? What does Rush have to do with this?"

"Until this minute, I was pretty sure Rush was the blackmailer."

"Rush? Why would he bother to blackmail me? I'd already given him money—long before he married that malamute. He always knew he could just ask and get more. We were friends. He wasn't much good for anything else after he got married." She began to quiver. "I miss him."

"Did Dougie know you were still friendly with Rush?"

"Of course."

"Was he jealous?"

"Well, yes. What's the use of having old boyfriends if you can't use them to rouse the current one?" Claudine's mouth dropped open. "You don't think Dougie—? No, no. That's impossible. Dougie would never hurt— Oh, just get me the money, will you, Lexie? My head is going to explode!"

"Dougie could have confronted Rush, couldn't he?" I asked. "At the hunt breakfast."

"No! Dougie might have been peeved about Rush and me, but he's too much of a ninny, really, to hurt anybody. Lexie, please!"

Lexie said, "Claudine, I'm sorry, but I won't help you this time. And if you light that cigarette in here, I'll have you thrown out."

"But—"

"If you give me a direct order, of course I'll arrange your financial matters because it's my job. But you're pouring your future down a rat hole, and I'm damned if I'm going to—"

"I need it!"

"You need an FBI agent."

"I know a cop," I volunteered. "He's reliable and smart and very discreet. Let's go see him now, and I'll—"

"No, no, no." Claudine stood up. "I want the money. I need it by Friday."

Lexie was on her feet, too, looking stony. "From where would you like me to get it?"

"I don't know!" Claudine wailed. "You're in charge of all my accounts, Lex. How do I know what to do? I just need—"

"You don't have that kind of cash sitting in your checking account. What would you like me to transfer?"

Claudine frowned, clueless about her financial situation. "What about some kind of fund?"

"Which one? You'll have to go home and look at your statements."

"What statements?"

"They come in your mail every month."

"All those envelopes? I never open them!"

"It's time you did," Lexie snapped. "I'm not going to hold your hand through this again, Claudine."

"Fine. Fine!" she cried. "Have it your way. I'll go home and open every one of those stupid envelopes. And when I finish, you'd better do what I say."

"Of course." Lexie strode to the door and opened it. "I look forward to your call."

Claudine grabbed her bag and bolted for the door. At the last second, she turned and swept the office with a disdainful glance surely learned from an overly melodramatic stage director. Then she departed in high dungeon.

"Exeunt, pursued by a bear," I said, when the door was closed behind her.

Lexie was still angry. "I give the performance average marks. She's a magnificent dancer, but a mediocre actress."

I grabbed my coat. "I'm leaving, too." I gave my friend a fierce hug. "You've got your hands full, and I've got things to do."

"Tell me you're not going gunning for Tottie Boarman."

"No. But I have just learned that Rush Strawcutter wasn't killed because he was blackmailing people, so everything changes. Look, I'll try phoning Claudine later. Convincing her to go to the police is worth another try. I'm sorry I interrupted. Oh, and good luck with the museum thing, too."

She helped me into my coat. "Oh, God, don't remind me. Look, you're pals with Hadley Pinkham. If you see him looking like he's been coldcocked, give him a little TLC, will you?"

"Hadley?" I repeated, my arm halfway into my sleeve. I turned to stare at Lexie. "Hadley's the one you're tossing off the museum board?"

"I shouldn't have said that, I know. Lord, I'm more upset by Claudine than I should be. Yes, it's Hadley, but—"

"He's broke?" I demanded. "He can't pay off his pledges?"

"The museum depends on the board to raise money,

and a big chunk of our operating expenses comes directly from the board. Hadley can't pull his weight anymore, so we—"

"I thought the Pinkham estate left him rolling in dough."

Lexie shook her head. "With so many heirs, even a huge estate makes for meager monthly allowances. Hadley's been living beyond his means for years, and it's finally caught up with him."

Chapter 14

Confused and desperate, I found Detective Bloom's various telephone numbers in my book. He sounded surprised to hear from me and even more astonished that I wanted to see him.

"I'll pick you up," he said. "Where are you?"

I gave him the address of Lexie's office.

He said, "Give me five minutes. Can you wait that long?"

I must have sounded frantic, so I forced myself to calm down. "Yes, of course."

Five minutes later, he came walking toward me on the sidewalk. Instead of his black trench coat, he was wearing a blue hooded sweatshirt over a blue chambray shirt and jeans. The breeze tousled his hair. He still seemed young, but at least he'd stopped looking as if he were wearing his dad's raincoat.

He took my elbow in hand. "Are you okay?"

"Why does everybody keep asking me that?"

"You look scared."

"I'm cold, not scared."

"That's good." He kissed my forehead.

Now I'm scared, I thought.

He put his arm around me as if to warm me up. "I live a couple of blocks from here. Let's get some coffee."

We found an Internet café around the corner. Hoping to steady my racing heartbeat, I ordered a cup of decaf. Bloom didn't need to ask the teenage girl at the counter before she drew him a fat-free caramel macchiatto and handed it over with a shy smile he pretended not to notice.

He took my coat and put it over the extra chair at a table near the Internet bar.

I sat down. "Am I interrupting your workday?"

"It's my day off. I'm glad you called."

"Tell me what you're working on besides Rush Strawcutter's murder."

He understood I needed something benign to talk about. He sat opposite me. "Nothing very exciting, really. We've got a scam artist running around—a guy who impersonates people for a few weeks before he moves on. We're double-teaming with the sex crimes department here in the city."

"How does someone impersonate a sex crime?"

"He poses as a police officer or a lawyer or someone who works with the public, and he lures his victims into—you know. Weird stuff."

"Is he dangerous?"

"The women don't think so. They're mostly annoyed when he leaves. I guess he's a real charmer. We've had a few husbands complain, though. It's an entertaining case. A good stress buster."

He didn't look very stressed, sipping his sweet coffee and looking at me with something new in his soft brown gaze. Something less law-abiding than usual. I tried to decide if I was afraid of that expression.

I said, "Have you learned anything more about Rush Strawcutter's death?"

"A little, yes. Did you read this morning's paper?"

"Not yet."

"We found the murder weapon. A polo mallet."

"So it wasn't Emma's riding crop?"

He had the grace to look embarrassed. "No. The crop wasn't heavy enough to inflict lethal injury. We think somebody used the mallet on the victim and threw it into a burn barrel near the service buildings around the hunt club. It's partially destroyed, so no physical evidence."

"Where did the mallet come from?"

"From a display in a tack room near the stall where Strawcutter was found. There used to be two mallets crossed on a wall with some photos and ribbons and junk. One's missing, and this one's a match. We think the killer took it down from the wall, hit Strawcutter with it, then dumped it in the barrel."

"And nobody saw anyone take it?"

"It was dark. People were busy getting ready for the hunt. We're still asking around."

I removed the plastic lid from my cup of coffee, and several seconds of unintentional silence slid by. It was enough time for him to absorb more information than I wanted to reveal, so I stupidly said, "I don't know why I called you."

He waited, not moving.

"I feel silly. I don't— I'm not sure what I'm doing here."

"It's okay. It's nice, actually. I'm glad you feel you can call me like this."

"I'm just— I have a lot of things happening right now. I want to tell you about them, but I can't."

Bloom moved into the chair closest to me. He forgot about his coffee and leaned closer. He touched my hand. "Because of your sister? Or are you protecting Abruzzo now?"

I was protecting a lot of people by not speaking, I realized. Emma and Michael and Tim. And now I was keeping secrets for Claudine and Dougie, too. I couldn't look at Bloom, but I said evenly, "You were right to suspect blackmail. There's been a lot of it going on, as a matter of fact. I think it affects Rush's murder, but I can't figure out how. Several people have been blackmailed."

He let out a tense breath of air. "Who?"

I looked into his eyes. "I can't tell you that without violating their confidences."

"Strawcutter?"

"Actually," I said, "Until today, I thought Rush was the one doing the blackmailing."

"What changed your mind?"

"Someone received another demand—after Rush's death."

He sat back slightly. Bloom's gaze took on a keen glitter as he thought about what I'd just told him.

I said, "Remember the white envelope you found with Rush's body? Have you learned anything more about that?"

"It's a standard photographer's envelope. They're very common. I imagine your newspaper uses them, along with most developing labs in the city. So the blackmailer was sending pictures?"

"Yes."

"Can you describe them?"

"They were taken by the same photographer as the pictures you have."

"What kind of money are we talking?"

"Ten thousand dollars to start. But increasing with each demand."

He grabbed his coffee cup so hard I thought he might crush it. "That's serious dough."

"Yes."

"Lots of people involved?"

"I don't know how many."

He couldn't contain his excitement. "Will anyone come forward? All we need is one person."

"That person will undoubtedly pay a price," I said. "Secrets will have to come out."

"We can protect people. We can—" He stopped himself and looked at me. "Nora." His voice changed. "Are you in trouble?"

I gave him a shaky smile and put my cup on the table. "You mean besides trying to help my sister escape a murder charge?"

He put his arm on the back of my chair and edged closer. "Are you being blackmailed?"

"I don't have any money," I reminded him. "You saw my house. It's falling down around my ears. My paycheck doesn't come close to covering my expenses. A blackmailer would be pretty stupid to choose me, wouldn't he?"

"That's not what I asked." Bloom covered my hand with his again. "Are you in a jam? Tell me what's going on, and I'll help you."

But I couldn't. The thought of turning Tim Naftzinger's life upside down made me feel physically ill.

"Nora."

I wasn't sure when it happened, but suddenly he touched my chin and tilted my face toward his. He radiated steady dependability. He was someone I could relinquish my problems to. Someone I could trust.

Next thing I knew, I was kissing him. It was a relief, almost. His mouth was sure, and his tongue tasted like caramel. I slid my shaking hand up to his smooth cheek. I realized we were breathing in unison—quick and shallow. I forgot about murder and just let it happen. My mind went blank, but the rest of my senses shivered awake.

When our lips parted, I asked softly, "Do you have a gun?"

He blinked. "What?"

"Do you carry a gun?"

He laughed uncertainly. "Why are you asking now? I never took you for the kind of woman who wanted to see—"

"I just need to know."

"I'm a police detective. Of course I have a gun. Why?" His hand tightened on my shoulder. "Do you need that much protection?"

"No. I—I don't know. I'm afraid of guns. I—"

"It's locked up," he soothed. "It's in my closet. It can't hurt you."

"That's not what I mean."

"What, then?"

Clearly, I was confused. Scared, too. Maybe I was desperate. Maybe I was furious enough at Michael to permanently break off whatever we'd been doing together and experiment with someone new. Maybe it was time to trade in a sexy, funny, tender, infuriating man for a younger model.

Bloom said, "You're really upset. Let's go back to my apartment. I live a few blocks away."

"Wait," I said.

"I've waited," he said. "There's a lot going on between us. We can work this out. Let's go to my place. Let me take you to bed. You're so beautiful."

His fingertips brushed the buttons on my blouse.

That did it. I was definitely not up for this. I pushed his hand away. My face was very hot.

He toyed with a strand of my hair and didn't move away.

"I'm sorry," I said. "Going to bed with you—it would be a shortcut. I don't know you. Not like— Not as much as I should."

"We can get to know each other better. Come on."

"No, I can't. I'm sorry."

"Why," he said. "Are you afraid of me, but not of him?"

I looked up into Ben Bloom's dark eyes and I knew what kind of pillow talk he hoped for. He was prepared to take me to bed to learn more about the blackmail. He didn't care about me, and I wasn't entirely sure he was sexually aroused by me either. The moment felt calculated. I had been sighted in his crosshairs for something more than a tumble on his bed.

"I think you know," I said.

I got my coat, went out onto the street. He watched me through the window, but I turned away hastily.

I hurried several blocks and found myself on Logan Circle looking down the length of the Ben Franklin Parkway towards the Rodin Museum, home of Rodin's most popular work, *The Thinker*. I wished I could summon up some useful sequence of thoughts, but no luck. My head was whirling.

Beyond the Rodin lay the Museum of Art. From it, a freezing wind blew down the avenue, and I stood for a long time looking at the buildings—constructed and maintained by vast donations from generations of generous supporters. My own family had contributed, as did the families of many friends. The result was a city laid out with precision, designed with grandeur and great beauty. But the side streets and old neighborhoods each possessed their own nuanced complexity—with dirt and confusion and character—that fashioned a city people could claim as their own. It had its faults, but we loved it.

I shivered in my coat.

Finally, too cold to think, I cut across to the Four Seasons. In the lobby I found a telephone.

Michael answered on the second ring.

"It's me," I said, my voice sounding strangled.

"I can't talk," he said. "I'm at a deposition."

But he didn't hang up.

Neither one of us said a word for a long, tense moment. We listened to the silence that stretched between us, infused with so many unspoken emotions that I thought my heart would burst.

I swallowed hard and finally said, "I need to see Emma. It's important."

Another silence, even more painful than before, laden with disappointment.

"Call Reed," Michael said at last. "He knows."

"Thank you."

"Nora," he said.

I squeezed my eyes shut and tried to breathe, but it came out like a hiccough.

Half a minute later, I hung up without saying anything more.

Blindly, I searched my handbag for more coins for the phone, using the time to compose myself.

At last, I called Reed. When he answered, I said, "I need to talk to Emma. Michael says you can help me."

"Where are you?"

I told him.

He said, "Give me an hour."

I went into the Swann Café. The host recognized me and gave me the best table in the house when I would have much preferred the darkest corner. I was so hungry that I ordered a club sandwich and ate the whole thing practically without taking a deep breath. I took a longing look at the dessert display, but remembered the ballet gala was only a few days away.

Soon, Reed pulled the town car in front of the hotel and got out cautiously. "Where's the dog?" he asked.

"You're safe. He's with my sister."

When he was behind the wheel and the car was heading past City Hall, I asked, "Did you talk to Michael?"

"The boss is busy today. Meeting with a bunch of lawyers."

A deposition, he'd said. Something he didn't want me to know about.

Reed drove into a parking garage and left the town car on the top deck. We walked down a flight of stairs, and he put me into the back seat of a different car and we went out onto the street again. I should have been amused by this extra step in securing my sister's safety, but today I was unnerved.

After the switch, Reed drove me through the thickening afternoon traffic until we reached the Mutter Museum.

"Oh, not here," I groaned. "Whose idea is this?"

"Your sister's," Reed said. "I'm not going in there. Place gives me the creeps. Call me when you're ready to leave."

The Mutter Museum was one of Emma's favorite spots, and one of my least. Originally founded to house a collection of medical specimens, it had evolved into a graphic display of frightful curiosities hyped to the visiting public as the perfect Halloween outing. Everything from the most gruesome obstetrical gadgets and deformed human skeletons to trephinated Peruvian skulls and the liver shared by the so-called

Siamese twins Eng and Chang, submerged in liquid in a jar, was on display to be gawked at by tourists. A plaster cast of their conjoined bodies was a visitor favorite. The term *gross anatomy* was particularly apt.

As a ten-year-old, I had been dragged into an exhibit of deformed babies and, overcome, upchucked into Libby's handbag. Libby threw the ruined bag into a museum garbage can, but a guard found it minutes later and kindly returned the bag to my appalled sister, having naturally noticed the sexy girl with the striped handbag as soon as she strolled through the doors.

Emma, of course, loved the place.

I found her now in the gift shop, poking through a display of novelty items. She was bouncing a pair of eyeballs in her hand and turned to me with a grin. "Think I should get these for the twins? And maybe Lucy would get a kick out of that squishy human heart?"

"Go for it," I said. "Those kids are a lost cause, anyway."

Emma tossed the eyeballs back into their bin and turned to me. She had gotten some sleep, and the bruise on her cheek had begun to turn green and fade, but the sight of it still made me catch my breath. She was dressed in an oversized parka I didn't recognize and wore a knit Flyers cap over her hair. I gave her a hug and was surprised to discover she wanted to hug me, too.

"Great disguise," I said once we were out of the shop and standing in the high-ceilinged lobby. "You look ready to sell ten-dollar Rolexes on a street corner in Alaska. How are you?"

"Life's a bitch," she said cheerfully "Except for

Libby. I talked to her an hour ago. She seems her usual lunatic self. Who's the new boyfriend?"

"A doctor."

"Have you met him?"

"Barely. Why? Has there been a development since this morning?"

"No, just—well, he sounds like a typical Libby acquisition. A sexual theme park with a major personality disorder."

"Oh, no, is she having sex with him?"

"Depends on what you consider sex, I guess." Emma slid her hands into the pockets of the enormous black parka. It had several zippers and a dozen extra pockets suitable for carrying supplies on an Arctic mission. "What about you?"

"I'm not having sex with him, either."

She studied me. "Are you having it with anybody else?"

"Let's talk about you, shall we? Can we go for a walk outside? This place gives me the creeps."

She stared at me and swore softly. "It's true, then, isn't it? Mick was right."

"Right about what?"

Emma didn't move to go outside. "He thought maybe you were going to do something drastic. It's that boy detective, isn't it? That kid who moons after you."

"He does not moon. And I didn't do anything with him, so relax."

"Your blouse is unbuttoned."

We were alone in the lobby, so I fastened the undone button, wondering how Bloom had managed that trick.

"You know," Emma said seriously, "if you push

Mick away often enough, he'll eventually get the message."

Hard-voiced, I asked, "Did he show you his gun, Emma?"

That took her by surprise. "What?"

"He's carrying a gun now. Whatever trouble he's in at the moment requires him to have a weapon."

"How do you know?"

"I saw it. It fell out of his pocket."

"Are you sure it's his?"

"Well, why would he have it otherwise?"

"I don't know. I just— I can't believe he'd—"

"Believe it. I can't be around him anymore, Em. I've had enough violent crime, thank you, and I don't want to be a part of it again. If he's going to get himself killed—"

"He won't get killed. He's indestructible."

"Nobody is indestructible. We both know it. In fact, that should be our family motto."

She shook her head in wonder. "Wow, this is hard to believe."

"So you understand?" I demanded. "Sure, I care about Michael. Most of the time I think I'm in love with him. But I'm not going to set myself up for another catastrophe. I've almost got my life back on track, and I don't think I could survive. Not if something happened to Michael."

She touched my arm and didn't say anything. Maybe this was what I had needed when I called for her. Some sisterly solidarity.

"I'm not going to cry," I said.

"Okay."

"I'm trying to be strong."

"Right."

"I'm trying to do the smart thing."

"Good. Men are a dime a dozen anyway. We'll walk around the block and find somebody worth spending a night with, I'm sure."

"Shut up."

"Whatever you say."

We stood for a silent moment, and then I said, "Can we talk about something else now?"

"What do you have in mind?"

"How about Rush Strawcutter?"

She took her hand away. "My turn to be the target now?"

We went outside together. The raw cold cut through my coat, but Emma looked unfazed. I said, "I need you to remember everything you can about that morning, Em. Any little detail might help."

"I already told you everything."

"Then let's back up. Tell me what you knew about Rush before he died."

"Like what, exactly? The color of his socks?"

"Did you learn the color of his socks?"

"No," she said. "The God's-honest truth is I never slept with him. We fooled around a little, but he was— I think he truly cared about Gussie. He didn't want to hurt her. I pushed him, and that was wrong, I know, but he— We only played around a little. Mostly, I liked being with him."

We started walking.

She began to talk then. It was aimless, but she told me about her friendship with Rush and I could sense she had longed for a real relationship with him. Even before her husband's death, Emma had been on a wild ride. Now I listened and wondered if we had both managed somehow to struggle our way out of the center of the storm. Maybe we were both on the edge of peace and quiet. Emma had found something in

Rush—something that cut some of the pain in her heart. Except now he was gone, and she looked worse than ever.

After we'd walked several blocks and she quit talking, I said, "I'm sure Rush wished things could have been different with you, Em."

She shook her head. "I don't know. He was always on the lookout for a stray puppy to rescue. Maybe I was just one of a long line of salvage projects for him."

"He felt that way about Gussie, didn't he?"

"Yeah, she was his ultimate project."

"Do you know how she felt about him?"

"She must have loved him once, but she couldn't trust him. She was always worried about the money. Is that nuts, or what?"

"Do you think Rush married her because he wanted to rescue her, or because he also wanted her fortune?"

"He was concerned about cash," Emma admitted. "He had to scramble to raise the capital to start Laundro-Mutt when Gussie refused to invest. He went to banks all over town, but nobody wanted to give him anything if he didn't have the Strawcutter guarantee standing behind him."

"If Gussie had just volunteered to do that much, he would have had an easier time."

"I don't think Gussie wanted to make anything easy for Rush. That was part of their relationship. She needed to test him all the time. He had to constantly prove he wanted to stay married to her."

"So he went the venture capital route to raise money for Laundro-Mutt. Why did he choose Tottie, of all people?"

"Well," said Emma. She stopped at the traffic light and didn't look at me.

"Well?" I asked.

"Because."

The light changed, and Emma hustled into the street. I followed her hastily.

"Em?"

"Do you know anything about Rush's family?" she asked.

"Not really."

"He grew up in foster homes around here. Never far from Philadelphia. I suppose that's why he was always adopting those dogs of his, because he was a foster kid."

"I had no idea."

"His mother couldn't support him, so he bounced around from family to family most of his childhood. I think it was hard on him, but he managed to survive. That's a testament to his real personality, isn't it?"

"Yes, it is."

I started to feel what was coming. It was a tidal wave, building in size far off shore.

"Em, if Rush's mother couldn't support him, where was his father?"

"Rush didn't know who his father was until just a couple of years ago when he married Gussie. He wanted to find his mother to invite her for the wedding, if you can imagine that. But she was dead, and he could only locate a sister of hers. The sister told Rush who his father was."

"Oh, my God. Tottie."

"Tottie Boarman," Emma confirmed.

"Did Rush go to see Tottie?"

"Not at first. Rush had already experienced the Strawcutters' reaction to a poor, unconnected young man in their midst. He figured Tottie would see him as a greedy opportunist. So he stayed away. But when he needed money for Laundro-Mutt, Gussie pushed him to go to Tottie."

"So Gussie knew of the connection?"

"Yes. It was only fair, according to Gussie. Rush was due some of Tottie's fortune—at least, to her way of thinking."

"Oh, God," I said again. I stopped walking.

Emma pulled me out of the pedestrian traffic and under the awning of a corner market. A display of fall apples stood beside us.

"What was Tottie's reaction? Did he know Rush was his son?"

"It's pretty obvious, when you think about it. They might be opposites in character, but they look alike. How could Tottie deny it?"

Of course they looked alike. How could I have missed it before? Tottie's rude personality had blinded me, of course. Rush might have had Tottie's odd walk and similar features, but they were so different in manner that no one could have guessed they were father and son.

I said, "Tottie didn't welcome Rush with open arms, did he? It wasn't in his nature."

"No, Tottie acted like a son of a bitch, of course. He told Rush not to expect any prodigal-son treatment. I think Rush was pleased, though. Something must have given him hope. The eternal optimist, he probably figured he'd eventually win Tottie's affections."

"And Tottie did give Rush the money to start Laundro-Mutt."

"Yes, and plenty of it. Maybe he wanted to prove to Rush that he wasn't a complete jerk. Money was Tottie's way of doing that."

"But lately Tottie needed some of his cash back to save himself."

Emma nodded. "Tottie's own business was falling apart. He needed help, so he started pressuring Rush. Of course, Rush had already invested the money into Laundro-Mutt, and he didn't have any cash left to give back to Tottie."

What had Tottie done? I wondered.

Emma had been watching my face. "What are you thinking?"

"I need to know what the terms of Rush's life insurance policy were. Does Gussie receive the death benefits, or does the money go to paying off Laundro-Mutt's investors?"

"Hang on," Emma said. "You don't think Tottie murdered his own son? For a few dollars?"

"Tens of millions of dollars."

"Oh, hell," Emma said. "This is starting to sound very dangerous."

Chapter 15

Reed picked up both of us and dropped Emma at a parking garage from where I presumed she would be whisked back into captivity.

"Where will you go?" I asked her.

"My home away from home is now a lovely student apartment near Penn," she said grimly. "It smells like pot and has a stolen stop sign on the wall."

I blanched. "I hope it won't be much longer."

"Who knows. Maybe the ever-charming Mr. Pescara will move me into a flop house for a change of pace. Let me tell you, the life of the modern gangster has no glamour. Their primary food group is beef jerky, and they mostly sit around in disgusting places watching the Home Shopping Network and popping anabolic steroids. Oh, and talking to their mothers on cell phones."

"Emma, about Danny—"

She waved off my concern. "Don't worry about him. He'll end up in the slammer someday soon and have lots of time to think about his shortcomings."

"No," I said, not sure I should tell her there might have been a connection between Danny and her husband, Jake. "I mean—"

"Listen," she said, "I appreciate what you're doing. I'd be going nuts if you weren't asking questions for

me. I mean it. I can put up with Mick's crew of hood-
lums for as long as it takes."

"I'm glad I can help," I said. "But about Danny—"

She closed the car door on my protest and walked
away with a wave over her shoulder that dismissed
the subject.

I checked my watch and discovered it was nearly the
cocktail hour. As much as I wanted to learn more about
Tottie, I had a party to attend for the *Intelligencer*.

The holiday entertaining season had gotten off to a
fast start after Thanksgiving, and I knew it would build
to a crescendo on Christmas Eve. We'd have a few
days off before the New Year's Eve festivities started,
then the long January lull. For the next couple of
weeks, I was going to be very busy. Every night of
the week I had at least two events to attend, including
the ballet's annual fund-raising gala on Friday night.
I hoped to put my questions about Rush on hold—at
least during my work hours. My miserable paycheck
depended on it.

Tonight, however, the parties were much less
exalted.

Reed drove me to a private home on Delancy Street
where two doctors were hosting a cocktail party for a
visiting colleague who had come to town to help raise
money for a scholarship fund. Their home was a narrow town house on a picturesque street, with the main
living quarters on the second floor. The rooms were
sparsely decorated with primitive American furniture.
As I walked into the living room, it was impossible to
miss the Grandma Moses painting, colorful and beautifully lighted, hanging over the mantel.

The deceptively simple décor hinted subtly at the
alliance of two of the city's most powerful medical

families. The living room was already very hot, crowded and loud with laughter—sure signs of a successful party.

"We should have waited until January," confided my host, Tomas "Tack" Estrada, when he greeted me. In a turtleneck with a medallion around his neck, he looked like an elegant Spanish grandee. "We could have avoided all the holiday conflicts, but what can you do? Dr. Powell was in town, so we're going for it. It's a good cause."

"Thanks for letting me crash the party, Tack," I said. "As soon as the photographer gets here, we'll snap a few pictures of Dr. Powell with the scholarship candidates, and we'll be out of your hair in no time."

"Stay as long as you like, Nora. I wish we could see more of you. Olivia often says she's sorry you don't still live close enough to have your brunches anymore."

He pointed out his wife across the crowded room, and Olivia Estrada, still blond and very pale-skinned thanks to her dermatologist husband's insistence on sunscreen, waved at me over the heads of the guests. She had been chatting with a tall male guest.

I waved back. "Is that Tim Naftzinger?"

"Where?" Tack craned to see. "Tim said he'd try to stop in after seeing patients to schmooze for his promotion, but yes, that's Tim."

"Think he'll get the Chief of Pediatrics job?"

"I hope so. He's good at administration and it will mean more time for his daughter. He has my vote, but it's a political scrum, and he's not the best good ol' boy."

I tried to make my way toward Tim through the guests, who were hungrily digging into the caviar blinis Olivia was known for. I didn't recognize many of the contributors who had turned out on short notice for the Estrada's fund-raiser, but mostly they seemed to be physicians from the various city hospitals. A few smiling faces appeared to recognize me, but turned away before they had to remember my name. Or before they had to remember that one of their own kind had slid down the slippery slope of drug abuse. Obviously, the two years that had passed since my husband's death caused the medical set to gladly forget who I was.

At last, I reached Olivia Estrada and hugged her.

"Nora, it's been too long! How nice to see you."

"Livvie, I've missed you, too. I have a stack of books I've been saving for you. When can we have lunch?"

"After Christmas," she said promptly. "Right now, I'm up to my elbows in women who want their Botox injections in time for New Year's Eve."

"Maybe I'd better make an appointment for myself."

"You? Don't be silly." Smiling, she gave my face a professional once-over. Olivia conducted the cosmetic side of the family practice, while Tack dealt with the surgical patients. "I'm glad to see those laugh lines again. I'll call you the first of January, I promise, and we'll go some place decadent for lunch."

"Sounds great. Did I just see Tim Naftzinger talking to you?"

"Tim?" Olivia glanced around. "Yes, he was here a minute ago."

"He probably had to run home to his daughter."

"He said he suddenly wasn't feeling well."

I spotted the *Intelligencer* photographer then, and we put our heads together to plan a photogenic moment in front of Grandma Moses with the guest of honor and some slightly tipsy scholarship candidates from the nearby medical school. Afterward, I wished my hosts a merry Christmas and ducked out. The *Intelligencer* photographer, Lee Song, came with me and reloaded his camera in the car.

"Lee, have you met Kitty Keough's new intern yet?"

"Andy Mooney?" Lee grinned. "Yeah, I tripped over him in the elevator."

"Have you ever seen any of his photographs?"

"Nope. You?"

"Not yet, but I'm going to catch a glimpse."

Lee laughed. "You think he's going to put us both out of our jobs? Just in time for Christmas?"

"I know you don't have anything to worry about."

Lee snapped my picture just for fun and smiled. "Neither do you, Nora."

Our next stop was a wine tasting, thrown by a law firm, at a very pricey French restaurant. They had thinly disguised their office party as a benefit for abused spouses. As soon as we stepped through the double doors, I heard the cool bebop of jazz musicians having a great time. The scent of wonderful food wafted with the fragrances of many expensive perfumes.

Guests had already seized glasses of wine and were flowing in clusters. I recognized a handsome former governor, two Philadelphia television personalities, a wacky artist who built erotic sculptures out of recycled plastic bottles and a Hollywood actor no doubt home to visit his parents and serendipitously making the scene. I gauged the party in an instant, and knew I'd walked into another very successful Delilah Fairweather event.

Sure enough, the crowd parted in time for me to

catch a glimpse of Delilah, cooing sweet nothings into the ear of the only annoyed guest in the restaurant. She patted his arm consolingly and headed in my direction through the crowd.

"Shoot me now," Delilah commanded, already pulling a cell phone from the pocket of her red satin suit. "One pissed-off guest can ruin the whole night."

"Delilah, isn't that your dad?"

"Yes, and he's fussing that I didn't order ribs. Barbecued ribs, for crying out loud! I've got the city's foremost French chef busting his balls in the kitchen, and my old man wants soul food. I should send him to the nearest pretzel cart. Give us a kiss, honey."

I did. "This party looks great."

"I'm redeeming myself after the Boarman fiasco." She checked her cell phone for messages. "Did you hear we had a rat attack one of the children? I'm never using that hotel again."

"Uhm, how awful."

"No harm done." Delilah didn't notice my embarrassment. "Turns out the kid has a history of bad behavior and the hotel admits it's had a rodent problem since they opened. Listen, I have your dress. The one from the prom party. It's in a box at the coat check."

"Thanks. I'll get it on my way out. I'm here for the newspaper. Can we grab a photo and hit the road? I have another stop to make."

"Me, too. I'm only staying here long enough to— Damn, I've got to take this call. Hysterical caterer. Do you mind?"

While Delilah plugged one ear and listened to her caterer with the other, I rounded up some of the celebrities and ferreted the chef from the kitchen to pose in front of a display of spectacular food and wine bottles. I jollied everyone into interacting. The actor was especially gracious and even put his arm around Delilah's grumpy father to coax him out of his very un-holiday spirit. Delilah came over and convinced the former governor to also lend his face for the good cause, and Lee snapped a dozen pictures in no time. Soon Delilah's father was laughing with a lovely young television news anchor.

"You're a godsend," Delilah told me.

"Your party is terrific," I assured her. "You're still the best in the city. Kitty will be sorry she didn't stop in."

"I'd much rather have you. Where is Kitty tonight?"

"An A-list shindig, I'm sure. I'm strictly the junior varsity team."

"Which one of you will attend Rush Strawcutter's funeral?"

"Has it been scheduled yet?"

Delilah nodded. "I heard it's going to be Thursday. A friend of mine was asked about doing the food afterward, but get this: the family said she was too expensive. I think they're going to get takeout from Kentucky Fried Chicken."

I knew she was kidding. "I'll probably attend. But Kitty may decide to go, too."

"Are you still going to the ballet gala on Friday?"

"Wouldn't miss it." I smiled. "What are you going to wear?"

"I bought just the thing in Bermuda last summer, believe it or not, and it only cost me fifty bucks, but don't tell a soul. Remember how I said somebody wants to buy your dress? Well, she called me again."

"Delilah, that dress is so old and fragile, it will fall apart if someone tries to wear it. It's better suited to a mannequin."

"That's what I told her, but she insists she wants it."

"Anybody I know?"

"Claudine Paltron, the one who wants everything she sees. She thinks it's just the right dress for her to make a triumphant entrance at the gala. I told her I thought you'd never part with it, but she phoned me again this evening."

"I can't sell that dress. It belonged to my grandmother."

"She's willing to pay big bucks, honey."

I was afraid to ask how much.

Delilah saw the conflict in my face and put her arm around me. "Don't worry. I won't give her your number. Unless you want me to?"

Her cell phone trilled, and she made an always-working shrug before she took the call. I used the moment to grab a plate of savory treats from the buffet, then went to the coat check and picked up the oblong box with my grandmother's Mainbocher inside. Lee helped me carry everything to the car.

I shared the food with Reed, who seemed unimpressed by French cuisine. He drove us across town to a hotel where another party was just getting started—a dinner honoring a very solemn feminist author. I was glad I didn't have to stay for the rubber chicken and suspected Kitty had requested I attend just to punish me. Lee got some photos and I scribbled down some quotes. We parted ways around eight o'clock.

While Reed drove me home, I wrote my stories and then fell soundly asleep in the backseat.

I woke up when the car hit the first pothole in my driveway. A bright blue tarp was hanging on the side of the house like a giant shower cap that glowed in the dark.

"That looks cozy," Reed said.

"Let's just hope it's watertight."

I said good night and staggered inside. The lake in the kitchen was gone, thank heaven, and another foil-covered plate of food from Mrs. Ledbetter awaited me on the table. I peeked and found she'd made stuffed peppers, enough for two. I put half in the fridge for tomorrow.

I e-mailed my stories to my editor and listened to my answering machine while the microwave worked its magic on my dinner. Libby, Hadley, my mother, my editor, my dentist's receptionist, two hang-ups, my tax man, who reminded me that my quarterly payment was due by Monday or penalties would be imposed, and Libby again.

"Don't call back," she sang, sounding as happy as a cheerleader who'd just come home from the big game. "I'm going to bed early. Spike's fine, but you owe me a new kitchen rug and two pairs of sneakers."

I ate a stuffed pepper while I looked through the mail. Three Christmas cards, a few bills and a terse letter from the local tax collector's office just in case I didn't listen to their daily phone messages.

I opened my checkbook and discovered that my next paycheck would cover the utility bills, but only if Mrs. Ledbetter continued to feed me.

My family didn't come over on the *Mayflower,* but they caught the next bus, so to speak, and they quickly prospered. By investing in banks and railroads and safety pins, the family fortune expanded. The family expanded, too, however, and eventually so many cousins were dipping into the well that the cash began to thin out. My grandmother had amassed a nationally-renowned collection of silver, but later in life she began to secretly sell it off, teaspoon by teaspoon, to support the family in the style to which we had become accustomed.

Grandmama's years of buying couture clothing had resulted in one of the country's finest collections of exquisite designs, too, which should have gone to a museum, I suppose, but I needed something to wear now that I was employed. I took great care not to ruin any of the many Chanels, Diors and Givenchys, which were each worth tens of thousands.

I played the message on my answering machine again and listened to the sonorous voice of my tax man.

Afterward, sick at heart, I looked up Claudine Paltron's telephone number.

The Zapper Czar answered rudely and told me that Claudine was out for the evening. He gave me her cell phone number.

I caught her at a restaurant.

"Nora!" She sounded surprised. Then, "Are you calling to lecture me like Lexie?"

"If I thought I could convince you to go to the police, Claudine, I would."

"Well, you can't. And I'm switching all of my accounts out of Lexie's company, so I don't have to listen to her, either."

I considered making another pitch to change her mind, but I could hear noise in the background and knew the time wasn't right.

Instead I said, "I hear you're interested in my grandmother's Mainbocher."

Chapter 16

The next morning, Claudine sent a messenger to pick up the dress.

He also dropped off a check for the purchase price.

And the envelope of photographs I'd requested in addition to the money.

I opened the envelopes of photos and spread them out on my kitchen table. Mind you, it was not an appetizing sight. The pictures showed Claudine's unmistakably long legs wrapped around Dougie Forsythe's bare behind. Her ugly dancer's feet were instantly recognizable.

I pushed my morning coffee aside and marveled at the strong stomach of the photographer. How had he or she managed to watch the event, let alone have the presence of mind to snap such telling photographs? These photos were much more graphic than the ones taken of Tim and myself, and the similarly soft-focus pictures of Emma and Rush. Yet they had the same greeting-cardlike quality.

Libby arrived with Spike.

"This animal is not a credit to his species," she announced as he raced into the kitchen and leaped joyfully into my lap. "Do you know what kind of poop comes out when a dog eats a whole bag of marshmallows?"

"Why in the world would you give him a bag of marshmallows?"

"I didn't! They were innocently sitting on the counter, which is nearly four feet over his head, so I assumed they were safe. But he managed to levitate himself somehow and—well, you owe me for more rugs than you can imagine." She dropped her handbag on the floor and sat down at the table.

"On the other hand, Lucy wants to come live here so she can be near him. They're soulmates. Her imaginary friend has decided to cut up all the draperies with scissors. I don't have a decent window treatment left in my house. And the twins are still filming a horror movie, so they make blood out of corn syrup. It looks as if Charles Manson has been living in my basement, and it's so sticky we have ants coming out of the woodwork—in December!"

"How is Rawlins?"

Libby avoided my gaze. "We just had a horrible fight, so don't ask."

I could see she was ready to blow, so I asked a safer question. "How is the baby?"

Her lower lip began to tremble. "Beautiful. But he still doesn't have a name."

"What about your new boyfriend?"

Her nose turned pink and tears began to glisten in her eyes.

"Libby?"

"He—he wants me to—well, restrain him."

"He what?"

"I'm beginning to think he's a little peculiar, Nora."

"What kind of restraining?"

"You know. Tying him up. And Melvin's always talking about discipline. I thought he meant improving the children's behavior, which I admit could use a little attention, maybe, but I'm starting to worry he—well, he might not be quite normal."

"Oh, for God's sake Libby! You haven't really had sex with this man, have you? He hasn't tied you up, has he?"

"No, no, *he's* the one who wants to be controlled, you see, and I'm supposed to pretend I'm the prison warden or the angry policewoman or the stagecoach driver."

"The—?"

"He gave me a pretty little buggy whip. I thought it was an antique, something I could display at Christmas with some nice holly branches and a Currier and Ives print, but—"

"Libby, I think it's time to break things off with Melvin."

"But he's so sweet!"

"Bringing you flowers and candy, that's sweet. Bringing you a whip is something entirely—"

"You can afford to say that!" she cried. "You have a man coming around, paying attention to you, wanting to sweep you into bed. But I'm this f-f-fat housewife with too many children and no hope of a fulfilling sex life again for the rest of my life! I'll be that old woman who lives in a shoe! Only my shoe is covered with corn syrup and doesn't have any curtains!"

She was blubbering then, with huge sobs heaving her Hindenberg bosom. Spike sat up in my lap and stared at her, fascinated.

I put the dog on the floor and gave Libby a hug, and brought her a cup of coffee and made soothing noises. She howled and bawled and wept until she was wrung out. Eventually, she accepted a damp cloth, which she applied to her face to cool down. When she sat up again, she looked as beautiful as Elizabeth Taylor in her most vibrant youth.

I said, "I can't believe how amazingly gorgeous you are, Libby. And you're such a sexy, smart woman with a wonderful sense of humor."

"Do you really think so?"

"Nobody makes me laugh the way you do," I said honestly.

"Well . . ."

"You don't need a nut like Melvin to make your life complete. Just wait until your hormones calm down, and things will start to feel good again, I promise."

"But . . ."

"There's a man out there with more than buggy whips to give. Take some time for yourself first. Let Placida help you—uhm—find serenity."

My sister nodded and dabbed her eyes. "You're right. I should have trusted Placida. I shouldn't be in a rush. Maybe I'll go back to watching Dr. Phil for a while."

I gave her a kiss. "Whatever it takes, Lib."

She smiled wanly. "Thank you, Nora. You're a good sister. And you won't mind moving back to my house to help me, will you? You've been such a godsend during my time of need."

Spike voted for not moving back to Libby's house by lifting his leg and peeing on her purse.

While I cleaned up the mess, Libby finally caught sight of the collection of Claudine's photographs spread out on my kitchen table.

"Good heavens, who's this?" she asked, picking up the photograph of Claudine and Dougie. "It's that ballet dancer, isn't it? Surely she could get a pedicure now that she's retired."

"I don't think that would help."

"Probably not." Libby turned the photo sideways. "Not a very imaginative position, is it? I always assumed creative people were creative in all aspects of their lives. Where was this taken?"

"At a private party. This is the bedroom where the host put the coats, I assume. See the headboard?"

She nodded. "A brass bed. Very pretty. Stick with the classics, I always say."

I retrieved the rest of the blackmail photos and spread them in front of her. "Notice anything these pictures have in common?"

A painter herself, Libby devoted a long minute of study to the array of images. "Well, they're all taken by the same photographer, of course. But . . ."

"Look at the hotel coatroom. And the coats on the bed under Claudine."

Libby chose two of the pictures that showed the best view of the coats. Her brows lifted. "That silk scarf with the fringe. There's just a hint of it here. It's the same scarf in both pictures, right?"

She had made the same discovery I had. "I think so, yes."

"So the owner of the scarf attended both events." She looked at me. "Who is it?"

I took a deep breath. "Hadley Pinkham."

"What does it mean?"

"Just that Hadley was a guest at both parties."

"But—" Libby's face slackened with shock. "My God, you don't think Hadley is your blackmailer? Why, in heaven's name? He's surely got more money that the Sultan of Brunei!"

"Maybe not anymore."

"What do you mean?"

"The Pinkham fortune may have been divided too many times, just like ours."

"I can't believe he'd be capable of preying on his friends! Our circle! Not people he's known since childhood!"

"I'm not jumping to any conclusions yet. But it's possible, don't you think?"

"What about the misspelled word on the note? Hadley would never—"

"He wouldn't misspell anything, but he's proud of being a klutz with anything mechanical—like a typewriter."

"Or a camera?"

"I know, I know." I gathered up the photographs. "He claims he doesn't know a camera from a hair-dryer. This isn't enough evidence to prove anything. But I have an instinct."

"Are you going to speak to him about this?"

"Not yet. There's someone else I want to talk to first."

"Who?"

I told her.

"Oh, God," Libby said. "Be careful, Nora!"

She drove me to the train station. Spike climbed out of my handbag once I'd taken a seat, and he braced his paws on the train window. With a panting smile, he watched the scenery fly by, snarling at the occasional school bus or noisy tractor trailer.

The train deposited us many blocks from the *Intelligencer* office. With Spike on his leash, we hiked up to the Pendergast building. The day was cold, and although I had dressed for an evening of party-hopping in a little black dress by Dior, I wore a favorite Italian knit sweater over it and was glad to have my wool coat and a pink pashmina to ward off the wind.

Oblivious to the cold, Spike was careful to leave threatening messages all along our route.

I put him back into my handbag while we rode the elevator, and he fell soundly asleep by the time I reached Stan Rosenstatz's office. The features editor was on the phone, so I waved at Mary Jude—hard at work at her computer and surrounded by boxes of cake mix—and headed over to the desk I was currently sharing with a part-time fashion writer. A stack of party invitations with a pink memo slip from Kitty lay on top of the computer monitor. The memo said only, *Reject these.*

I was flipping through the invitations while my e-mail program loaded when Andy Mooney suddenly materialized like Rumplestiltskin at my elbow. An enormous camera swung from a thick strap around his neck, and he held a lumpy briefcase in one hand. "Hi, Miss Blackbird! You look really pretty today."

In my seated position, I was nearly eye to eye with him. His shirttail was coming untucked, and it looked as if he hadn't combed his hair since getting out of bed. But he had a vaguely Spike-like look of wide-eyed interest in anything that moved. "Thank you, Andy. You're here early."

"Oh, I'm just running a few errands for Miss Keough. But I have some free time. What are you working on? Anything I can do for you?"

"Actually, I was hoping to bump into you today."

"Really?" Quickly, he grabbed a swivel chair from a nearby desk and wheeled it close to mine. He dropped the briefcase on the floor with a thud and sat down. "What's up?"

I pulled the white envelopes from my bag without

disturbing Spike. "Can I trust you with some sensitive information, Andy?"

He perked up. "What kind of sensitive information?"

"You know that a journalist sometimes has to keep secrets, right?"

He nodded. "Right."

"Even from your friends and family," I said darkly. "And sometimes even from your boss."

"Gee, Miss Blackbird, you're not in trouble, are you? Everybody's been saying you're involved with that Godfather guy, but I never thought—"

"That's not what I'm talking about, Andy. I'm fine. I have some information here that I can't show you unless you promise to keep it to yourself. You're not to tell anyone. Even Kitty."

He blinked at me from behind his Harry Potter glasses. With less certainty, he said, "Okay."

"Tell me first what pictures you've taken for Kitty."

"Party pictures," he said promptly. "You know—important guests, that kind of thing."

"Any other pictures? Things Kitty wanted personally?"

He began to look squeamish. "Well . . ."

"It's okay. You haven't done anything unethical. Right?"

"I did take some shots of Miss Keough and . . . her friend. Just for her to keep."

"Pictures of Kitty with Tottie Boarman?"

He nodded. Without being asked, he opened the briefcase at his feet. He glanced around the room to make sure we weren't being observed before he pulled out a sheaf of photos and spread them on my desk. Lousy photographs with bad lighting and the subjects badly centered. I was immediately assured that Andy was incapable of taking the blackmail pictures.

These, however, were indeed pictures of Kitty cuddling up to Tottie Boarman.

I had imagined that their relationship might be like a pair of mating alligators—all claws and teeth and bad tempers. But the expression on Kitty's face was unlike any I'd ever seen before. She actually looked girlish. And fond of her companion.

Tottie didn't look displeased, either. His hand looked almost tender as he cupped one of her elbows and appeared to pull her closer to him.

I shuddered and pushed the photos away.

"Is there something wrong?" Andy asked.

"No, Andy." I looked at him. "You didn't take pictures of other people at Kitty's request? Secret pictures, maybe?"

He frowned and gathered up his pictures. "I don't know what you mean."

"Okay," I soothed, confident he wasn't lying. "Just promise you won't mention these to anyone." I tapped the envelope in my lap. "Do I have your word as a journalist?"

"Scout's honor!"

Reassured, I took out the least damning of the blackmail photographs of Claudine and Dougie, then one of the photos of Tim and me.

Almost unwillingly, Andy leaned forward to look at the pictures. When he finally realized what the image of Claudine and Dougie was, his glasses began to fog.

"Wow," he said. "Those are really ugly feet."

"That's not really my point, Andy."

"Uh, no, I suppose not."

"It would take a skilled photographer to take such pictures in the dark, don't you think?"

He nodded uncertainly.

"You didn't take these pictures, did you, Andy?"

"Me?" He paled. "Oh, no, Miss Blackbird, not me."

"Have you seen them before?"

"No! Should I?"

"I suppose not."

I knew he was telling the truth. His open face lacked the cunning to conceal a lie. He was an innocent, but he wasn't stupid, so I asked, "Is there anything you can observe about these pictures, Andy?"

"What do you mean?"

"I'm trying to figure out who took them."

"Oh, the photographer?" He was flattered to be asked and picked up one picture. He flipped it over. "Well, it's not one of the *Intelligencer* camera guys. The paper always stamps the back. See? No stamp."

"Is there any way a picture could be taken by a staff photographer and escape receiving a stamp?"

"I don't think so." He looked at Claudine's feet again. Then he looked at the other photo carefully, too, as if he were taking a crucial examination. He removed his glasses and held the photo close to his face. "Do you have the negatives?"

"No," I said.

He handed the picture back to me to look at. "See that trophy case in the back of the picture?"

"Behind the coatrack, you mean?"

"Yeah, way back. See? There are trophies lined up on the shelf behind the glass doors." He pointed a stubby finger at a very small figure, distorted around the Grecian-inspired shape made of silver. "Is that the guy taking the picture? Reflected in the trophy? It looks like somebody holding a camera, doesn't it?"

I felt a thrill of adrenaline in my heart as I peered at the tiny yet unmistakable figure. It wasn't clear enough to anyone who didn't know the man in question, but I was sure. "Yes. Yes, it is! Andy, would you mind if I kissed you?"

Startled he said, "You're kidding, right?"

"Only a little." I gathered up the pictures. "You've just made my day. I'm not kidding. You're aces in my book, Andy."

He began to blush. "Really?"

"Really. Thank you. Thank you very much." I got to my feet and impulsively smooched the top of his head.

"Where are you going?"

"Out to see somebody.

"Can I come, too?"

I hated to disappoint him, but I said, "Not this time. But you'll definitely have to come to a party or two with me. That is, if Kitty can spare you."

"Oh, that sounds fantastic, Miss B. Just let me know when and where, and I'm ready to party!"

I grabbed my bag and heard Spike give a little sleepy sigh as I headed for the elevator, envelopes in hand. I checked my watch in the elevator. I had a couple free hours before I had to go to work. I knew just where I had to go.

But in the lobby, the guard manning the security station spotted me and broke off his conversation with two big men in dark topcoats.

"Oh, Miss Blackbird, these gentlemen are asking for you."

Me?

I didn't recognize either of them, but I stepped closer. "Yes?"

"Eleanor Blackbird?" The taller of the two pulled his wallet from his trouser pocket. Except when he opened it and showed me what was inside, it wasn't a wallet. It was FBI identification.

I faltered to a stop. "Yes, I'm Nora Blackbird."

"We'd like to talk to you."

"About?"

He tried to smile winningly. "We hear you might be able to tell us a little bit about Michael Abruzzo."

Spike popped his head out and told the FBI to get the hell away from me.

Chapter 17

While Spike kept the FBI at bay, I called my own lawyer and old friend, Tom Nelson.

"Bring them up to my office," he said. "And don't say anything between now and then."

I'd known Tom since a ballroom dancing class when his primary goal had been kicking shins, not learning the finer points of the waltz. At age nine, I wore many a pair of white knee socks to cover up bruises he'd inflicted. In his teens and twenties, Tom enjoyed beer drinking, football and carousing, until an accident sobered him up and landed him in a wheelchair. He settled down after that, gaining a sense of humor and a better concept of how he fit into the world. Miraculously, he married a wonderful young woman and was working on becoming one of the most respected lawyers in the city. As a couple, they championed wheelchair marathons for kids and hosted warm, friendly dinner parties.

He asked the FBI to wait in one of the firm's plush lounges while conferring with me in his office.

"What's this about?" He poured me a glass of water from the pitcher on his desk. "Are you okay?"

"I'm fine. Just shaken up. Thanks for making time for this, Tom."

"No problem. Is that a dog or some kind of ferret?"

I pushed Spike back into my handbag. "He's a rare Mongolian rat chaser."

"Uh-huh." He gave me a dubious look with raised eyebrows. "I gather the fellows outside have come to ask you about your friend the mobster?"

"He isn't— Look, Tom, I know what everyone's read in the papers and the rumors that have been floating around town. It's true that Michael Abruzzo and I were seeing each other off and on for a few months. But I don't know much about his business except when it got mixed up in mine, and he was careful not to tell me anything he didn't think I should hear."

"Let's back up," Tom interrupted gently. "How does your business mix with his?"

I told him how Michael and his silent partner, Rory Pendergast, had purchased a small corner of Blackbird Farm, which allowed me to pay the original installment on my colossal tax bill and reorganize my finances so I didn't have to sell the farm. His leasing of farmland from me to grow grass for his Marquis de Sod company also helped me keep my head above water.

Tom whistled. "You owe two million dollars in property taxes? Jesus, Nora."

"Less than that now. I know, it's crazy to keep trying, but I can't—I won't—sell the farm until all my options are used up."

He smiled grimly and made notes on a legal pad. "Okay, let's leave that out for now. Tell me what you do know about Abruzzo."

"I understand client privilege, Tom, but I can't go blabbing information about a man who clearly wants to keep his own secrets, even from me. He's too private."

"Do you think he's a crook?"

The blunt question took me by surprise. "In my heart? No."

Tom said, "Has your heart or your head come to that conclusion?"

"He has tried to separate himself from the Abruzzo family. But there are other people around who are different."

"Different how?"

"Scarier."

"I've seen pictures of your friend. He looks pretty scary himself." More gently, he asked, "What do you know about money laundering?"

"That it doesn't involve detergent and water. Other than that, I don't have a clue."

Tom doodled on his pad. "Does Abruzzo keep his savings under a mattress? Has he ever bought a car or a boat or a big-ticket item using quarters? Does he run off to Caribbean islands frequently?"

"No, nothing like that."

"Does he sell drugs?"

"Oh, my God, no."

"But he has a lot of little enterprises that all bring in a cash income?"

"Yes."

"And what does he do with the money?"

"I don't know. For a while, he was paying off a debt to Rory Pendergast, but when Rory died, the debt was forgiven."

"A big debt?"

"One large enough to start a couple of his businesses."

"Nice deal if you can get it," Tom said lightly. "What does he do with the cash now?"

"He probably reinvests in other schemes. He's al-

ways got something under construction. He's very
smart, very . . . uhm, creative. He's got half a dozen
businesses going."

"Such as?"

I told him about Gas 'n' Grub, the Marquis de Sod,
Mick's Muscle Cars, the limousine service, the motor-
cycles and the Delaware Fly Fishing Company. And,
more reluctantly, the tattoo parlor. Tom managed to
remain straight-faced during the whole list.

"Okay." Tom put down his pen. "I'll try to keep
this simple. Banks are required to report cash deposits
of more than ten thousand dollars. A few currency-
transaction reports start adding up and a red flag is
raised. My bet is that he's run up a bunch of red flags
and the FBI wants to find out if he's legit."

"But don't other businesses deposit large amounts
of cash in banks?"

"Of course. But they aren't owned by members of
the Abruzzo family."

"Isn't that harrassment?"

"I'll bet that's what his lawyer calls it."

We talked for a few minutes about gambling and
money laundering and organized crime in general.

At last, Tom said, "My advice? Don't talk to the
FBI. Before you know it you'll be on a witness stand
with your hand on the Bible."

"But what if I can be useful?"

"Nora," he said, "you've got a lot of personal feelings tied up with this guy."

"Not at the moment."

"Okay," he said steadily, "then we don't have to
discuss the wisdom of your seeing this person on a
romantic level. But I've got to assume he's got a thing
for you, too. Don't you think he's kept you in the
dark for a reason? Abruzzo wanted to spare you this.

You say he's smart, so let's assume he's made the right decision on this, too. Let me take care of the FBI today, and we'll plan a strategy for when they come back. Because they're going to come back, you know. And next time, they won't be as friendly as they pretend to be today."

The FBI agents were ushered into Tom's office. They seemed unimpressed by his commanding view of the city and the displayed photos of Tom posing with two former presidents of the United States and mobs of kids in wheelchairs. They got down to business fast.

Spike quivered with rage in my lap, ready to hurl himself at an FBI jugular at a moment's notice.

"No," I said in answer to the first question. "I don't know which banks he deals with."

"No," I said. "I have never seen large amounts of cash sitting around."

"No," I said. "He has never asked me to deposit any money in any of my own bank accounts."

"Miss Blackbird, we have currency transaction reports that show Mr. Abruzzo making large deposits into accounts in two different banks. We'd like to establish if, in fact, Mr. Abruzzo made these deposits himself or required an acquaintance or employee to do so."

The agent passed a stapled set of papers across the smooth table to me while Tom made disapproving noises. "Will you look at those dates, please, and tell us if you were in Mr. Abruzzo's presence on any of those days and times?"

I looked at a year's worth of bank transactions and blinked. "I can't do this off the top of my head."

"Do you keep a social calendar?"

"Of course I do."

"So perhaps you'd allow us to look at your calendar

and establish exactly when you were with Mr. Abruzzo?"

"Gentlemen," Tom said firmly, "I think we're all intelligent adults here, and we know Miss Blackbird is not going to throw her life open to the FBI. I suggest we agree to disagree right now and allow Miss Blackbird to get back to her job." He cast me a look that said he knew how badly I needed that job. "If you want her cooperation in the future, you're going to need a subpoena."

The FBI agents did not appear astonished by this suggestion. They gathered up their paperwork and politely declined to make me a copy of the dates in question. They departed with friendly handshakes and smiles that promised we'd meet again.

The second agent reached out to give Spike a friendly pat.

Spike took the opportunity to bite him.

I lingered to thank Tom and then took Spike down to the street, where he lifted his leg on the curb, looking pleased with his day's work.

I said to him, "That was a federal employee, you know. Which probably means you committed a felony."

Checking my watch, I discovered there wasn't enough time to run out to Bryn Mawr as I'd hoped, so I hotfooted my way back to the newspaper offices. There I made some phone calls and responded to the fresh influx of invitations that had arrived in the mail. Then I repaired my makeup and called Reed to pick me up.

By the cocktail hour, I was walking into a venerable private club that might have been founded before the Magna Carta. A few founding members seemed to be still sitting behind their *Wall Street Journal*s in the smoking room. The cracked leather furniture hadn't been reupholstered since Harry Truman visited, and the Oriental rug looked as if a family of Persian cats had enjoyed a claw-sharpening contest. The mantel sported a dreary portrait of the club's first president, whose expression indicated he'd eaten too many pickled herrings.

I tiptoed past, careful not to wake anyone.

The creaking elevator dawdled its way up to the fourth floor. I left my coat in the musty cloakroom and went into the paneled ballroom, where a few dozen of the city's most elderly citizens leaned on their canes, sat in chairs or teetered precariously on their orthopedic shoes while straining to communicate with each other. I heard the squeal of many malfunctioning hearing aids.

My arrival caused everyone in the room to turn and go silent. I felt like the ringmaster arriving in the center of a slow-motion circus. The average age of the party guests around me was a hundred and twelve.

Pasting a bright smile on my face, I plunged in.

"Merry Christmas, Mr. Bartholomew!" I shook the hand of the first frail curmudgeon in the receiving line. "How is your great-grandson Arthur?"

"I had another colonoscopy!" he bellowed back. "The doctor says it doesn't look good!"

His spidery-thin wife shouted, "I finally had my thyroid removed!"

The next couple wanted to discuss his and her mysterious stomach pains.

A trio of doddering women asked if I had regular breast examinations, because I couldn't be too careful.

At last I came upon Dotty Dubose, huddled in a rump-sprung wing chair and waving her cane to flag me down.

"Get me out of this damn chair," she said. "I'm stuck like a pig in the henhouse door!"

I grabbed her arthritic hands and hauled Dotty to her unsteady feet. She had shrunk to barely five feet tall, but the look in her eye was Amazonian. "Thank God you're here," she said. "I'm bored to tears, not to mention starving. Is there anything besides strained baby food on that buffet?"

"Let's find out." I put my hand under her arm and helped her hobble across the ballroom floor.

The city's social strata included a variety of levels, but at the summit, or very close, was a very small, elite group of elderly widows—patrician, sedate ladies who lived lives of unparalleled privilege. They had inherited great fortunes on their own and had also enjoyed the tremendous accumulated wealth of their powerful husbands, now dead. Some had successful careers on their own, but their foremost accomplishments were in more rarified arenas. Their days were very detail-oriented. Things were just so in their homes, as with their clothing and jewelry as well as with their precise, hands-on and generous philanthropic work. Each had chosen a particular cause or institution upon which they bestowed financial largesse and their leadership in matters of taste, networking and fund-raising. To a woman, they were intelligent connoisseurs with generous spirits, and I felt privileged to know many of them. There were no greater role models.

Dotty Dubose was one such woman.

Known as dotty Dotty, she had cut a colorful figure in my youth. Always competing with her friends to dress more extravagantly, Dotty had been among the first women of the city to wear hot pants and go-go boots. As years passed, she inherited her father's steel fortune and the proceeds from her husband's oil ventures. She kept exquisite homes in the city, Florida, Wyoming, Maine and Provence. In her seventies, she had climbed the Great Wall of China and ridden camels around the pyramids of Egypt. Now in her eighties, she still regularly paid for medical supplies that she personally accompanied to South American communities destroyed by hurricanes.

While her husband was alive, she devoted herself to the study of Chinese porcelain. Now, I had heard, she was arranging matters with the museum to donate her collection after her death—and the donation would include the construction of a satellite facility for research and appreciation.

Meanwhile, dotty Dotty was still a good-time girl.

"While we eat," I suggested, "you can give me all the details on this wingding. I hear you're on the organizing committee."

"You think we rate any coverage in the newspapers? All of us mothballed antiques?"

"Of course you do. What are you raising money for? A city architecture foundation? What a good cause."

"You can't snow me, young lady. You're as bored as I am. Life's too short, so let's talk about what really matters."

"Okay, Dotty, that's a magnificent dress."

She sent me a twinkly wink. "Schiaparelli. Your grandmother and I bought a matching set. Hers was blue."

"I know. I've worn it." I smiled down at her. "It looks so much better on you."

"Hogwash. How do you like my bling bling?"

The string of diamonds around her wrinkled throat could have blinded P. Diddy himself, and her triple bracelet might have made a significant improvement in the national debt. "They're astonishing, Dotty."

"Thanks. I get them out of the vault every few years for exercise. See this ring? Your grandmother gave it to me when I was just about your age. We raised some hell, your gramma and I. At a Paris fashion show, we once threw spitballs at Twiggy. Did she tell you that?"

"I believe she did, yes. And a movie star was sitting next to you."

"Vivien Leigh. That was years earlier. She offered me a Benzedrine. God, look at this food! It cost us ten thousand dollars apiece to walk into this room tonight, and all they've got is leftovers from the lunch special downstairs. Christ on a crutch, is that macaroni and cheese?"

"I don't know." I looked at the forlorn display of easily digestible fare. "Do you want me to try some?"

"God, no, why risk being poisoned? They never keep these steam trays hot enough, and someday some old fossil is going to keel over from botulism. Knowing the management of this dump, they'll blame it on a heart attack. Tell me what you're doing these days, dear. My son says you got a newspaper job. Are you using Rosalind Russell as your role model?"

"No, I'm just winging it."

"Well, I'm sure you're good at your work. You're not talking to rapists and pornographers, are you? No? Well, that's disappointing. What do you do, exactly?"

"I'm helping Kitty Keough. Right now, we're trying to cover all the Christmas parties."

"Kitty Keough. Is that bimbo still sucking up to any breathing man with a big portfolio?"

"Well . . ."

Dotty cackled. "Come clean! She always had an eye for the single men with money. Who's she chasing now? I have no pleasure left in life except good gossip. So tell me. Who is Kitty's victim?"

"Tottie Boarman," I admitted. "But you didn't hear it from me."

"Tottie Boarman!" Dottie scoffed. "That old softie! I had a little fling with him myself, you know."

"You? Dotty!"

I was floored and must have looked it, because she laughed. "Help me over to that settee and I'll give you all the gruesome details. I was tarty in my younger days, you know. And he didn't seem to mind that I was a few years' more experienced than he was. He didn't mind a bit, in fact."

"How in the world were you attracted to a man like Tottie?"

"Oh, don't let appearances fool you, Nora. He might act as if he's got a swarm of bees in his boxer shorts, but he's as sweet as pie underneath."

"Are we talking about the same man?"

Dotty flumped down onto the settee. "Oh, he was a randy rascal in his youth. Quite the lady's man. Very handsome, but rather sweet, really. Shy, if you can believe it."

"Sounds as if you know Tottie very well. And I haven't known him at all."

"Oh, ancient history is dull as beans to you young folks. Tottie's known his share of ladies over the years. It's a damn shame that he's only got Kitty Keough to stand by him when he's going through this awful financial mess. He deserves better."

"Not many people would agree with you."

"Well, what do most people know?" Dotty challenged with a fiery look in her eye. "Surely nobody ever thanked him for all his good works. But Tottie hates public displays of generosity."

"I can't imagine Tottie being generous."

"No? Well, you have a limited imagination, then. Tottie's as generous as any of the old coots in this room. Maybe more so. But he never allows his name to be associated with his charitable work."

"Are you serious?"

"Of course I am. Anonymous benevolence is considered old-fashioned these days, but it's still classier than all the self-serving chest-thumping that's taken over. I hate those lists with people's names and a dollar amount beside each one. You know that new section of the children's hospital? The new section they call the Freedom Wing? Tottie gave that."

"That was a hundred million dollars at least! From Tottie? I don't believe it!"

"He wouldn't allow them to name the wing after him. But he gave the money. I know. I was on the board at the time. We were sworn to secrecy."

"Dotty," I said, looking into her keen face, "you're telling me now for a reason, aren't you?"

She smiled sweetly. "I haven't had champagne in months. I would love a glass of champagne right now." She was looking perkier by the minute and sat up straighter. "Do you suppose a little bubbly would interfere too much with my medications? Oh, what the hell. You only live once. Waiter!"

A passing waiter—at least as old as most of the guests—limped to Dotty's side and presented her with a tray full of glasses. I was afraid he'd never be able to straighten up again, but when she chose a tall flute of gently fizzing champagne, I heard his back give a crackling noise when he straightened and hitched away from us.

When he was out of earshot, I leaned closer to my elderly companion. "Dotty, are you suggesting the *Intelligencer* reveal who donated the Freedom Wing?"

"I'm not suggesting anything." She sipped from her glass and smiled with satisfaction. "I hate to see a man go down in flames, that's all, when he's been more philanthropic than half the bums in this town."

I thought back to the moment I'd seen Tottie storm into the Koats for Kids Christmas party. He'd been furious, and I assumed he didn't like the party. But perhaps he'd simply been angry about being "outed" as the charitable sponsor of the event.

I shook my head. "Dotty, there are some strange things going on right now, but that information is certainly some of the strangest."

She grinned. "Okay, your turn. Doing anything naughty these days? Give me a vicarious thrill, would you?"

"Sorry. I'm behaving myself."

"A lovely young thing like you? Don't waste time, Nora, dear. Take my advice and grab the sexiest man you can lay your hands on and have a fling you can brag about when you're my age. Enjoy life. Before you know it, all your chances will be gone." Dotty suddenly looked her years again. She drank down the last of her champagne. "Grab life while you can, dear."

I left the party soon thereafter and went down to the street again.

"Where to?" Reed asked, holding the end of Spike's leash while the puppy tried to climb up my leg.

I wanted to go home. I wanted to stop thinking about murder and blackmail and self-serving people.

But I had miles to go before I slept, so I told Reed about our next stop and we took off for another party.

In the car, I mused about Tottie Boarman, the secret altruist. What else had I been wrong about?

Chapter 18

At midnight when I got home, there were four blinks on my answering machine. One message was from Hadley— "Call me, kitten! We'll have some eggnog!" Another from the tax man, one hang-up and one from Rawlins.

I phoned Hadley and left a message on his voice mail. He was out partying at someone else's expense, I was sure.

My nephew sounded surprisingly hesitant in his recorded message. "Uh, Aunt Nora? I need to come see you soon. Can you call me?"

It was too late to phone Libby's house, so I went to bed and lay awake for a long time. I tried to plan my next move, but my hand kept drifting to the other pillow and I ended up dreaming fitfully about Michael.

*   *   *

Early in the morning, Thomasina Silk arrived with a horse trailer marked with the hunt club logo, so I left my half-eaten toast, put on my parka and went outside into the wind. Barking madly, Spike ran circles around Thomasina's truck until it rumbled to a stop near the barn. I didn't hear any of the telltale signs that usually accompanied Emma's horse when he was confined to a trailer—enraged neighs, thunderous kicks and cursing human beings.

Diminutive Thomasina, dressed in breeches and a

Polartec vest, climbed down from her truck, all business. "I brought Emma's jumper," she reported, adjusting her gloves. "Have you started training that puppy yet?"

"Oh yes." I snapped my fingers authoritatively. "Spike!"

The dog ran over and discovered that because Thomasina was so small he could almost sniff her crotch. He made a valiant effort.

Humiliated, I grabbed him. "Thanks for bringing Mr. Twinkles, Thomasina. I know Emma will be relieved that he's home."

Thomasina obviously thought I was beneath contempt because she told me to stay out of the way while she set about unloading Mr. Twinkles herself. The usually rambunctious horse came down the ramp as obediently as a child who'd been promised ice cream. In my arms, Spike barked joyously to see his favorite subject of torture. Mr. Twinkles behaved himself, but when Thomasina wasn't looking, he flashed a kick in Spike's direction.

When Mr. Twinkles was safely in his paddock, I approached Thomasina. "I know you've competed against Emma for years. You must have gotten to know her pretty well."

Thomasina shoved her gloves into the pocket of her warm vest. "Sure, we've had our moments."

"She helped at your barn after your accident, if I recall."

I had her full attention then. "Yes. Emma kept my horses in good shape. I'd have sold off most of them if she hadn't continued their training."

"She's in trouble now."

Thomasina eyed me coldly. "I like Emma. And maybe I owe her a favor or two. But her life is over if she killed Rush Strawcutter, Nora, and I can't do anything about that."

"She didn't kill Rush," I said firmly. "All we need is some proof."

Thomasina flushed, but she didn't bend. "Well, good luck," she said shortly.

Thomasina departed without another word, and I felt bitterly disappointed. "People can be jerks," I said to Spike.

While Spike and Mr. Twinkles took turns chasing each other around the paddock, I got a rake out of the barn and began collecting some of the leaves that had scattered across the lawn. The skiff of snow had melted and the work was cold, but I was glad to have something useful to do with my hands while I thought about what to do next.

Rush Strawcutter had not been murdered because he was blackmailing people. That much I now knew was true.

But a lot of other people had been terrorized by the blackmailer. Claudine Paltron, for one, had assumed her extortionist was Rush Strawcutter. Maybe others had, too. And one of them preferred to kill him than give him money.

Tottie Boarman wasn't the son of a bitch I thought he was. But could he have murdered his own son for an insurance policy that might make him solvent again? Or might Kitty Keough have done the killing on behalf of her wealthy boyfriend?

Could Claudine have whacked her former lover with a polo mallet? Or more likely, could she have sent her doltish boyfriend to do the deed?

And Gussie. Had she been more furious to learn Rush was having an affair with Emma or to suspect that Rush would need to dip into the Strawcutter fortune to pay his blackmailer?

And I could not ignore Emma's belief that she had heard Tim Naftzinger's voice on the morning of the murder.

I heard a car in the driveway.

I went around the house and saw Hadley Pinkham's classic MG evade the potholes and roll to a stop by the backdoor. He climbed out, looking dapper, and swept his arm wide to indicate the blue tarp, the sagging fences and Spike rolling in fresh horse manure.

"My dear kitten, are you vowing to never go hungry again? This place looks ready for the carpetbaggers!"

I leaned on my rake and waited until he picked his way across the muddy lawn to me. "Is that what you're here for, Hadley? To take my plantation for the back taxes?"

"Of course not, kitten. I have my own derelict shanty to maintain. I got your message and came as soon as humanly possible. Good morning." He bent to kiss my cheek, but his scarf blew between our faces and prevented it. "How lovely you look working al fresco this morning. So this is how you keep your figure."

"Why don't you take a picture?"

He laughed handsomely. "Well, I like to think I'm even more photogenic, but after you comb your hair, perhaps—"

"Did you bring your camera?"

"You know I'm missing the photography gene. My forebears all had the eye, of course, but I am sadly—"

"You can cut the act, Hadley. I know all about your talent behind a lens."

He put his hands into the pockets of his great coat

and regarded me with an oblique sort of smile. "Talent?"

"I expected more, actually, despite your claim you're no good with gadgets. To be truthful, I'm surprised your photographs are so ordinary."

"You're angry."

"I'm more than angry, Hadley. Do you know what you've done?"

"I've survived," he said lightly. He leaned against the fence and gazed at the ruined roof of my house. "Looks as if I'm doing better than you are."

"At least I'm not screwing my friends to do it."

"Screwing? What an indelicate word, especially from you. Kitten, I didn't pick on anyone who couldn't afford my rates."

I suppressed the tremor of anger that shook my whole body. "What about me, Hadley? Does it look as if I have an extra ten grand lying around?"

"I thought you were ready to sell the grange and come back to the city where you belong, suitably enriched by the profits and willing to share a little. If you called a realtor right now, you could be moving your four-poster into a lovely condo by nightfall, and you know it. I even gave you a little extra time to consider the matter."

"I made my own decisions long ago, thank you."

Spike had heard something in my voice and came over. Silent, he crouched at my feet, his beady eyes fixed on Hadley's face.

"You're a rat, Hadley."

He said, "Can I help it if I have expensive tastes?"

"You could have gotten a job."

He laughed brightly. "Good heavens, remember who you're talking to. Can you see me waiting tables?

Filing returned library books? Suggesting wines at Sabu? I'm suited for no useful work at all."

"But you're perfectly suited to extortion?"

"Another harsh word! Is this the result of hanging around with the criminal element? Because it's not attractive—"

"You are the criminal element, Hadley. And don't you dare compare your idea of civilized behavior to Michael Abruzzo."

"Oh, Lord, you're not going to start quoting bad romantic novels next, are you?"

"I think you'd better start quoting the fifth amendment," I said. "Because you're going to need it."

"Do you think so?" he asked archly. "I don't. I don't believe you'll find a shred of evidence against me. Nothing that will convince judge or jury, at least. I chose a crime that's very difficult to prove, you see. I'm cleverer than you think. I didn't stoop to murder."

"Yes, you did. You were the cause of Rush's death."

He waved his hand to dismiss the accusation. "Impossible to prove."

"The only thing I haven't figured out yet is why you blackmailed Tottie. What secret did you discover about him?"

He tried to look surprised. "You haven't learned yet? Then you're not the detective I thought you were."

"Tell me now. Why did Tottie feel he needed to pay for your silence?"

"He didn't pay, actually. That briefcase he left in the square? It was empty. He told me to take his dirty laundry and—well, it was another crude expression, so I won't use it. I managed to get the briefcase despite

Kitty Keough's interference—she didn't remove it from the park, by the way, but was merely checking to see if Tottie had followed my orders. When I got the case home, I was very disappointed. It seems Tottie would rather have the truth come out than pay me the pittance I requested."

"What was the truth?"

"That he was Rushton Strawcutter's natural father."

Spike looked anxiously up at my face.

More calmly than I thought I could manage, I said, "How did you know?"

"An old auntie of mine was one of Tottie's girlfriends back in the stone age. She knew there was an illegitimate child floating around, and I asked her to gossip amongst her ancient friends until she learned the truth. It wasn't hard. Surely you were near the truth yourself."

"I can't believe you're so heartless."

"I figured if Tottie was crazy enough to loan huge sums of money to a child he never knew, he could spare a few thousand for me."

"And instead of paying you? Do you think Tottie might have attacked Rush in a rage? For—"

"Honestly, kitten, I couldn't care less who murdered Rushie. He couldn't come up with the cash to pay me, so I sent the photos of him necking with your sexy sibling to Gussie. And who knew what a hot button philandering was for her? I received my first installment from her last night. Even now that her husband is dead, she wants to keep his affair with Emma quiet."

The triumph on his face was too much for me. My hands were tight on the rake handle. It took all of my self-control not to swing it at his head. Spike began to growl very softly.

He continued. "I figured you had started to guess I was behind my little money letters. So I thought I might offer you a deal."

"Little money letters? Is that how you make blackmail sound well-bred?"

"Do you want to know why I didn't pressure you to pay me? I have an offer."

"I don't want to hear it."

He looked at me frankly. "We could be partners, Nora."

For a second, I thought I might be physically ill. "You are despicable."

"Think of all the secrets you know. You're even more connected than I am! With your insider knowledge and my willingness to exploit it, we could—"

"Shall I call the police to kick you off my property," I said far more calmly than I felt, "or will you go peacefully?"

He regarded me again, and we communicated our farewells in that moment.

He said, "I'm sorry you feel this way. Maybe if you think it over—"

"I don't need to think. I am no longer your friend, Hadley."

"Nora—"

"I'm going to see the FBI today, anyway. Shall I tell them about you?"

"I will make your life miserable"—he cocked an eyebrow at me—"if you tell the FBI or anyone else what I've been doing. I could make the lives of your family and friends miserable, too. I guess that's what counts with you, isn't it? See? I know what strings to tug."

"Go away," I said.

He shrugged.

We both heard another vehicle enter the driveway. Libby's minivan rounded the side of the house.

Hadley tightened his scarf and sauntered attractively toward his car. Spike followed, hugging the ground like a lion stalking prey. Hadley got into the car and started the engine. Spike began to bark at him.

I called Spike, but he didn't listen.

Hadley put the car in gear and revved the engine.

"No," I said. "Spike!"

Hadley's car jerked and swung hard toward the dog. By then I had dropped the rake and started to run. Spike leaped to escape, but he was too small and the car too fast.

I heard him yelp, and then a bloodcurdling howl. Hadley swerved back onto the driveway and accelerated, narrowly missing the minivan.

I reached Spike and fell to my knees. He thrashed on the ground, his jaws snapping convulsively. I put both hands on him, and he immediately bit me. His teeth punctured the muscle of my hand just below my thumb, and then he rolled his eyes up to me for help. He hung on to my hand, and I let him.

An instant later, Rawlins was beside me on the ground. "Aunt Nora, Aunt Nora!"

I was cursing and soothing at the same time, talking to little Spike and trying to hold him still.

Rawlins ripped off his coat. "Here," he said. "Wrap him up in this. We'll take him to the vet."

I managed to ease Spike onto the nylon jacket, but he cried and yipped with every move. He began to pant, and I knew he was dying.

"Come on," said Rawlins.

My nephew hauled me up by my elbow and bundled me into the front seat of the minivan. I cradled Spike, still letting him hang on to my hand with his teeth.

There was blood on Rawlins's jacket, but I didn't know who it had come from.

Rawlins spun the minivan in a tight circle and thumped over the potholes. In a minute, we were speeding on the road, heading south. Rawlins drove fast, grimly clutching the steering wheel. I murmured to Spike, but the puppy's eyes had begun to glaze and his breathing was shallow and pained.

We arrived at the vet's office in a spray of gravel. I climbed out with Spike in my arms and ran to the door. I'd been to the vet once before for Spike's shots, and I knew my way inside. Rawlins burst in ahead of me, calling for help. The nursing staff rushed out from behind their counter and took Spike from me. He held on to my hand until they pulled him loose. I heard him yip weakly as they rushed through a set of swinging doors.

Rawlins held me in the waiting room, pulling me to a windowed corner. "It's okay, it's okay," he kept saying. "Spike will be fine. Don't worry."

But Spike wasn't fine, and I knew it.

A mother and young daughter watched us from the waiting room chairs. The mother held a cardboard cat carrier on her lap, and a kitten mewed inside the box. The little girl looked at me with her face ready to crumple into tears of sympathy. A wave of sickening blackness washed over me. I put my head between my knees.

"It's okay, it's okay," Rawlins said, patting my back.

I sat up finally. "It's not okay, Rawlins. Hadley did it on purpose. Did you see? He deliberately ran over an innocent puppy!"

"I know. I couldn't believe it. He didn't even stop."

The chief nurse came out and told us the veterinarian was with Spike and doing his best. But I could see by her expression she was doubtful my dog would live. And there was an accusatory gleam in her eye, too, telling me I could have avoided hurting Spike if he'd been on a leash or better trained. She gave me an ice bag for my hand.

I sat down unsteadily and applied the ice to my bleeding hand. Rawlins sat beside me and awkwardly patted my arm.

At last my mind began to focus. I wiped my nose on my sleeve and cleared my throat. "What are you doing driving around on a school day? Have you been expelled again?"

"No." He looked at his lap. He had various bits of jewelry pierced through his lip, eyebrow, nose and ears. The little girl sitting a few feet away was fascinated. But for all his effort to look like a dangerous man, Rawlins still had soft hands and gangly legs and slumped teenager's shoulders. He said, "I had to talk to you."

"Well, thanks for bringing us here. If you hadn't come along, I don't know what—"

"It's okay."

"No, I mean it, Rawlins. If you hadn't—"

"Hey, I feel like a shit already, okay? Just leave it alone."

I turned my attention to Rawlins at last and realized he was gnawing on his fingernails as if they were his last meal. "What's the matter?"

He shook his head.

"What's going on?" I asked. "Is it your mother?"

"No, she's fine. If you think it's okay for her to be dating this weird doctor guy."

"Is she still seeing him?"

"Who knows? I hardly ever go home anymore."

"Rawlins—"

"Look, I got to get this off my chest," he burst out. "Plus she says she'll kill me if I don't tell you, so here goes."

"What in the world . . . ?"

"I admit I haven't always been smart, but really, I didn't think it was such a big deal. Mick went with me and made me tell Mom, but then she went ballistic and everything got—"

I had no idea what he was talking about. "What does Michael have to do with anything?"

He sighed. "Here's the thing. I have this friend. And he gave me something to keep for him. So I kept it. But Mick noticed I had it, and—"

"Just what exactly are we discussing?"

"A gun," Rawlins said. "I had a gun."

I stared at him.

"I had this gun," he went on, "when I went to the airport to pick up Mick from Paris. We put his gear in the trunk, and he found my friend's gun in the—"

"Wait a minute. Are you saying Michael took a gun away from you?"

"I know I shouldn't have had it." Rawlins looked miserable. "But it was only supposed to be for a couple of days, see? But Mick took it and said I had to tell my mom, and she said I had to tell you, so—"

I put my face into my hands. I felt like crying, but somehow it came out like a sick laugh. "That was your gun? And Michael took it away from you?"

"No, it was my friend's gun. See, that's what I'm trying to explain. I didn't plan on keeping it, and maybe I shouldn't have had it in the first place, but—"

"Rawlins," I said. "Stop."

He stopped talking.

"Rawlins, my husband was shot to death."

"I know," he said, sounding tired.

"He made a bunch of mistakes in his life, but the biggest one was starting to associate with people who carry guns. It got him killed, Rawlins."

Rawlins sighed.

"For me, there is no *maybe* about having a gun or being with friends who have guns. A person with a gun is never, never your friend."

He nodded.

I took his hand in both of mine, and the two of us looked down at the blood all over my hands and clothing. "If your sister or your mother or one of your little brothers got hurt, do you think you could live knowing that you brought a gun into the lives of people you love?"

He shook his head.

"Promise me you won't carry a gun ever again, no matter who wants to give it to you."

"Okay."

"And can you stand it if I say one more thing?"

He allowed a tiny hint of a smile. "Maybe."

"I love you."

He choked on a little laugh and bumped his head against mine, which was as close to declaring love as a teenage boy could get, I suppose, considering we were being watched by a woman and her daughter and their kitten.

The nurse came over and told us we could step into the doctor's office. I held on to Rawlins's hand, braced for the worst news. We sat down in front of a desk decorated with paw-print stickers and a framed photograph of a young family, each child holding a beagle puppy. A moment later, Dr. Gilley came in. He was almost as small as a beagle himself, with the same guileless expression. He wore sneakers and a set of blue hospital scrubs, flecked with blood.

"I'm sorry," he said. "Spike's in very bad shape. We've sedated him, and we need to take some X rays, but he's got multiple broken bones, probably including his spine."

Tears sprang into my eyes. I barely managed to speak. "Should we— Is it cruel to keep him alive?"

Dr. Gilley sat on the edge of his desk. "Let's not talk about that yet. We'll take the pictures and decide what needs to be done. We can do some surgeries here, but we may have to send him to a facility with more technology at their disposal. Let me keep him for a few more hours before we decide anything drastic. He's young enough that his bones are still flexible, and we all know he's a fighter."

I tearfully thanked the doctor, and we promised to communicate again in a few hours. I asked to see Spike one more time, but Dr. Gilley assured me he would be better off if we didn't disturb him. I must have looked awful, because Dr. Gilley gave me a hug before I left.

Chapter 19

Rawlins took me home, where I washed my hand and bandaged it. Then I changed into a no-nonsense suit and boots. Dressed for business, I let my nephew drive me first to my doctor's office for a tetanus shot, then to the train station. I didn't lecture him anymore, but gave him a big kiss in the minivan and told him I was glad he was safe. I took the train into the city, trying not to think about how much Spike had enjoyed the trip just a day earlier. But my throat clogged up anyway, so I tried to study my calendar instead.

Rather than going to the *Intelligencer* offices, I consulted the address on the card given to me by the FBI agents. I took a cab from the station and reached their security checkpoint a few minutes before noon. When the agents were alerted of my unexpected arrival, they chose to skip lunch in order to meet with me.

"Show me the list of bank transactions," I said when we were seated in a bare-bones conference room. "I'll confirm whatever I know to be true."

They bumped into each other trying to get the papers fast enough.

My lawyer did not approve and tried to convince me by phone not to give the FBI any information at all, but I spent the next three hours carefully consulting my calendar to establish that Michael Abruzzo did not make suspicious bank deposits in my presence.

Nor did he pose as someone else to make deposits illegally. I could not address all the dates in question, but I was surprised to discover how much time I had spent with Michael in the last six months.

The FBI seemed disappointed with my information.

When I finished in the late afternoon, I called the vet's office. The nurse told me Spike was still sedated and they were looking at his X rays now. I raced off to two cocktail parties and called again. Spike, I was told, had been sedated for the night. Phone again in the morning. They would decide on his treatment then, if he survived.

Gulping, I headed for my last stop for the evening, a Christmas dinner at the private home of an old friend of my grandfather. The thirty-two pillars of the community who sat around the grand mahogany table set with heavy silver and lavish flowers wanted to discuss the ethics of American foreign policy since FDR. I felt as if I was choking down dinner on Mount Rushmore. I sat between a jowly federal judge and Hartz Calloway, the bow tie–wearing, tin-pot conservative columnist for the city's most widely read newspaper, who lectured me about nuclear proliferation. I found myself more worried that we all might imminently be destroyed by the two-ton chandelier that swayed ominously over the table. I developed a splitting headache.

Reed took me home, and we were both subdued during the drive, thinking of Spike. I stayed up late, writing my stories and e-mailing them to my editor for him to insert into the weekend edition. Afterward, I fired off a note to a friend at the other newspaper, offering her a tip I thought she would best know how to plant.

Then I wrote a carefully worded e-mail to Joe

Crawford, the news reporter who'd been following the Abruzzo money-laundering story. I waited until after midnight to send it, so the information wouldn't be rushed into the morning edition. Joe needed a day to absorb my statement and find other sources to make a rounded story.

Satisfied I had done what I could, I went to bed.

Two hours later, I got out of bed again, took two more aspirin and made one phone call.

Detective Bloom woke up fast and agreed with me.

On Thursday morning, I phoned the vet first thing and learned that Spike had two broken legs, a crushed pelvis and three broken ribs. One lung had been punctured, but was reinflated. His spinal cord was undamaged, but he had two injured vertebrae. With my heart beating so hard it hurt, I asked again if it would be kinder to put him down.

"Let's give him a few more hours," Dr. Gilley said. "But I'll be honest. If his liver is damaged, we may have to make a difficult choice."

I dressed in a somber black Karl Lagerfeld suit with leather piping. The matching coat buttoned Nehru-style around my throat. Reed drove me to Rush Strawcutter's funeral.

The first person I saw when I stepped out of the car was Kitty Keough, in her scraggly fur coat. Behind her stood Andy Mooney, looking sorry he'd gotten out of bed that morning. His dark suit revealed a bad case of dandruff. Kitty spotted me and steamed over.

"Do you think it's appropriate for you to be here?" she demanded, loud enough to be heard by arriving mourners. "After all, your sister killed a very promising young man!"

She swept past me and into the church. Andy cast me an apologetic glance and scuttled after her. I was too numb to feel embarrassed. More important issues weighed on my mind.

I slipped into the church and sat in the back row. From that vantage point, I studied the crowd. Gussie sat up front, alone in a straight-backed pew, facing the coffin, which was draped with a small spray of ordinary red roses. Gussie appeared to be reading listlessly from a prayer book. Or was she contemplating the circumstances of Rush's death?

A furnace clanged beneath our feet, and I felt a blast of heated air against the back of my neck. The organist had already begun playing an uninspired selection of Protestant hymns. "Rock of Ages," for heaven's sake. The crowd was surprisingly small, considering the influential Strawcutter family. I wondered if half the people might be company employees. As the heat increased, I unfastened the top buttons on my coat.

At eleven, a last person entered the church as the service began. Tottie Boarman. From my seat, I thought he looked very ill—ashen and furious. He made no effort to locate Kitty in the sparsely filled church but sat down in the row directly in front of me, alone. He forced his shoulders square.

I tried to think about Rush during the dreary service, but the music and the spoken words did not celebrate his life or uplift my heart. I felt sadder than ever that Rush had not been appreciated during his too-short time on earth. Except perhaps by Emma, who was prevented from saying good-bye to the first man she truly cared about since her husband's death.

When the congregation stood to drone through "Amazing Grace," I couldn't stand it anymore. I slipped out the back door. The fresh air was cold, just what I needed.

A moment later, I was surprised to hear footsteps behind me, and I turned. Tottie Boarman came toward me, obviously also driven out by the banality of the service.

I paused under the stone portico of the church. He nearly strode past me without a word, but suddenly realized who I was and stopped. He seemed startled to find himself willing to linger.

Equally surprised, I didn't know what to say. But here was a man like every other in my family—incapable of expressing emotion and substituting stern control in its place. I had stood in silence with my grandfather in many times of crisis, and mute endurance had always been the preferred method for coping.

I took a chance this time and said, "I'm sorry for your loss, Tottie."

His fierce eyes fixed on my face, and I saw his jaw tighten. He drew a long breath and mastered whatever he had been feeling inside. Then he said, "Thank you."

And he walked away.

I didn't stick around, either.

I stopped for a bite of lunch with a friend at Rouge where we discussed Red Cross committee work and her eight-year-old daughter's rapid progress in her Suzuki violin class. I was glad to put all other thoughts out of my head for a short while. Afterward, my friend invited me on a January getaway to her New York pied-à-terre.

"We'll spend a week hitting the after-Christmas sales," she suggested. "And there's an orchid show, too, I think."

I made no promises and kissed her good-bye. Next I headed off to the Dollar Bill Club. A hundred years ago, a feisty band of ladies gathered to discuss a woman's right to vote. They eventually established a club, moved their headquarters out of their suffragette leader's parlor and into a lovely brownstone. They had flourished ever since, and were still a hot-eyed bunch eager to discuss politics and world affairs over their Earl Grey tea and mushroom sandwiches. My grandmother had been a member, and I had a soft spot for them all. I was only sorry that so many such active women's clubs were dying out. Young women had careers and busy family lives and little time to devote to organizations like the Dollar Bill Club, founded by women from another era. I wondered how much longer the group might remain vital.

Their Christmas tea wouldn't rate even half an inch of space in any newspaper, but I enjoyed myself. Looking at all those elderly, intelligent faces, full of energy and life, I was glad I'd come.

Reed drove me to two more parties that evening. Neither made me feel especially festive.

That night, I spent the night at my friend Lexie's house.

"Sweetie!" she cried when she opened the door. "You're here for our annual slumber party!"

I mustered a smile and held up my overnight bag. "I brought my pajamas, but I didn't have time to buy *Tiger Beat* magazine."

"We'll make do without somehow. I've got everything else we need coming first thing in the morning— my manicurist, Seth the orgasmic masseur, and the wonderful new girl from that crazy rock and roll hair salon. I've got all my lotions and potions ready. By tomorrow night, we'll be stunning. We'll be the belles of the ballet gala!"

The ballet gala was the Christmas party of all

Christmas parties. The *über* event. Always the affair to remember. It was the most glamorous party of the season and attracted the beautifully dressed, the most connected and the oldest and newest money in town. Everybody came for the razzle-dazzle, and nobody went home disappointed. People from the arts, the medical community, politics, professional sports, the financial world and charitable institutions put aside their petty differences and came together for the ballet gala every year to see and be seen. Powerful CEOs danced with kooky artists, malpractice lawyers drank with their doctors, and everyone admired the lush flowers, the extravagant decorations, the world-class entertainment and the sumptuous food.

For the gala, Lexie took her beautification process very seriously. She actually refused to go to her office for the day—although she made dozens of phone calls just to "keep tabs." Otherwise, she hired the best beauticians and devoted herself to relaxation. I spent the night at her place so we could start the beauty treatments early.

"Breathe," she advised when I called the vet for the third time and still received no satisfactory answer. "We're going to get rid of those circles under your eyes if it takes every tube of Preparation H in the city. How about a nap while my dressmaker makes the final nips and tucks in my dress? You can't help your poor puppy by working yourself into a state, so let's concentrate on calming down."

Her doorbell rang, and Lexie's assistant Samir called me to the door. A large package had been delivered with my name on it. The elderly chauffeur said he'd been to Bucks County to drop the package at Blackbird Farm, but "some crazy woman" told him I was staying in the city, so here he was.

"Libby," I guessed.

When we'd thanked the driver and he went back to his Rolls Royce, Lexie leaned close. "What is it?"

I read the card. "It's from dotty Dotty Dubose. She says I'll get more use out of these than she will."

"I love presents from rich people with good taste. Open it!"

We look the large package into her dining room and put it on the table. Samir brought scissors, so we cut the packing tape and opened what turned out to be a faded box marked PATOU.

"Oh, my God," said Lexie.

Gabrielle, the dressmaker, began to murmur in French, and when I lifted the lid she was soon babbling incoherently.

Packed in the thinnest tissue paper lay six opulent vintage dresses, two fine suits and something made of lace that looked like a body stocking. The fabrics were weightless silks, airy chiffons, burnished taffetas and the finest wool I'd ever touched. Overwhelmed, I ran my trembling fingers along shimmering embroidery, iridescent beadwork and invisible stitching.

"See?" Lexie cried. "You can't regret selling that old Mainbocher! You've got all these glorious things to choose from now."

"They'll never fit me!"

Gabrielle cried, "We will make them fit!"

"Fashion show!" Lexie yelled. "I want to see them all!"

Samir fled as they stripped me down to my underwear right in the dining room. For the next hour, they threw dresses over my head, fastened buttons, adjusted bodices and hemlines and demanded pirouettes.

It was not difficult to make the choice for the gala.

"That's the one," said Gabrielle.

"It's superb," Lexie declared when I stood by the windows in the last dress. "You'll look like a bride while the rest of us schlepp around in our gloomy velvets and brocades."

I tugged at the flimsy silk. "But it's—"

"Leave the tailoring to me," Gabrielle said firmly. "It will be an honor."

I telephoned Dotty Dubose immediately. She was full of laughter and glad to hear that part of her collection might go to good use.

"I chose some things I thought would flatter your lovely figure, dear. Now go out and get down!"

"Dotty, you are so very kind."

"Nonsense," she said. "Call it a thank you for planting that hint in today's paper about Tottie's hospital wing. It won't take long for people to figure out the truth, thanks to you."

"I hope it doesn't make Tottie angry."

"Everything makes that old goat angry. This will do him good."

After I gave her more profuse thanks for the vintage dresses, she added, "It's nice to see those wonderful clothes going to parties, like they were meant to. I hate shriveled rags hanging in museums! Play your cards right, dear, and I'll put you in my will. You can have them all someday."

The hairdresser swooped in to finish our hair, and Lexie and I dressed and made up our faces side by side at her bathroom mirror.

When she declared herself ready, Lexie looked gorgeous in simple black velvet with her hair pulled up and enhanced by chandelier diamond earrings.

By contrast, my white dress, hardly more than wisps of silk cut on the bias with infinitesimal upside-down pin tucks beneath my breasts, gave the impression of clinging to my body by magic. The thin overlay of sheer white fabric over a slightly pink layer beneath created an effect as lustrous as freshly bathed bare skin. Gabrielle's adjustments fine-tuned the fit so that I was very glad I'd skipped dessert for weeks.

Perhaps I should have accepted the pearls Lexie offered me, but I had always shied away from borrowed jewelry. I liked my naked throat better tonight, anyway. To cover the red and swollen effects of Spike's bite, I slipped on a pair of over-the-elbow kid gloves.

When Reed arrived to take us to the gala, he looked at me as if he wasn't sure who I was.

He said, "Is that your nightgown?"

"It's a dress, Reed."

"Where's your coat?"

"I'm using a wrap." I held up the rectangle of perfect white cashmere. "It's warm enough. I won't be out of the car more than a few minutes."

"I wasn't thinking about the cold," he muttered.

Chapter 20

The Christmas gala was usually held in whatever location seemed the most avant-garde, the most luxurious, the place best suited for over-the-top set decoration. In recent years, the ballet's big fund-raiser had been staged at the museum, in a magnificent barn and on the stage of the symphony hall, decorated as if for a full-scale opera.

But this year, an excellent hotel had stepped forward and offered their recently refurbished ballrooms for free, and the ballet board had jumped at the gift.

The music swept up to us as soon as we entered the ornate lobby. A trio of classical Spanish guitars played intricately interwoven melodies. The gala theme was Velasquez, and we were greeted by matadors in red and black with frothy white lace at their throats. I should have guessed Lexie had insider info about the theme. Her black velvet was stunning.

The receiving line began with the executive director of the ballet company, his wife and the Zapper Czar himself, Osgood Paltron, Claudine's husband and the chairman of the ballet's fund-raising committee. In high fund-raising mode, Osgood was Prince Charming. He thanked us for coming and paid homage to Lexie as the museum's unofficial delegate to the night's revels. He pointed us toward the ballroom, where cocktails were being served before dinner.

In contrasting black and white, Lexie and I went down the grand staircase together. Below us, the growing crowd mingled festively, turning to look as each new arrival descended the marble steps. We heard cheers and applause when we started down, so we linked arms and did the royal wave to much laughter.

On the mezzanine level, we paused. The mezzanine ran around the ballroom like a balcony, with dozens of Palladian archways, each featuring a partially clothed Roman statue.

Lexie reached up and pinched the bare bottom of the nearest alabaster figure. "Let's find a drink and hang out here to gawk for a bit. Do you mind? I want to see the clothes as everyone comes down the steps."

A waiter with champagne materialized, and we lightened his load by two glasses.

From our vantage point, we snagged the most entertaining friends for quick chats and watched the parade of arriving guests—elegant women in their finest finery accompanied by affable husbands in cummerbunds and an assortment of festive neckwear. I much preferred black-tie to white-tie, since it gave the men a way to be creative.

"Hot dog," said Lexie. "Check out that babe. Looks like she sprayed herself with glue and rolled around in a pile of sequins."

"I think she's a baseball player's wife."

"And that one? Nobody her age has boobs that shape."

"She's a partner in a law firm, I believe."

"Order in the court!"

Next came a grand dame in brocade with a mink-trimmed hem and her regal husband in long tails. Both of them very chic, arty and ninety years of age.

"Nora!"

I turned and saw my college flame Flan Cooper shouldering his way through the mezzanine throng. "Flan! Merry Christmas!"

"You look like you belong on a wedding cake." He kissed my cheek and held my hand at arm's length to admire my dress. "Or one of those round honeymoon beds. You're beautiful tonight. And very, very sexy. Did you bring your boyfriend? The crime boss? I want to meet him now that he's avoided jail time."

My heart skipped. "He's avoided jail?"

"It's on the evening news. They've dropped the investigation. Guess he dodged another bullet. Is he here?"

"No," I said.

"Damn. Bring him around sometime. I'd like to meet him."

Dougie Forsythe brushed past us then and accidentally knocked shoulders with Flan. He gave Flan a nasty look before sending me a slit-eyed glare meant to intimidate.

When he walked away, Flan said, "Who's the jerk?"

"Claudine Paltron's latest," I reported. "Pay him no mind."

"Whatever. Want another drink?"

"Sure."

"I'll be back." He took my empty glass.

Thomasina Silk appeared beside me next, hardly recognizable out of her horse clothes. She wore a simple pillar of chocolate taffeta that flattered her small size and hid her bowed legs. A diamond necklace lay delicately on her collarbones. I had no idea she was so feminine underneath her barnyard persona.

We complimented each other on our dresses, then she cut to the chase.

"I've been thinking about what you said about Emma. Like you, I know she didn't kill Rush."

"All we need is some proof," I agreed.

"I thought about everything. And here's the thing." Thomasina held my gaze steadily. "I know how much Emma wants to ride the Grand Prix horses again."

"Yes . . . ?"

"So I hesitate to reveal what I know, even to you."

"Thomasina, Emma is the prime suspect in a murder case. If someone doesn't come forward with evidence to clear her name, she'll never ride any kind of horse again."

Thomasina nodded shortly. "All right, here goes. She hasn't recovered from the broken arm she had over the summer."

"What?"

"She tries to conceal the extent of her injury so everybody will think she's fit enough to ride, but I can see it plain as day. She can't lift that arm over her shoulder. There's no way she could swing a polo mallet hard enough to hurt a flea, let alone a tall, able-bodied man like Rush."

"Are you sure? Thomasina, this is important."

"My horses are important, too. And there's no way I'd trust Emma on a single one. Not now, anyway. She's not strong enough to manage them."

"Have you talked to her about it? Can you be certain—"

"I don't have to talk to her, I can see it clearly. Besides, you know how touchy she is."

"Somebody has to tell the police."

Thomasina frowned uncomfortably. "I hate to go behind Emma's back."

"There's a detective I know. I'll have him call you

tomorrow. If you tell him what you told me, Emma can come forward."

She shrugged. "Okay. I'll be in the barn first thing in the morning."

"You're a godsend, Thomasina."

She hesitated again, not ready to leave. "Look, when Emma is ready, I'll let her ride for me. When she's in top form, she's hard to beat. She'll get strong again. But she's got to stop the drinking, too."

"I know she'll appreciate that vote of confidence."

Thomasina went off into the party, and I clutched the marble balustrade to stay on my feet. The first ray of hope. I almost burst into tears right there.

I decided to find the ladies room to compose myself and threaded through the people to the edge of the ballroom. A discreet sign pointed the way, and I soon reached a carpeted hallway. A few yards further, and I entered the lavishly appointed lounge. The attendant and I exchanged smiles, and I went to the mirror to pretend to check my hair.

"Miss Blackbird?"

In the mirror, I saw Merrie Naftzinger's shining face. I turned.

"It is you," she said shyly. "You look really pretty tonight."

She was nicely dressed in a prom gown suitable for her age—a slim, high-necked, sleeveless dress that brushed the tops of her sparkly sandals. A more discerning eye might have put her into something with a bit more shape to it, so I suspected she had either chosen the dress herself or had her father's help. Her hair was wound up in a complicated do, and good drop earrings finished her look.

I said, "Honey, you're lovely tonight! What a pleasure to see you."

She smiled more gamely, and I noticed she had changed the rubber bands on her teeth to green and white for the season. "Dad brought me. It's supposed to be a big Christmas treat."

"Aren't you having a good time?"

"Oh, sure, but—well, I thought it was going to be a real ballet. I take lessons myself, you see, along with the horseback riding, and Dad thought we'd have fun seeing something besides *The Nutcracker* this year. But I guess he didn't understand this is a party, not a performance."

I laughed and hugged her shoulders. "That's a man for you! I'm sorry you're not having fun."

"Oh, it's fun," she said, clearly fibbing. "But I don't know anybody."

"Well, you can't hide in the bathroom all night. Come on, let's go find someone you can talk to."

"Is Emma here?"

I saw the hope in her eyes. "No, she isn't. Fancy parties aren't really her thing."

Merrie nodded and looked away to hide her disappointment. "They're not mine, either. But I thought she might—you know. I really like her. She's not my mom, but she's fun."

I wanted to take Merrie in my arms and hug her hard, but I knew I'd burst into tears if I did.

"My dad likes her, too," she continued. "He doesn't talk about it, but I can see that he does. Not anything lovey-dovey, you know. Friends, maybe."

I thought I had detected more than a friendly interest from Tim for my sister, but I didn't say so. Things were bad enough already.

I said, "Let's go find some young people for you. You can't hang around with the old folks all night."

She smiled again, and we went out to the ballroom.

I found Flan Cooper again almost immediately, and he reported his nephews were in the crowd somewhere. We soon had Merrie talking with some of the naughty Cooper boys—a new generation from the same hard-partying gene pool. Merrie blushed with the pleasure of their attention.

I saw Tim Naftzinger then, standing apart from the crowd, holding a glass of champagne and gazing at his daughter with an unhappy expression. He caught sight of me watching and wiped the emotion from his face.

"Hi," I said, going to him. "Merrie looks lovely tonight."

"Did she tell you what a mistake I made? Bringing her here?"

"Maybe it was serendipitous. Now that she's met some teenagers, she'll have a good time. She's a wonderful girl, Tim. So many great qualities wrapped up in one young lady."

"She's strong, too."

Although we were standing in the middle of a party, I had never seen a man look so shattered. The very essence of him had vanished and left Tim pale and uncertain—a different person from the vibrant young doctor I used to know.

I took a deep breath. "But is Merrie strong enough?" I asked. "To understand what you did?"

"No."

The party whirled around us—noise, laughter, music and the vivid, flesh-and-blood colors of Velasquez— all an incongruous maelstrom with the two us at its silent center.

"Nora," he said hoarsely. "She's too young to be by herself."

"I'm sorry, Tim."

He brought one trembling hand to his face and covered his eyes. "I'm sorry, too. I hate what I've put Emma through. I just can't—I haven't found the courage to turn myself in."

"I'm sure it was an accident."

"It wasn't." He dropped his hand away. All the color had drained from his face, and he stood rigidly, still holding his champagne flute but stiffly now, as if he had just discovered it was a ticking bomb. "I knew what I was doing. I heard Rush and Gussie arguing, but I didn't go into the stall until Gussie ran out. Rush was furious, and he hit Emma. I'd never seen him like that. I—I went looking for a weapon. When I came back, he was shaking her. Hard. I had to stop him."

"Tim—"

I wanted to pull him out of the ballroom, take him somewhere private, where nobody could overhear us. But I was afraid to touch him. He looked as if he might break like glass.

He said, "Emma was drunk. She couldn't defend herself. I thought Strawcutter was going to hurt her, maybe kill her. He was so desperate, so angry. I hit him with the mallet. I only meant to stop him."

I could imagine Gussie's meltdown, and Rush's helpless rage taken out on the most convenient target: Emma.

"He'd had a fight with his wife," I said. "She'd just learned about the blackmail."

Tim looked at me as if I had just spoken in a new language. "Blackmail?"

"Rush was being blackmailed. That's why he and Gussie were—" I suddenly realized what his shocked expression meant. "Oh, Lord, did you get a blackmail letter? With pictures of you and me?"

"Yes," he whispered, staring at me. "I paid. I

couldn't risk another disaster, not with this promotion at stake, so I— My God, I thought it was you."

"You thought I was the blackmailer?" Suddenly his recent behavior made sense. "No wonder you avoided me!"

"Everyone said you were broke and I thought—" He swallowed. "If it wasn't you, who? Who would do such a thing? I can't—" He almost laughed. "Listen to me. I can't understand how anyone could blackmail another person, yet I'm the one who killed Rush Strawcutter."

I took his arm. "Don't say that, Tim. Don't, not yet. Don't tell anyone."

"I have to." His voice was strained. "Emma will be arrested if I don't. Ironic, isn't it? I wanted to save her, and she's the one who ended up ruined."

"She'll come out okay. I'm serious, Tim. Don't say anything to anyone. You have Merrie to think about. If you go to jail, what will happen to her?"

At last tears began to well in his eyes. "I don't know. I don't have any family left. It's just the two of us."

"Then hang on," I said, low-voiced and urgent. I caught hold of his arm. "Just wait. Will you promise me? Say you won't tell anyone yet."

Dazed, Tim said, "God, I don't want to ruin her life, too. All because I had a stupid crush on another woman."

I had no more words of comfort.

"First, do no harm," he said. "That was my oath as a physician. It's so meaningless now."

I heard someone calling my name, but I was afraid to leave Tim. I thought he was in shock. He began to tremble as if overcome by a cold wind.

Lexie slipped through the crowd and grabbed my

elbow. She was laughing. "Nora, you've got to see this. Come on."

Tim turned away from her.

"Really, you've got to come." She jiggled me. "It's hysterical. Claudine's dress is falling off."

Tim staggered away.

Lexie glanced after him. "Has Tim had too much to drink? I never took him for the type."

"Yes, he must be a little drunk."

"Well, come on now. Wait until you see."

She dragged me through guests to the edge of the balustrade. She leaned down and pointed. "See? Claudine is dribbling!"

Sure enough, the Mainbocher dress I had sold Claudine was shedding dozens of tiny beads by the minute. As I predicted, the old fabric was too dry and delicate to wear, and the threads were giving way from the weight of the beads. As Claudine intently lectured Dougie Forsythe, her clothing was slowly disintegrating on her body. Around her, the floor was dancing with flashes of tiny glass droplets.

While Claudine reamed him out, Dougie took a pace back and stepped on the beads. One foot slid out from under him, and he went down on the floor like a circus clown. But he grabbed Claudine to save himself at the last instant, and ripped her sleeve completely off her dress. Mouth open, Claudine stared at the shredded fabric dangling from her wrist.

Other guests began to notice her predicament. A ripple of laughter ran through the crowd.

"Oh, shit!" Claudine held up the torn sleeve. "This damn dress is rotten!"

Dougie scrambled up again, and she snapped, "Give me your coat!"

"But Claudie—"

"Take it off this minute!"

Dougie removed his jacket, whereupon it was immediately apparent that he had used safety pins on the back of the shirt to improve the way it clung to his chest.

Claudine rushed up the marble stairs to leave, and she spotted me in the crowd. "You! You sold me a worthless sack!"

"She told you not to wear it, Claudine," Lexie spoke up. "She told you it was too fragile, but you wanted to buy it anyway."

Claudine pointed at me. "I want that dress! Give me that one!"

I melted back into the laughing crowd. Around me, people seemed to surge into a blurred mass. For an instant, I thought I was blacking out. But through the tide of people, I saw a familiar scarf and my attention sharpened. I craned my neck to get a better look and suddenly found myself staring into Hadley Pinkham's smugly smiling face. He raised a glass of champagne to me.

I spun around and shoved through a knot of surprised guests, making my way to the staircase. Halfway up, I encountered a waiter and told him what I needed. He dashed up the stairs, and I went back down into the crowd.

I found Hadley again, chatting in his most mocking tones to a young man I didn't know. He saw me and turned.

"Kitten," he said, feigning surprised delight. "What a fragile beauty you look tonight. Sweet heaven, is that Patou? It's a masterpiece, but it pales beside your loveliness this evening."

"Did you crash the gate tonight, Hadley?"

His companion blanched and eased away.

Hadley said, "Let's not get ugly, kitten. Not in public, anyway."

"I'd like to shout it from the rooftops, but breaking into a party uninvited seems so petty, doesn't it? Compared to everything else you've done."

"Lower your voice, please."

"Afraid I'll make a scene? And spoil your reputation as the smoothest operator in town?"

"Kitten—"

"I don't need to make a scene, Hadley. Because you're about to make one all by yourself."

We were surrounded then by men in uniform. Ben Bloom was with them.

"Hadley Pinkham?" Bloom reached for Hadley's wrist. "You're under arrest."

"For crashing a party?" Hadley objected. "This is ridiculous."

The dinner gong sounded and the guests around us began to move toward the dining room. Everyone glanced curiously at Hadley as the police officers took him into custody, but nobody had the bad manners to ask what the problem was.

Hadley's affront began to give way into something more mortified. "Kitten," he said. "What have you done?"

"Not nearly enough," I replied.

The police took him away in a degrading parade that even Hadley couldn't carry off with panache. Only a few party guests glanced up to watch his humiliated exit. Politely, everyone else moved away. Perhaps Hadley's worst punishment was this: society's cool rejection of his offensive behavior. I intended to make sure he would be shunned by everyone forever.

Suddenly, I didn't want to stay. The thought of having dinner and remaining to dance and drink was all wrong. While the throng moved toward the dining room, I ran for the staircase like Cinderella leaving the ball.

I telephoned Reed from the lobby.

"Call Michael?" I said. "Ask him to come for me."

Without pause, Reed said, "He'll be there in five minutes."

I ran to the cloakroom to get my wrap, and when I came out again a waiter walked by, still carrying a tray of champagne. I accepted a glass and wished him Merry Christmas.

Flute in hand, I headed across the hotel lobby and realized the man waiting for me by the door was Ben Bloom. He couldn't stop himself from looking me up and down.

I said, "Are you going to stay for the party?"

He didn't smile, but met my eye. "No, they're going to book Pinkham now. I thought I'd go along."

"On what charges?"

"Animal cruelty, like you said. And the city's got him for the parking tickets. The son of a bitch owes almost fifteen thousand dollars in parking fines."

"Will that keep him in jail?"

"Not for long. We'll need something else to hold him."

With determination, I nodded. "Okay."

"You going to give me a clue?"

"No, I need time to think, that's all. And to convince some people to help. If you can hold him for a day or two, I'll see what I can put together to help indict him on extortion charges. Meanwhile, there's someone you need to call. Her name is Thomasina Silk. You might remember her from the hunt breakfast. She has some information you will want to hear."

"What information?"

"It won't mean as much coming from me. Call her."

Our business was concluded. But neither of us was ready to leave. The music from the party below was muted but rose to us, sounding sentimental and meaningless. Ben looked like a kid who'd lost his favorite pencil box.

He spoke first. "Nora." He no longer sounded like a policeman. "I'm sorry about what happened."

"With Hadley?"

"You know what I mean. I came on too fast. I thought you were ready. I assumed too much."

"It was my fault," I said. "I was feeling confused that day."

He touched my bare arm. "What about now?"

"Now I'm going home," I said. I didn't believe the naïve act he put on anymore, but I didn't blame him for trying it. He had a job to do, after all, and he'd hit upon a technique that worked for him. Just not with me. I smiled up at him. "Good night, Detective."

The doorman opened the door, and I went out into the night. There was a church across the street with an old car illegally parked and idling in its shadow. With the champagne still in my hand and the cashmere wrap over my arm, I dashed across the street, oblivious to the cold.

He was sitting on the church steps, surrounded by kernels of rice. He wore a dark suit with the tie loosened around his neck.

Breathless, I stopped at the bottom of the steps.

He said, "Should I go looking for your glass slipper, princess?"

"I'll save you the trouble." I kicked off one shoe and tossed it to him.

He caught it one-handed. "Does the rest of that outfit come off so easily?"

"No. I'm going to need some help."

He lifted his chin to indicate the hotel behind me. "Detective Gloom is watching from across the street."

"Shall we give him something to see?"

Michael got up and came down to the sidewalk, taking off his coat. I went up one step, and he slung the coat around my shoulders. Then we were nose to nose, and I suddenly felt as if I'd had far too much champagne. I gave him the glass and slipped my arms around his neck.

He drained the glass in two swallows. When the champagne was gone, he wrapped one arm around me and smiled. "I made my first million today."

His smile filled me with pleasure. "You did?"

"Yep. So where do you want to go? Venice? Fiji?"

I tried to match the lightness of his tone. "Did you make your million by selling old cars? Or gasoline? Or was it truffles?"

He laughed then, and looked very pleased with himself. "There's money in all of it. How did you guess about the truffles?"

"It's taken months, but I'm finally starting to understand how your mind works. And Rawlins let it slip that you were in Paris."

"I made a little detour on the way home from Scotland. The fishing wasn't all that good, anyway. Wrong time of year."

"So that's what you were delivering to the restaurant? A package of truffles?"

"Did you think it was cash? That I was laundering money? I brought some truffles— illegally, yes, but I have all the right permits now."

"I didn't know what to think, then," I said with complete honesty. "The FBI has been under the impression you were illegally moving currency in and out of bank accounts. But I checked my calendar and it turns out you were making risotto in my kitchen."

"Nora," he said, finally serious, "you shouldn't have talked to the FBI. Tomorrow your name will be in the papers with mine, so you know what everybody's going to think. You've put yourself in harm's way for me. You'll never live it down."

I touched his mouth with one finger and let his concerns go unacknowledged. It was my turn to be serious. "Why didn't you tell me you had taken that gun away from Rawlins?"

He sighed. "It wasn't my place. He had to tell his mother first, and it was their decision to talk to you about it, not mine. I thought maybe your sister would want to keep it quiet."

"Libby? Quiet?"

He smiled, and I kissed him. I tasted champagne along with something definitely more potent. I don't know when Detective Bloom left, but if he had stayed to watch us, he would certainly have turned away by the time we broke our kiss.

I eased a curl of hair off Michael's forehead. "Come inside and meet my friends. You'll like some of them."

"I left my tuxedo hanging in the closet. Let's go home." Michael put my shoe back on my foot and tucked me into the front seat of his car.

On the way out of town, I broke the news about Spike.

"I'm gonna stop now," he said, sounding dangerous again. "If nobody's at the vet's office, we'll break in."

"We're not going to break in anywhere, ever. We'll call first thing in the morning. He's being well taken care of. Dr. Gilley is excellent."

"How can you stand not knowing if he's alive or dead?"

"I think I'd know if he were dead."

"You've got a psychic connection with a dog?"

"He's not a dog, he's Spike. He's our first baby."

Michael glanced over at me and let his gaze slide down my body. "That's a very fetching dress, you know. But how come it makes me think about how naked you are underneath it?"

Of all the compliments I'd enjoyed that evening, this was the one that made my toes tingle. I began to strip off my long gloves. "You know, we've never had the health discussion."

"The what? Oh, Jesus."

I folded the gloves and laid them demurely in my lap. "After Todd died, I had all the tests, just to be sure he hadn't brought home anything horrible. And I'm perfectly healthy."

"I can see that," he agreed. "Okay, I had to take out a life insurance policy when I expanded Gas 'n' Grub last month. I passed the physical—blood tests and everything. My cholesterol isn't too bad either."

"Michael, will you pull over, please?"

"What?"

I pointed. "There's a parking lot."

He peered out through the windshield. "It's The Home Depot. It's closed."

"I know. Just pull into the parking lot, will you?"

A minute later, the car came to a stop and he asked with concern, "Are you okay?" Then, "What are you doing?"

I had kicked off my shoes again and wrestled around for a minute. At last I handed him my panties.

He stared at them, and then at me. "What are you doing?"

I pulled him out from under the steering wheel and halfway across the seat. I undid his tie, tugged it off and threw it onto the backseat. His shirt was unbuttoned in a flash, and he was laughing, but his hands were on me.

"Wait a minute." His mouth was against mine. "I thought you wanted to go away someplace romantic?"

"Unfasten my dress. Here, feel the hooks?"

"I'll tear it!"

"Just the top few and I'll wiggle out."

"You're crazy."

"No, I'm just not wasting any more time."

He tried kissing me for a while as a diversionary tactic, but then it became evident that he was just as ready as I was, maybe more, and things really went to hell. We were wrestling and he was growling, and pretty soon I was out of the dress and straddling him on the seat. I liked the shape of him, and he wanted to taste every inch of me within reach.

"Wait." He was out of breath and I could feel his pulse racing beneath my hand. "A tuxedo isn't the only thing I'm not wearing."

"It's okay. I think it doesn't count in a car."

"Is that like calories from cake you eat standing up?" He held my face in his hands, smiling and making sure I was intent.

"Michael," I whispered. "I love you."

Chapter 21

In the middle of the night, too energized to sleep and too physically spent to make love again, we talked quietly in my bed about Tim Naftzinger.

"I don't know what to do," I confided.

"You're sure he killed Strawcutter?"

"Yes, I've known it for a day or more, but tonight he told me himself. He only meant to stop Rush. He was protecting Emma."

"But if Emma blacked out and can't remember what happened, there's nobody who can corroborate his story."

"Exactly. Can he possibly be acquitted?"

"Doubtful. And you don't think he should go to jail," Michael said, slowly tracing my lower lip with one finger. "Do you?"

I sighed, glad I had shared my dilemma, but feeling no closer to reaching a decision. "It's not black and white, is it?"

"Usually, yes."

"But not this time. Tim isn't a violent man. Far from it."

"What do you want to do?"

I propped myself up on one elbow and looked at him in the candlelight. "I don't know. All along, I just wanted Emma to be cleared of Rush's murder. In a few hours, Ben Bloom will hear that she can't have killed Rush. Her arm hasn't healed as well as she pretends, and she couldn't have swung the polo mallet."

"So Emma can come out of hiding today?"

"Very likely, yes. But that leaves the murder unsolved, as far as the police are concerned."

"So what else is new in law enforcement?"

"But it's so— I feel torn. On one side are Rush and Gussie. On the other is Tim's daughter. She's such a wonderful girl, but so vulnerable. First her mother is taken away, and now this. Tim has tried his best, of course. He's a sweet and gentle man, a good father."

I studied Michael's face, lined and bruised from years of hard experience and so often shuttered to keep the world from guessing what he had done and seen in life. His misspent youth was gone and in its place was the thing I'd fallen in love with—a bittersweet sort of hope for a future born out of the ashes. I asked, "Could a gentle man like Tim survive in prison?"

He touched my throat very lightly, but did not answer.

My heart swelled. I couldn't make sense of the tangled motives anymore, but I knew there was one person who was guilty. "This is all Hadley's fault." My voice trembled. "Maybe he didn't swing the murder weapon, but he set it all up like dominoes. He turned people against each other, used their weaknesses and fears for his own gain. Growing up, we always thought he was a scamp. But now I see he's grown into a monster. He deserves . . ."

"What do you think he deserves?"

"Something terrible." I closed my eyes as if to shut out the thought. "I should feel guilty for wanting him punished more than Tim. Maybe you've lured me to the dark side."

"I'm sorry."

I shook my head. "This calls for street justice, doesn't it? If the police have their way, Emma will be free, but Tim will suffer every day of his life. And Merrie, the innocent one—well, I don't want to imagine."

"What about Rush Strawcutter? What about his justice?"

I slid against him and put my head on his chest. "I don't know. When my—when Todd's— killer was caught, it didn't make me feel any better. Michael, please tell me what to do."

"I can't, and you know it." He stroked my hair. "Maybe tomorrow things will be clearer."

We slept in a warm tangle that felt as natural to me as if we'd been together all our lives. In the morning, he woke first and made quick and quiet love to me before I was fully conscious. Then he covered me up, kissed me and slid out of bed. I heard the shower start, but I lay in the bedclothes, half dreaming, half brooding.

What to do? If I caved in to my instincts and allowed the police to forget about Tim, was I setting down the same path of corruption Hadley had traveled? I wanted to do the right thing, but Merrie's face kept swimming up from the bottom of my swirling mind.

And I thought of Todd, weirdly enough. Here, at last, I was cleaving to another man and allowing the forces of his life to wrap around mine. Was I letting Michael's moral code dictate my own, or was I allowing mine to evolve into something more complex than simple rules of law? Was I wrong? Was it hubris to think I could make the choice?

I thought I heard a door slam downstairs and it woke me up completely. I lay still and listened.

Definitely voices. Definitely coming up the stairs.

I sat up in the bed and groped for something to wear.

Libby and Emma burst into the bedroom in time to see me snatch the sheet against my breasts, hair in a tangle and my lips no doubt swollen from the most passionate of nights.

"Well, well!" Emma poked her head in first with a wide grin on her face. "How bad was the fall from your pedestal, Sis?"

"Oh, my goodness!" Libby waltzed past Emma into the room and looked around in mock dismay. "What happened here last night? There is a magnificent dress thrown over the sofa downstairs, and other unmentionable clothes are scattered from the back porch all the way up the staircase." She picked up one of Michael's socks from the floor and dangled it as Exhibit X.

"Do you two have any definition of *privacy* at all?" I asked.

"We wondered about the etiquette of calling on you this morning," Emma said, still in the hallway. "Do we have to wait until next week for you and the love machine to take a refueling break?"

"Why don't you just come back next month?"

Her grin broadened. "I don't think you want to wait that long. We brought you something."

"Spike!"

Emma carried my puppy into the room. He squirmed and whimpered, but he was alive, firmly encased in a white plaster cast that covered the entire rear half of his body. His front half had been partially and unevenly clipped so that his hair stuck out at all angles, and his left eye was swollen as if he'd won a prizefight.

I burst into tears and gathered him up. He licked my face so frantically that he eventually peed on the sheets, which meant his body cast wasn't completely sealed.

"Nice," Libby observed. She climbed into the bed beside me, avoiding the wet spot. "Next time, why don't you just adopt one of my kids? They'd be less messy."

"Is he okay? Will he be able to walk?"

"He's probably going to limp." Emma sat on my other side and scratched Spike's head. "Which will be the least of his appearance woes. He's incredibly ugly, isn't he? Oh, and he bit Dr. Gilley on the way out."

"The first thing I'm going to do today is find an obedience class."

"Well, the vet doesn't hold any grudges. He said to bring Spike back in two weeks for a checkup and to make an appointment for him to be neutered."

At that moment, Michael came out of the bathroom rubbing his head with a towel and demonstrating that he had not been subjected to the sort of emasculation soon to be suffered by Spike.

He caused a minor miracle, however, by striking both my sisters completely mute.

He stopped buffing his head and transferred the towel elsewhere. "We're changing the locks," he said.

"Look who's home!" I cried.

He came over and gently took the dog from me. "Hey, buddy!"

Spike happily chewed on his nose.

"How come he doesn't pee on you?" I asked.

"Mutual respect. Hey, Em. Glad to be a free woman?"

"Your cousin is a pig. And I think he's running some kind of half-assed gambling operation. But he's such an idiot that he's going to get busted soon."

"Yes, I know. We'll just let it happen, and you'll never have to see him again. In fact, I can guarantee that, if you want."

"That's okay. You seem to have him suitably terrorized already."

"How's the arm?"

"My arm? Fine." She flexed it, but I noticed she didn't raise it very high. "Great. See? No problems."

Libby said, "The police have decided she's not a stone-cold killer."

"Yeah, this morning's papers say the cops have determined I'm no longer a suspect."

"Question is," Libby said, "who did kill Rush? Have you figured it out, Nora?"

Michael looked at me. So did Emma. Libby blinked expectantly.

"No," I said. "I haven't."

"What a disappointment. I guess you're not much of a detective, after all."

Emma continued to study me. She said, "The police are sure it wasn't me. I bet I have you to thank for that."

The right time would come to tell Emma everything I knew. She would be relieved to hear she had not caused Rush's death. But she would be devastated to learn Tim had been bent on rescuing her when Rush died. I needed to be alone with her when she learned the truth. For now, I said, "None of it was your fault, Em."

"Certainly not," Libby said. "But that means there's still a criminal on the loose! A woman is hardly safe anywhere anymore, is she?"

"And some criminals aren't safe from you," Emma said. "Tell Nora about Doctor Discipline."

Libby looked very frosty. "Turns out Melvin wasn't a doctor after all. He was faking! I spoke to the chief of security at the hospital, and he thought Melvin's behavior was highly unprofessional, not to mention suspicious, but he complimented me on my intuitive good sense—"

"Melvin?" asked Michael.

"It's a long story," I said.

"—which I immediately attributed to my recent acceptance of Placida into my life, so the chief of security went to the police." Energetically, Libby continued. "And he learned that Melvin has been defrauding people all over the state, posing as all kinds of things and using soap opera names to prey on attractive, available women. And Philip said—"

"Who's Philip?" we asked in chorus.

Libby looked prettily surprised. "Philip is the chief of security at the hospital. Didn't I say that? And he's a very sensitive person, I might add. He was shocked to hear what an ordeal I've been through, and thought I must be having a very difficult time learning to trust men again after this dreadful experience, so he—"

"Oh, Lord," said Emma.

"What?"

"Libby," Emma said, "isn't it time to nurse the baby? I think you're leaking again."

Libby grabbed her breasts and stood up. "You're right. Let's step on it."

"Does the kid have a name yet?" Michael asked. "Or is that another dangerous subject?"

"Well, Philip has a pleasantly royal ring to it, don't you think? Or maybe Zeke. I knew a very charming Zeke once—"

Emma grabbed her. "C'mon, Lib. Let's give these three some privacy."

"Thank you for bringing Spike," I called as they headed downstairs.

Michael had lulled Spike to sleep, and he put the puppy on the bed. He began to dress like a man who wanted his breakfast. I enjoyed watching.

When he got his pants on, he said, "I'm not crazy about marrying an entire family, you know."

I smiled. "Who said anything about marrying anyone?"

"I did, just now. I don't want to marry all three of you."

"Michael, I can't marry you."

He put on his shirt and looked at me. "You don't still believe in the Blackbird widow's curse?"

"Of course I do. If you marry a Blackbird, you'll be dead in no time. It's been happening for generations. You and I can't get married."

He gave up dressing and crawled back into bed. "Nora, sweetheart, let's review. Last night we definitely made a sibling for Spike. And no child of mine is going out into the world without my name on it."

"That's a medieval attitude."

"I know," he said. "Despite that, will you marry me?"

I kissed his mouth. "Get dressed and we'll talk about it over breakfast."

"Okay." He got up again.

I climbed out of bed, too, and located my bathrobe. As I slipped it on, I found myself staring out the window at the barn. Emma's horse was there, nose to the ground and tail swishing. The window was closed, but I felt a sudden draft—a ghostly whisper that stirred the curtains and slid past my skin.

I still didn't know what to do about Rush's killer. Let him go, or tell the police everything I knew? Ruin more lives now that one was irretrievably lost?

I turned around quickly, fastening the tie on my bathrobe. My voice was strained. "Should we take Spike downstairs with us?"

Michael had been watching me, I saw, and he knew where my mind had gone. He finished buttoning his shirt and said, "You know what they say about sleeping dogs."